Deep Secret

'This is Doherty at her best
and her many fans will love it' *Guardian*

'Berlie Doherty has a magic in her... [she] uses
words as if language had just been invented'
TES

'We should treasure writers like Berlie Doherty
who are incapable of writing a mediocre
sentence' *Sunday Telegraph*

'Berlie Doherty is a superb writer' *Scotsman*

'Berlie Doherty writes with an authority that
brings life to all she describes' *Independent*

'Excellent... what could be an unbearably sad
tale is made compulsively readable by a writer of
grace and skill' *Independent* (on *Abela*)

Other books by Berlie Doherty

Abela: The Girl Who Saw Lions

Daughter of the Sea

Holly Starcross

Treason

Deep Secret

Berlie Doherty

ANDERSEN PRESS
LONDON

First published in 2010 by
ANDERSEN PRESS LIMITED
20 Vauxhall Bridge Road
London SW1V 2SA
www.andersenpress.co.uk
www.berliedoherty.com

First published by Puffin Books, 2003

British Library Cataloguing in Publication Data available.

ISBN 978 1 849 392 358

Typeset by FiSH Books, Enfield, Middx.
Printed and bound in Great Britain by
CPI Bookmarque, Croydon CR0 4TD

To Jacqueline Korn, in appreciation of her
encouragement, advice and support

1

Are we beautiful? Madeleine looked the question at her sister's reflection in the mirror. Grace's identical reflection looked the answer back, *We think so.*

They had no need for words. It was a slight frown, a flicker of smile, a raised eyebrow, movements that no one else would perceive. Madeleine loosened the blue ribbon that tied back her hair, and Grace did the same, her red ribbon twining round Madeleine's. They scooped back their hair and allowed it to fall again and again, lustrous.

The reflected room behind them was dark with their moving shadows. They could see the pine dresser, their bed, the old chair with its green silk cushions. Grace put out her hand, almost touching the mirror. Her image did the same.

There's another world in there.

It's like ours, but it isn't ours.

Turning the world inside out.

We could float in and out of it.

Madeleine stepped aside, so her reflection disappeared. Grace laughed at her own image.

Is it you in there?

Or you?

Come and see.

Grace allowed her fingers to touch the cold, golden glass. She pressed her palm against it.

Can't go in.

Can't follow.

Lonely.

Madeleine appeared again next to her sister. *I'm always here!*

So am I!

They held hands and swivelled each other round, shrieking with loud laughter. Downstairs in the kitchen their mother and father looked at each other. 'Twins are awake!' Sim Barnes laughed. 'That's today's peace and quiet gone.'

2

Old Aunt Susan woke badly. She often did, these days. She heard a girl's laughter in the farm across the yard outside, and went to her window. 'Is that the twins?' she called. She peered out. A girl with dark red hair was leaning on the gate of the farmyard, laughing across at the young farmer.

'No, it's only their cousin,' Susan muttered. 'Elspeth! I can hear you, Elspeth!' she called out.

The laughter stopped, held on a listening breath.

'And is that Ben you're flirting with?'

Susan tutted, annoyed with herself, and softly closed the window. 'There was no need to say that, you crusty old bird,' she told herself. 'Just because you lost your chance.'

'Will you marry me?' Ben asked Elspeth, suddenly, just as he was opening the gate into the pigsty. He

3

blurted out the words as if he had been holding them so tight inside him that they were no longer particular words with individual weight and significance, but bubbles of wind. 'Pass me the broom,' he might have said or, 'Mind your feet.' Instead it was, 'Will you marry me?'

And when Elspeth gasped and paused behind him, halfway between laughter and astonishment, he put down the swill pail he was carrying and asked her again, but gently this time. 'Elspeth? Will you?'

She hardly paused to take his kiss, but ran till the breath was bursting out of her to get her little brother ready for school, hugging her happiness. Her twin cousins would be the first to know.

Ben went on to the sties. The sow screeched at him, shoving her snout into the bucket before he had time to tip out the swill. 'Garn, you bummer!' A hen bustled round his boots and he toed her out of the way. He glanced across at the windows of old Susan's cottage, frosty with white sun, and cursed her for spoiling his morning.

'He was feeding the pigs!' Grace screeched. She toppled backwards off the low boulder she was sitting on, clutching at Madeleine and bringing her down too. She wiped her eyes on Madeleine's skirt. 'Poor old Ben! What a romantic fool he is!'

'And Aunt Susan spying from her window,' Madeleine giggled. 'I hope you told him you're waiting for his Lordship's nephew to ask you.'

Elspeth smiled, listening to her cousins' teasing laughter. Far up on the side of the hill she could see Ben, working the sheep down with his dog.

'I'm going to marry his Lordship's nephew!' the twins' younger sister Louise said. 'I'm going to live in the Hall and have nine children. And Grace is going to teach them needlework, and you're going to teach them French and music.'

'And where are we going to learn all that?' demanded Madeleine. 'We could teach them how to milk cows, and make—'

'Bramble jam.' Grace put in, 'but that's about all.'

Louise pouched her cheeks and buffed them gently with her fists, making little bursting boufs of contempt.

'But what did you say to him, Ellie?' Madeleine asked. She glanced quickly at her sister then, a teasing smile flickering quickly in her eyes. 'I can just imagine him, poor old Ben, with his mouth hanging open.'

'And his eyes popping out of his head,' said Grace.

'I said...' Elspeth paused. 'I said...'

'Go on,' Grace urged her. 'You said no.'

'I said I'd see,' said Elspeth quietly. The laughter stopped. Madeleine and Grace exchanged glances, primming up their lips.

'Oh, you're never going to marry Ben!' Louise blurted out. 'You know what you have to do, don't you, when you're married? You have to kiss him. And he'll be all mucky and sweaty and smelling of pigs. And you have to do other things, much worse things.' She swung her head so hard that her plaits smacked her in the face.

'At nine years old you know more than is good for you,' said Grace. 'If Mum heard you—'

'—she'd make you wash out your mouth with soap,' Madeleine finished.

'But not Ben!' wailed Louise.

'I said I'd see, that's all.' Elspeth looked away from her cousins. From where they were lying, in the hay meadow, they could see the farm that Ben rented from Lord Henry. It was the biggest and oldest in the valley. The sun was striking the stone walls so they glowed as if they had been brushed with gold. *I could live there*, she thought to herself. *I could live there and be happy for the rest of my life.*

'He's a good farmer, our Ben,' Madeleine thickened her voice to make it sound like Ben's mother, Joan. 'He comes home with mucky boots from when he's been feying. That proves it.'

Elspeth giggled with her. She had often watched Ben spreading the patches of horse dung and cow muck with his feet, like all the farmers did, inching its goodness over the pastureland.

'And he's stubborn as a donkey,' Grace went on.

'As fat as his best pig!' said Louise, catching the game her sisters were playing.

'No he isn't!' Grace shook her head at her. 'Don't exaggerate. As pink as one, maybe.'

And, thought Elspeth, though she didn't say it out loud, *he's as loving and gentle as a pigeon.*

Madeleine and Grace carried on in Joan's voice, swapping the story from one to the other, 'He thinks nought of driving—' 'eight hundred sheep to Yorkshire—' 'does our Ben—' 'over the tops, come rain—' 'come wind—'

'—come snow,' they finished in a triumphant chorus.

Elspeth smiled. 'That huge house,' she said dreamily. 'The kitchen is bigger than the schoolroom! And there's just him and his mother in it. It should be full of children, every inch of it!'

'I'm going to travel the world and be cultured,' Louise flopped on to her back, cycling her legs fiercely, 'before I marry his Lordship's nephew. He's a fine soldier, Mum said. Even though the war's been over a whole year, he's still going to fight in Asia for King and Country. That's so romantic. I might just bump into him now, if I bob over and meet Mum.' She jumped up and ran off, skipping lightly over to the stepping stones that led away from the meadow to the rutted cart track below the Hall.

'We're never going to leave the valley,' said Grace. 'Are we, Maddy?'

'Never. We'll work in the Hall, like Mum.'

'And which of you is going to marry Colin, might I ask?' Elspeth teased. 'I know you're both crackers about the vicar's son!'

They looked at each other again, and this time their conversation was silent, shutting out Elspeth. She was used to it. As a little girl, not much older than them, she had tried to imitate their signs and glances, to enter into their silent language of looks and smiles, but it was too quick, too subtle, too exclusive.

'Neither of us,' the twins said at the same time. 'Or both. First one over the stones!' They jumped up and raced to the stepping stones, where the lazy brook trickled down into the valley from Black Tor. Grace jumped lightly from stone to stone, laughing and twisting away from Madeleine. Her sister tried to unbalance her and tip her in.

'He's mine, he's mine!' Grace screamed.

They pulled each other back, splashing and kicking, and both reached the far bank at the same time.

Louise ran past a dusty black car that was parked outside the Hall gates. Its chauffeur was slumped back in his seat, his mouth wide open and his chest rising and falling steadily. Her brother Tommy grinned at her from the running board. She ran up the steps and paused to stroke the stone lions, one on the left, one on the right of the main gateway. She crouched down so she wouldn't be seen from the Hall and made her way through the kitchen gardens to meet her mother. Her father was stooped over a row of cabbages, teasing caterpillars off the leaves and squashing them between his fingers. His Lordship's vegetables supplied the whole village. Sim was proud of that. 'There'll be good grub to carry home today,' he called to Louise. 'His Lordship's had a visitor.'

'I know, Dad,' she said. 'I've seen him. And he won't have ate much. He's right skinny.' Along with all the children she had peered out of the classroom window at the unfamiliar sound of the visitor's car bouncing over the rutted lane earlier that afternoon. A spiky stranger in a black suit had scrambled out, unbending like a folded pole. Miss Skinner, the teacher, had sent the children back to their seats and had spent the rest of the lesson giving them dictation while she gazed at the car, imagining it carrying her away to fancy places. 'He's a doctor,' Tommy had whispered. 'No, he's not,' said Louise. 'He's a bank manager, come to count his Lordship's millions.' The car was still there when they left school, and the boys had tumbled round it, wide-faced with rapture. And it was still there now.

As Louise ran towards the kitchens she was surprised to see old Lord Henry himself standing with his skinny visitor at the back of the Hall. They were deep in animated conversation. His Lordship was angry, she could tell that from his raised voice and the way his hands gestured sharply as he spoke. She hesitated but he had already seen her.

He nodded to her and then held out his hand as if he wanted her to go to him. She shrank back, shy.

'This is one of the village children,' he told his visitor. 'Both of her parents work for me at the Hall. How many of you are there in the school, Louise?'

'Twenty, sir,' she said, bobbing. 'The twins left last year when they were fourteen, but they help Miss Skinner out sometimes.'

'You see,' the visitor said. 'Tiny, tiny school. Too small to be viable anyway.'

Lord Henry snorted. 'And there's three farms,' he went on. 'All my tenants. Not to mention the hill farmers on the tops that use the valley for winter grazing. Then there's the vicarage, the shop, the sawmill. Six mill cottages. A young blind man up on the hill – he does a bit of handiwork round the place for me. Half a dozen other smallholdings tied to my estate.'

'And that's it?'

'And the Hall.' Lord Henry turned and gazed up at the house he visited every summer with his wife, Lady Charlotte. 'This beautiful Hall; 1641, it was built. It's a national treasure.'

'Very pretty.' The visitor scribbled down some notes. 'So how many residents in all?'

'In the village? Including my wife and myself, about sixty. Many of them are related to each other; their families have been in the valley for donkey's years. We lost three in the war. Tragic.'

'A tiny community.' The visitor snapped shut his notebook and slid it into his pocket. He fluttered his fingers at Louise, signalling to her to go away.

'But a community none the less.' Lord Henry put out his hand, which the visitor ignored. 'And therefore your proposal is unthinkable. I bid you good day, sir.'

'I assure you, it is your refusal which is unthinkable. We'll talk again.' The visitor raised his hat slightly and walked past Louise and down the main drive to his car. His chauffeur woke up with a start, jumped out and opened the door for him. The boys on the running board fell away like leaves spinning from trees.

Aunt Susan, sitting in the lane outside her cottage with a sketchpad on her knee, looked up and frowned. She was interested in the reflections on the side of the car, how the roses that tumbled over her wall caught themselves in it as if the car was painted with yellow flowers. She

12

would have liked to capture it before the visitor left the village.

Louise's cousin Mike had been lovingly stroking the rounded hubs and the boot and, as the driver backed round, his fingermarks shone like jewels. The boys ran alongside the car, waving excitedly, cheering and laughing, ignored by the visitor.

Lord Henry stood watching, tapping the side of his leg as if a fly had landed there to annoy him. The car swung away up the track and round the bend of the hill, out of sight. Dust settled on the track behind it and still he watched. Lady Charlotte came slowly down the path towards him, smiling at Louise. She touched her husband's arm.

'What did he want?'

'Mm? Nothing. A foolish project. Nothing at all. The man's an idiot.'

He took his wife's arm and walked on with her down the path towards the main lawns. They stood on the half-circle of steps between the lions at the gateposts as if they were posing for a photograph, silent and perfectly still, arm in arm.

Louise ran on towards the kitchen. Her mother came out of the kitchen door at that moment, with the remains of the skinny visitor's lunch in a basket on her arm.

'Who was that man?' Louise asked her, lifting up the cloth that covered the basket. Her mother edged her hand away.

'I've no idea,' she said.

'His Lordship doesn't like him,' Louise told her. 'And neither do I.' She lowered her voice. 'Guess what! Ben wants to marry Ellie!'

'Now that's good news,' said her mother. 'It's a grand old farmhouse, needs living in properly. If his mother will let her, Elspeth will make Ben a very good wife. But some mothers find it very hard to let go of their sons, and I fear Joan's one of 'em. Pity.'

'What d'you mean?'

'Nothing you'd understand. She's full of bitterness, poor woman.'

'Is that why her husband went away?'

'No, love. It's because he went away. Mind you, her heart's always been with someone else.'

'That's so romantic! She has always loved another!' Louise sighed. 'Why didn't she marry him then?'

'Ooh, you're a pest!' her mother laughed. 'He was an older man, that's why, and no doubt she thought she could do better.'

'And has always regretted it.' Louise sighed again.

'Now don't you breathe a word of it to a living soul. It's stuck in the past, that is.'

They went into their cottage, which was like a dark cave after the bright sunlight. Her mother called up the stairs to Madeleine and Grace to get the fire lit, and when there was no reply she sent Louise up to fetch them. Louise loved the twins' room, with its bulging walls and pale rosy wash. They spent hours there, whispering secrets, doing each other's hair, making up songs, practising dance steps. It was their world, and anyone else was a trespasser in it. Louise tiptoed right into its silence, touching their pillows with the tips of her fingers, imagining the girls there, watching her. It's not fair, she said to herself. They have each other, all the time. She caught her reflection in the old Victorian mirror and smiled fleetingly at herself. Then she ran noisily back downstairs again.

'I bet they've gone on to Auntie Susan's. Watching out for Colin when he comes over the packhorse bridge.' She giggled. 'He's back home from boarding school today. Have I to fetch 'em?'

'No, leave 'em be,' her mother said. 'Let's have a quiet few minutes on our own, shall we, Lou? Just us.'

'Just us in the firelight. The way we like it. Watching the shadows dancing on the walls.'

The twins were mixing paints in Susan's kitchen, and every so often one of them would glance over her shoulder to see whether there was any sign of Colin. At one time they would not have admitted aloud to each other that they knew that he was home again, or that they cared, or that they knew the other cared, even though nothing was hidden between them. But now the secret was out, whispered in an evening of confidences in their bulging pink bedroom, and then giggled over. The whole village knew by now, and smiled over it. The twins were in love with the vicar's son, and he with them, and he couldn't tell one from the other of them.

But Colin didn't turn up that afternoon, and after a time the girls stopped watching out for him and absorbed themselves in their paintings. Aunt Susan was in a strange, fidgety grumbling mood when she came in from the lane.

'Are you not very well?' Grace asked her.

'I slept bad last night,' Susan told them, pouting over her unfinished painting of the visitor's car. 'Can't wake my head up proper today.'

'Was it a nightmare, Aunt Susan?' Madeleine asked.

'No, Twinny, not a nightmare. It's a dream what keeps coming again and again, about the dam over the hill. That dam that bust when I was a girl. You'll have heard your grandad speak of it. Terrible flood it caused.'

'I would have built an ark,' said Grace dreamily. 'And we would all be safe.'

'No time to build arks,' Susan snorted. 'Not when water's got loose. Water's a monster.' And her voice snapped tight then, and there was such pain in her eyes that the girls looked at each other in alarm. She seemed to slip away from them as if she had forgotten they were there and was back in another time.

'Aunt Susan.' Grace recalled her gently, touching her hand. 'Tell us what you think—'

'—of our pictures,' Madeleine said.

Susan leaned forwards and peered at the painting Grace had done of one of the stone lions at the Hall gates.

'It's not bad,' she nodded. 'But it's same as hers,

in't it?' She glanced at Madeleine's painting of the other lion. 'Why do you both have to do same?'

'It isn't,' Madeleine pointed out. 'My lion's got his tail tucked round this way.'

'And mine's the other way.'

'But you've both painted the lions! You could have done the gates, or the steps, or the garden, anything, but you have to do same thing, always. And they look the same – you've used exactly the same palette as she has, same style – have you got the right colours on?' She tweaked Madeleine's blue hair ribbon. 'It is Madeleine, isn't it? Same as Grace, you always have to be same as Grace, and she always has to be same as you. You'll never be good painters till you get your own style. One day I want to look at a painting and say that was done by Madeleine, or that was done by Grace.'

'We can't help being the same,' said Madeleine. 'Can we, Grace?'

'It just happens.'

Susan splayed out her fingers in a helpless gesture and laughed. She still couldn't tell one twin from the other, except by the colour of their hair ribbons, and she was sure they switched those round to tease her. She found it easier to call them both Twinny. Even Jenny, their mother, admitted that she got them mixed up. Sometimes Susan wondered whether the twins themselves knew which one of them was which, but only saw their own reflection in each other. *Now there's a bonny thought*, she mused. *Madeleine looks at Grace and thinks, that's what I'm like; that's me. And Grace looks at Madeleine and thinks, that's what I'm like. They only know they're like each other.* The puzzle to her was that one of them was better at art than the other. But just when she thought she had it worked out that it was the one who she thought was Grace who was the better, the one who she thought was Madeleine would draw a beautiful picture or colour something just right. When she pointed this out to them they would just look at her thoughtfully and shrug.

'It's time you found out what makes you different from each other.' Aunt Susan looked at each of them in turn, searching the sweet identical faces, caught as they were at that moment between childhood and womanhood, at fifteen years old. The same physical features, the same voice, the same mind, it seemed. They were endlessly fascinating to her. 'I could try and paint you, and catch the difference. You could paint yourselves. Not each other – your own self-portrait in the mirror.'

The girls flicked smiles to each other. *What was the point*, the smiles said. *They knew which was which, didn't they?*

Aunt Susan started to gather in the brushes and paints, talking half to herself. 'Mind you, mirrors is the hardest thing to paint. Like water. Come another day and we'll think about painting water. Might as well make friends with it. We'll sit by the stepping stones and paint the brook. Full of trout and pebbles and sunlight. That's the colour of rivers.' She clapped her hands together. 'We'll have a storm tonight, I can feel it in the air. Rain'll fetch colours up lovely.'

Grace smiled at her. It was so like Aunt Susan to be sad one minute and happy the next, as if she was slipping between one self and another.

'Might Colin come?' Madeleine asked innocently.

'He might. I could ask him to fetch me some kindling. He'll come if he knows you'll be here.'

The girls exchanged glances and Aunt Susan smiled. 'I might just mention it, if I see him. Go home now. I'm tired. I are tired, as you two used to say when you were toddlers. Remember? I are tired.'

*

That night the twins lay in their bedroom listening to the rumble of the storm in the hills around the valley. A sudden flash of lightning lit up their room and they clung to each other in mock fear. The thunder cracked closer now, taking the sky in booming strides. Under it all they could hear the river streaming over the stepping stones. Madeleine jumped out of bed and went to the window, opening it wide, turning her face up to the green-black sky. Below her the trees in the churchyard tossed their heads like wild horses. The vicarage was a dark bulk, with here and there a glow of light; the dining room, the vicar's study, Colin's room.

'He's back! His light's on,' she said. 'He must be studying.' She leaned out, holding her face up to the cascading rain, laughing and gasping. 'Colin, we're here!' she called.

Grace pulled her back in.

'I saw him! He waved to me!'

'I don't believe you. He couldn't possibly see you from there!' Grace leaned out, but now she could see that a curtain had been pulled across Colin's window. She turned back to her sister, disappointed.

'What will you do,' she whispered, 'if he asks you to marry him?'

'I'd have to say no,' Madeleine said. She closed her eyes tight against the impossible thought.

'I would too.'

'It's better that way.'

'Promise.'

'I promise.'

'But what if he marries someone else?'

'Don't. We couldn't bear it.'

'It might be better if you married him.' Grace's voice was tiny. They had this conversation often, and sometimes it made them laugh and sometimes it made them cry. They climbed back into bed. 'Better than letting him go to someone else. But you won't, will you?'

'I'd have to say no.'

They lay listening to the storm, the one draping her arm loosely over the other, cradling her against the cold; and when they turned they changed the cradle, their soft breaths falling into sleep.

Colin had been called downstairs to have a late supper with his parents. He was still thinking about the twins and how he had secretly watched them coming home from Susan's, strangely shy to go up and talk to them. His mother was telling him about the visitor to the Hall and he half listened, letting the girls' names chant in his head. *Maddy. Grace. Grace. Maddy. Madeleine. Ah, Madeleine. His favourite.*

'He didn't look like one of Lord Henry's London friends, you know, the shooting party mob,' his mother said. 'More a business type.'

'I'm sure he came to admire the beauty of the scenery.' The vicar too was only half listening to his wife. 'We must open our arms to them, ramblers and sightseers alike, who spend their days in the smoky grime of the cities.' Then, forgetting the visitor completely, he pushed back his chair and folded his hands behind his head. 'What I would like is a new organ for the church. I thought I might have a word with Lord Henry about it tomorrow. Imagine filling the valley with music!' He hummed loudly, tapping his long fingers together. 'When I walked down from Marty's farm today, with all the colours of the fields around me and those broody storm clouds gathering up there, I could just imagine hearing Bach thundering across the valley.'

'You and your music.' His wife smiled at him fondly and stroked the back of his head, the bit that he couldn't see, where his hair was still black on the nape of his neck.

'We're lucky to live here,' he said. 'We have a preview of paradise.' He leaned forwards and pecked idly at his food, hearing again the imaginary organ rolling across the valley.

'I wish you'd eat more.'

'Food doesn't interest me,' he said. 'You know that. I eat to please you and to stay alive. No other reason.' He stood up and walked to the window.

'Sometimes,' she said to his back, 'I would like to be praised, just a little, for the work I've put in. Even Colin's gone temperamental about his food, moping about those two Barnes girls. He can't even tell which of them is which. I've never heard anything so foolish in my life!' Colin frowned at her from the other end of the table and left the room. It wasn't true. He was only in love with Madeleine, he was sure of that. And if he wasn't always sure which one she was, then it didn't affect his feelings, surely. He went up to his room at the back of the house. His theology books lay open on the table next to the list of written exercises his father had set him. He had finished at school now, where he was a weekly boarder. His father was tutoring him for a university entrance exam. He wanted Colin to follow his footsteps exactly: to go to the same university, to read theology just as he had done; to become a vicar. If Colin passed his entrance exam and got a place he would be leaving Birchen, and he wouldn't see either of the girls for months on end. He hated the thought of leaving. He didn't even know if he wanted to study theology. He felt he was being swept along in a river; fast, too fast, helpless. He sat with his head in his hands, listening to the growl of thunder. The girls filled his thoughts, with the same sweet, smiling faces, the same teasing eyes. They had always been his best friends and now, since his last school holiday, the friendship for Madeleine had grown into love. He had kept away from Susan's that day deliberately, knowing that they were painting there, sure that Grace – or was it Madeleine? – would laugh at him if he turned up, torturing himself for staying away. But he had watched them from a distance and knew that tomorrow, whatever happened, he would try to see them again.

He'll grow out of it, his mother said to herself downstairs. *Once he's at university he'll forget they exist.*

'We could paint this room green,' the vicar said. 'All over, ceiling and all. Imagine. With these big windows, it would look beautiful, the green of outside flooding in and over the walls. What do you think?'

I think you can paint your study green. You can write your sermons in a green room. You can smoke that nasty pipe in a green room. You can recite your poetry in a green room. But here, where I eat the meals that I have cooked for you, I will not have green walls. She said nothing of this aloud. She cleared the table in brooding silence. A sudden crash of thunder startled her so much that she dropped the jug she was holding. It shattered into tiny pieces on the stone floor. The rains came thrashing against the great windows, drowning out the words she might have said.

3

And in her tiny cottage overlooking Ben's farm, Aunt Susan dreamed her nightmare dream again.

It is midnight. A mighty wall of earth is crumbling; great gashes in it, wet stains darkening it like blood. Millions of tons of water are pressing against it. With a mighty, gasping roar the wall gives way, and like beasts of the night water plumes, leaps over, and devours it. There is no holding back the flood now. Rubble and stones, trees, houses are swept along with it. People in their beds wake from a dream of thunder and clutch wildly at nothing, at wet air, and are rushed to their deaths. Onwards the greedy tide rushes, black in the black night, and the cry of grief itself is drowned in the roar and growl of the water beast.

Susan woke in a sweat of terror and gazed round her. Dawn was pushing a pale light across her window, the morning birds were singing. She could hear the quiet stream trickling across the stepping stones; the light laughter of Ben and Elspeth courting before the day's work began. *You were dreaming*, she told herself. She plucked at the dry old skin on her wrist. *Nearly seventy years ago, and you still dream about it, you poor old thing*.

But she could not chase this dream away. It seemed to her that she was indeed a girl of seventeen still, wakened cruelly from her sleep by the shout: 'The dam's bust!' She had struggled out of bed to see her father running out of the house to inspect the dam that he had helped to build. Later, she and her mother had walked over the hill to see the harm for themselves, never imagining the utter devastation they would find. She had stood bewildered on the ravaged slopes of the lost dam. She watched where a sluggish river of mud oozed and bubbled through the vast gape where the wall had been, and still she didn't know. Slowly the truth worked through, in hushed hearsay and gossip, climbing up the hillside towards them. The violent rush of water had crushed all the houses in its path. The village of Beggar's Bridge, ten miles away, had gone completely. Two hundred and forty people were drowned in that one night.

'Battered to bits,' people whispered, aghast. 'Swept as far as Donham, some of them.'

But Beggar's Bridge was where Susan's sweetheart lived. It couldn't be true. How could it be true? Her heart went cold and still inside her, she was dizzy with panic, her moans sent spasms of unutterable grief through her whole body. Her mother put her arms round her and held her close. There was no comforting the girl, because she had lost forever the young man she was going to marry. Susan knew that at last. But what she didn't know was that the seed of his baby stirred in her womb.

Wake up, Susan, the old woman told herself again. *It's gone. It's past, girl. Over now, seventy years ago.*

4

After the storm, the valley was vibrant with washed colours. The leaves on the trees were bright flames of light; the grasses glittered with jewel drops. As Jenny Barnes went across to the Hall to clean the rooms she stopped on the pack-horse bridge, watching the heron as it flapped along the swollen river in search of sheltering fish.

'By, that river's fast,' she called across to her sister, Madge, who was coming back down from the Hall. 'It's washing the stepping stones today. Be careful on 'em.'

'You've to come quick, and fetch Sim,' Madge called. 'His Lordship wants the Hall closed up. They're leaving at once.'

'Today? They never said,' Jenny tutted. 'They usually stay till end of September.'

'Well, they're leaving,' Madge said. 'Something's happened to upset them, if you ask me.'

She put her hands to her mouth, as if she was trying to keep bad news in, then stepped cautiously across the stones to her sister and grabbed her arm. 'Jenny, I don't think they'll be coming back.'

'How d'you mean?'

'I think they're leaving for good.'

'For *good*?'

'He was stuck in his study all breakfast time making phone calls, and she was sat at the table as stiff as a poker. Never opened her mouth all morning. Then he came down to the kitchens with a face on him like last night's thunder and said, "Madge, we're leaving."'

'I can't believe it. They'd never leave here. They love this place, Madge.'

'Well, that's how it sounded to me, the way he spoke, the way he looked this morning.'

'Surely they'll be back for the Christmas party!' Jenny laughed. 'Can you imagine it, Christmas without the Hall party? All the holly and candles, and Lady Charlotte giving out presents! They'll come back for that, Madge!'

'I hope you're right. You'd better fetch your Sim, anyway,' Madge said. 'He'll need to get the trap ready.'

Jenny hurried home with the strange news. Her husband was just as puzzled as she was. 'Funny do. Her Ladyship said nought to me about leaving, and we were walking round the grounds yesterday, looking at plants. She loves the garden, this time of year. We always do a big sort-out, and she's said nought to me yet.'

'If you ask me, they've had bad news of some sort,' said Jenny.

'Oh, dear Lord, I hope it's not their nephew.'

He went round to the stables to prepare the pony and trap. In London Lord Henry had a car and a chauffeur, but here in their country home he liked life to be simple. Few cars ever visited the valley, and he preferred it that way. He had changed nothing in the Hall since his childhood, apart from having a telephone installed when World War II broke out.

Lady Charlotte walked carefully down the slippery garden path, clinging on to her husband's arm. 'Look after yourself, ma'am; you don't look well today,' Jenny said. Lady Charlotte smiled weakly. She spoke to no one, not even to give instructions about pulling the heavy curtains across so that her Chinese silk carpets wouldn't fade in the sunlight. She had no smile for the servants, no word for Sim Barnes about her beloved garden. As he whipped the pony on she turned to look at the Hall, a gloved hand on her husband's arm.

'Go on,' Lord Henry said curtly to Sim. 'No point hanging about.'

The track that led up to the road was already turned to mud by the rain, and the trap wheels spattered sludge on the watching servants. Madeleine and Grace had run across the pack-horse bridge to join their mother and stood with their arms raised in a wave of farewell. It wasn't returned.

'It's the queerest thing, them going off like that,' Jenny Barnes said, her voice tight with concern. 'I feel odd about this, I can tell you. You can help me with the bedding today, girls. Start work today, might as well.'

It was the first time the twins had been upstairs in the Hall. They followed their mother up the great carved staircase to Lady Charlotte's room.

'Beautiful, isn't it,' Jenny breathed, proud to show it off to them. 'All oak, these walls. All oak panels.' She left the girls to lift the heavy embroidered counterpane off the four-poster bed and to peel off the linen sheets. Grace bounced on to the bed and drew the curtains round her. 'It's stuffy!' came her muffled voice. When she drew the curtains back, her sister had gone.

'I know you're here!' she called into the silence, her voice querulous suddenly. 'Maddy! Maddy? Where are you?' She listened into the breathing emptiness. Nothing. She slid out of the bed, going round at the dark, gloomy walls, and caught a flicker of candlelight in the mirror. A figure in a long white gown was approaching her. She whipped round, her breath fluttering in her throat. It was no ghost, but Madeleine, Lady Charlotte's nightdress flung over her own clothes. They both collapsed into helpless laughter and their mother came running in, alarmed at the sudden noise. She looked aghast at the rumpled sheets and nightdress.

'Never, ever do this again!' she shouted at them. 'Have you no respect? This kind of thing could cost us all our jobs, do you realise that? And then where would we be? No home, no money, no nothing, if it wasn't for his Lordship and her Ladyship!'

Ashamed, Madeleine wriggled out of Lady Charlotte's nightdress. Grace drew the sheets carefully off the bed and folded them into the linen basket. Neither caught the other's eye. And Jenny Barnes, standing watching them with arms akimbo, knew that they didn't have to look at each other. They were shaking inside with suppressed laughter, and as soon as her back was turned, it would explode like bright fireworks round the ancient panelled walls.

When they left the Hall that day, rumours were already flying. It was the talk of the village, the sudden unexpected departure of Lord Henry and his wife. Louise Barnes knew more than anyone did what it might have been about, but because she hadn't understood any of the conversation that had taken place between his Lordship and the stranger, she forgot about it. And besides, something else was to happen that would take the villagers' minds off their rumours and suppositions entirely. It was the worst tragedy that had ever struck the valley.

5

It began with a game. Jenny had sent Grace and Madeleine to find kindling, as a punishment. As they climbed up towards the Ghost Woods they turned to look back down the valley. On the lane that wound into the valley was a small caravan, pulled by a donkey. They looked at each other, frowning *Stranger* with their eyes, then they both shrugged and carried on towards the woods. The grass was still very wet underfoot, spongy and slippery.

'Like it,' Grace smiled.

Madeleine pulled a face and tipped up her foot to show that the sole of her boot was leaking. Grace pouted in sympathy. They went on up to the Ghost Woods as far as the S and D stone, and made a heap of twigs and broken branches there, snapping the pieces into equal lengths for the fire. The little stone was carved with the initials S and

D, the letter S twined like ivy round the D. It had been there as long as they could remember, and they used it as marker, halfway through the woods, where home was still in sight.

'Guess what,' said Grace. 'I saw the white monks the other night.'

'You wouldn't dare come here on your own.'

Grace giggled. 'Who said I was on my own?'

Madeleine dropped her pile and stared at her sister. *Who were you with, Grace Barnes?* her look said.

Grace laughed across at her.

'I don't believe you,' Madeleine said. 'There isn't a minute when we're not together.'

'Believe what you like,' said Grace, solemn now. 'I did see them, Maddy. And I heard them, chanting a low, sad hymn.' She started singing in the back of her throat, making her voice wobble.

'Don't, you're as bad as Elspeth,' said Madeleine, laughing. 'Let's carry this lot down now before it rains again.'

'Before the monks come again, you mean.'

The girls were about to split the pile of kindling between them and stagger down with it when they saw Colin coming. He had his head down, pretending not to see them.

Shall we tease him or be nice? Madeleine's look asked.

Tease first, then nice.

That's what I thought.

Madeleine waved to Colin. 'If you can catch us, you can have a kiss!' she shouted.

Grace giggled. 'And if you can't, you can carry all the wood down!'

'I'll catch you both, then,' Colin laughed. He ran towards them, hopping from side to side to stop them in their tracks as they danced away from him.

'Which of us do you want, Colin?' Madeleine teased him. 'Me or Madeleine?'

And Grace echoed, 'Me or Grace? Or me and Madeleine?'

'Or Madeleine?' Madeleine chanted, and gave him her special smile, sure that this time he would know one from the other of them and say her name out loud. Surely that would mean that he liked her best. But there was only one person who could tell the twins apart, and it wasn't Colin. It wasn't even their mother, though sometimes she said she knew for sure, and sometimes she was wrong.

'But you'll have to catch her first,' said Grace,

dancing back and round him in that elfin way of hers, which Madeleine copied immediately. Colin laughed out loud, pretending to ignore Grace, and then when he turned towards her he caught her red ribbon. She twisted out of his reach and ran, head back, so her hair streamed. He grasped out for her again and Madeleine ran between them, letting her own hair loose, so her blue ribbon floated away and tangled with Grace's red one.

'Maddy? Is it you? It is, isn't it? Got you this time!' Colin laughed.

Madeleine lingered just for a moment, letting him nearly catch her; his arm just trailed across her shoulder and then she skipped away too. And the chase was on, that never should have been on. First it was Grace and then it was Madeleine, and Colin still darting after them, zigzagging from the one to the other, the three stumbling and giggling as they hurtled down the slope and on to the track to the river. The young blind man, Seth, was on the track, walking steadily up towards his cottage. He smiled when he heard the girls' voices and held out his arms as if he would catch them both. He started to say something as Grace sidestepped past him, and Madeleine took his hands and twizzled him round, laughing into his milky-white eyes, and by that time Grace was ahead and Colin was nearly with her, heading for the stepping stones.

Further up the river the little caravan was moving slowly towards the packhorse bridge. For a moment the youth leading the donkey paused to watch the golden-haired girl who was running towards the river. 'Hey, my beauty!' he called to Grace just as she reached the stepping stones. She stopped for a second on the tips of her toes, flinging out her arms for balance, and he laughed and went on his way, and saw nothing of what happened next.

I can tell them apart, said Blind Seth every night of his life. I think I'm the only one who can. Not their mother nor their father knows them like I do. I've known since they were only babies and I was a child of nine or ten; I could tell even then. Even when they're singing in church, and they let their voices wind round each other's, I know. Grace makes my skin grow cold with the slight tremble in her voice, and Madeleine's has a breathlessness about it as if there's laughter shaking inside her. I hear it when they sing, and when they speak, and when they laugh. People ask me sometimes, even their mother, 'Which one is it, Seth?' Sometimes I tell. But not if the girls don't want me to. I sometimes think they're just one person really. One person with two laughing souls.

No laughter now. No singing.

And that day, when young Colin was running down the stone field, crazy for the two of them, and driven wild by them both, I knew it was Grace who was in front. I knew it was Madeleine swirling me round, giving Colin a tease and a chance. And I tried to call out, but she took the breath out of me. 'Mind the second stone, Grace! The storm's loosened it!' That's what I tried to call, and didn't, because Madeleine was making me laugh. I wanted to dance with Madeleine that day, take her hands and dance.

I should have called out again, but Madeleine took my mind off it. The river was like a demon. The stepping stones weren't safe. I knew it. I should have warned her.

And by her scream, I knew. And by the other's shout of grief; I knew. I knew by their voices.

6

The younger children were just coming out of the schoolroom, pitching their high voices into the sky like birds set free. Louise and Tommy saw Colin walking up to their cottage from the river, carrying their sister in his arms. They saw their other sister beside him, white with grief. They saw Blind Seth hurrying behind them. They followed in terrified silence.

Colin stepped straight into the house with the girl in his arms as if she was his bride being carried over the threshold. He took her into the bedroom and laid her down on the bed that the twins shared. 'Fetch your mum,' he said, in a voice that was broken like crumbled stones, and Tommy twisted away and ran sobbing to the Hall, where his mother was cleaning up the kitchens. She took one look at him and ran in her work apron down to the cottage and up the stairs to the twins' room and stood in the doorway with her hand to her mouth, and was as still as stone.

Madeleine came to her and put out her arms, and her mother looked from her to the girl on the bed, and back to her, and in that moment Madeleine realised that her mother did not know which of her daughters had died.

It was my fault that you died. I started the game with Colin. I made him chase you. It was my fault that your foot slipped on the rocking stone. It was my fault that your skull cracked like an egg, that you turned your face into the rushing water, that you lay drowning even as Colin ran to scoop you up. It was my fault. It should have been me. Your other self.

Don't leave me. Grace, Grace, don't leave me.

But you didn't look dead, Grace. That was the worst part of it. You looked like the sleeping ghost of yourself, myself, tranced between life and death. If Colin could have kissed you out of your enchantment he would have done. And when I looked at you I looked at myself, a glass-cold image of myself. Yet down at the river's edge, before Colin lifted you out of the water, I saw the spirit rise out of you and I knew the very moment

43

that you slipped away forever, taking me with you.

'Mum, it's Madeleine,' Madeleine said. 'Madeleine is dead.'

I wanted to die instead of you. I wanted to give you your life back.
    And once the words were said, how could they be unsaid?

7

That night Jenny Barnes came into the girls' bedroom and rolled up her sleeves. She herself would wash her daughter down for the funeral. She would allow no one else to do it, or to be with her when she did it. Sim was downstairs in the silent kitchen with the other children and her sister, Madge. Colin was sitting on the outside step, his head in his hands, unable to move himself from the house.

The villagers had been and gone, aghast and helpless with the news, and the mother was alone with her dead child. She was weak with grief and pain, but she would not let anyone else touch her daughter. She looked down at the girl, wondering at her still loveliness, how perfect she was in death, not a mark on her. How strange that there should be nothing, even at this last moment, to distinguish the one daughter from the other. When they were standing side by side she knew, or felt she knew, that Madeleine was the taller of the two, just, and that Grace's smile was quicker. Madeleine was the leader, and Grace would look to her first before agreeing to do anything. Madeleine was bolder, Grace was shyer, Grace had a deeper laugh, Madeleine's eyelashes were slightly fairer. 'Oh yes,' she sighed, stroking her daughter's pale hair, 'there are many ways of telling my two girls apart. But when there is only one, there is only one. There is no measure, no marker.' She kissed her child. 'God bless you, Madeleine,' she said. 'My darling one.' She opened her throat and sobbed as only the mother of a dead child could sob; a cry that seemed to rise out of the earth itself.

I heard my mother in our room with you. I watched her come out, and I knew she had said goodbye to you, to me. I'm Grace now, to everybody. I have become you. I will do the things that you would want to do. And I won't let them plant flowers on your grave. I don't want stiff crocuses and tulips and daffodils sprouting over you. I will sprinkle the seeds of wild flowers that grow down by the river, the tormentil and bird's-foot trefoil, the forget-me-nots and the blue-eyed speedwell.

Those are your flowers. I will be able to see your grave from our bedroom window. But it won't be you, sleeping in the graveyard with the old folk. You're not there.

Madeleine went into the bedroom and looked down at her sister's wax-pale face, then turned and quietly drew the curtains. The room dulled for a moment and bloomed again. She could just make out the shape of their paintings on the walls, and her own reflection, in the mirror; her solitary self. She stared at the golden glass, and the face that stared back at her stared from another world. Outside she could hear the river, the insistent song of the blackbird. It was raining again, the sharp drops sparking against the pane.

Autumn will come and the leaves will shower over you. Winter will come and seal the earth over your grave. And then spring. When you have been dead for nine months the woods will be hazy with the smoke of bluebells, and the hawthorn hedges creamy with May blossom. And a year will come, and our roses will be out and the air will be full of their sweet breath. What will I do, Grace, without you? What will I do?

8

The men took the coffin awkwardly down the twisting narrow stairs, and out into the brilliant daylight. Madeleine clung to the side of her bed, unable to follow them down the stairs, unable to move. She lay with her eyes wide and staring, listening to the bump of the wood and the muffled remarks of the bearers. She heard the door being pushed back as the men stepped outside. It was her mother who came up then, who came to the bed and put her hand on Madeleine's shoulder. Still Madeleine couldn't move or speak.

'Come, Grace,' her mother whispered. Her voice was shaking. Madeleine stared up at the white face, at the blue eyes swimming with grief. She shook her head, bereft of words. 'You have to, my darling,' Jenny Barnes said. 'We have to do it. We have to say goodbye to Maddy. I need you with me.'

As if she was rising up out of the sea, Madeleine stood up and followed her mother down the stairs. She felt as if she was in a trance of some sort, that none of this was happening. She followed her mother out of the dark house and into the dazzling light of day.

It should not have been a day like this. The sun should not have been shining. It should have shrouded itself in mists. Her father and his brother and her boy cousins, all in the dark mourning suits of their fathers, walked with the coffin on their shoulders. Madeleine felt her mother gripping her arm tightly, and she moved with her, not knowing what it was that allowed one foot to step after another, not knowing how it was that the familiar brief way to the church stretched ahead as if it had no end.

And when they arrived and were ushered into the cool building, she noticed with a kind of detached awe, as if for the first time, the elegant stonework, the soft lights of candles. She looked with wonder at the coffin that had been left on its own in the middle of the aisle; at the flowers placed on it. She could sense rather than hear the shuffling of feet as the pews filled up behind her. She watched the vicar's mouth move and heard nothing of what he said. She heard gasps around her, her cousin Elspeth sobbing, her sister Louise wailing, her mother and father crying aloud and unrestrained.

At the end of the service she stood up woodenly and followed everyone outside for the burial. Louise clung to her mother, arms twined round her as if she was a baby again, as if she could never be separated from her. Her father put his hand on Tommy's shoulder, and Tommy put his hand up to Madeleine's, looking up at her with swollen red eyes. His sobs were torn from him like tiny explosions. And when it was over, when the burial was over and the soil had been scattered on the coffin and more soil had been heaped on it, and people made their sad ways back to their farms and cottages, Madeleine was gently nudged by Elspeth and knew that she had to move with them, back at the cottage, back to the room where Grace would never be again.

I can't cry. They expect me to cry and I can't. Is that wrong? Is that terribly wrong? I don't know how to cry. Forgive me, Grace. I am cold and dry and dead inside. I have forgotten how to cry. It used to be so easy. We used to cry together.

9

The long summer trailed through autumn and into winter. Jenny and Sim made work for themselves at the Hall as though the summer parties there were still happening. They were afraid to sit still and listen to the silence left by their missing daughter's voice. Sim harvested the vegetables from the Hall gardens and shared them all out round the village rather than see them wasted. Louise helped him to clear the lawns and the flowerbeds of old leaves, and they lit a bonfire and stood quietly together, watching the slow curl of blue smoke.

'It's better out here, isn't it, Dad?' she said.

'Aye, it is,' he said, understanding her.

When they went home again Tommy was hovering on the doorstep, watching the other boys playing. Sim touched his shoulder lightly, releasing him, and Tommy ran off, breathing deep draughts of the misty air, galloping after his cousins to collect hazelnuts in the Ghost Woods. They passed the little caravan that had been up near Marty's hill farm for weeks now. The donkey grazed in the field, flicking its ears against the flies and midges. The boys stopped for a moment to watch a group of men climbing up from the packhorse bridge, their voices carrying deep and full.

'What's they doing here?' Tommy asked.

'Dunno. There's more of 'em; there's a van by the Hall, look.' Mike cupped his hands round his mouth and hollered, 'Can't fetch vans over bridge, misters. Too narrer.'

'There's a whole gang of 'em up over valley top, me dad says. Up on Dyson's Fields,' another boy said. 'Reckon as they're sheep rustlers?'

'Dunno.'

'Ey, there's a gang up there, going up top. Let's foller 'em.'

They slapped their thighs as if they were lashing horses on and galloped up the hill.

'Garn!' Tommy shouted, making his voice rough and deep. It felt good to be running free again; it felt wild and wonderful. He galloped ahead of the others, smacking his thigh and hollering, and the men on the hill turned to look. They were carrying tripods over their shoulders and, as the boys approached them they lowered them to the ground and began to assemble them.

'They've got guns!' Tommy shouted.

'Reckon them's shoulders?' Little Billy Meakin panted.

'Shoulders?'

'Army shoulders. Bloomin' Germans!'

'Bloomin' Germans from the war.' The boys stopped, eyeing the men. One of them looked across and winked.

'They for shootin'?' Tommy asked, braver than the others. He could see that the tripods weren't guns anyway. He felt Mike knuckling his back, his breath splintering with scared laughter.

'Shooting?' The man grinned. 'These are measuring instruments.'

'What you measuring then?' Billy demanded.

'Oh, the valley, the contours, this and that,' the man said mysteriously.

'Hope you can swim, lads,' one of the others said, and the men laughed to each other, a private joke that excluded the boys. Even though they didn't understand, the boys laughed with them and ran off again, paddling their arms in front of them as though they were swimming through the mist.

When Tommy came back to the house again he felt a wash of guilt. The laughter was still in his head, loud as bells. He went inside quietly, his cheeks bright and the outdoors sharp on his skin and his clothes. His pockets were bulging with hazelnuts and he tipped them on to the hearth and crouched down next to his father, watching and waiting as if his sister might come home at any minute.

Sim Barnes moved suddenly in his chair, racked by the sudden memory of the twins running into the house on just such a day as this. They would stand together in front of the fire, telling a story about this or that, their eyes shining, their hands clasped. The one would begin the tale and the other would take it up, and then the other, in just the same laughing breathless way; the same voice, the same gestures, the narrative seamlessly running between them. He put his hand across his eyes.

Abruptly Jenny stood up and opened the door at the side of the fire. She brought out the bread that Madge had sent round earlier, tapped it smartly and put it back for a minute or two.

'Shall we bake?' asked Louise.

'Aye. Let's do summat,' Jenny said. 'Fetch the eggs from the larder. Time the Christmas cake was made.'

From her chair at the fireside Madeleine looked sharply at her mother. How could she think of such a thing? What did Christmas have to do with them now?

'You could help,' Jenny said, and Madeleine shook her head.

Sim took Tommy outside with him to chop wood for the fire. Madeleine could hear the *crack! crack!* of the axe on the wood, and the *chuck!* as Tommy piled them up for drying. The vicar hailed them; the chopping stopped. The men's voices rumbled on; ruminating about the strangers up on the hill.

'They're measuring or summat,' Tommy's voice piped up.

'It's Lord Henry's land, all that,' Sim said. 'Maybe he's building another house there. It's the cold side though, up near Marty's.'

Madeleine hunched in her corner, staring into the flames, seeing nothing, never moving.

Tommy hopped back into the kitchen. 'Vicar's here,' he announced.

Mr Hemsley tapped on the door and crouched through, awkward in a room that was too low for him.

'Sit yourself down, Vicar,' Jenny said. 'Louise, pour Mr Hemsley a cup of tea, child. Excuse me while I get on. I need to keep busy or...' she raised her floury hands in a silent gesture, and the vicar nodded and went over to the fire to sit by Madeleine.

She didn't stir. Grief takes its time, he knew that. His job all too often brought him into contact with mourning families, and he knew that every individual had to find their own way of coping. But this girl's numb silence was almost more than anyone could bear. In the vicarage Colin too was a ghost of himself: hardly eating, crying often, staying in his room all day, taking himself out for long walks on the moors under the bright cold stars. But his grief was tangible. You could talk to him about it. This girl was locked inside herself. The vicar took Madeleine's hand in both of his, rubbing it gently as if he was trying to bring life and warmth into it.

'It's you I've come to see. I have a plan in mind,' he said to her. 'There's a small window in the church that needs replacing. I have enough money in the funds to commission a simple stained-glass window to put in its place.' He let her hand slip away and took the cup of tea that Louise brought to him. 'Thank you, Louise. I would like to dedicate the window to Madeleine.'

'Oh, what a lovely idea,' Jenny said. 'It would be such a pretty thing. She would – she would have loved it.' She put her hand to her mouth, sorrowing again, her eyes brimming.

'And I would like Grace to design it.' He touched the cold hand again. 'Grace, would you like to do that?'

Madeleine looked at him blankly. It seemed to him at first that she hadn't even recognised her own name.

'Grace, answer the vicar,' her mother prompted.

'I don't think so.' Madeleine's voice was dull and completely without emotion, hardly sounding. 'I don't think I could.'

'Think about it, my dear,' the vicar said gently. 'It would be a way of celebrating your sister's life, and it would be a gift from you to her. It would always be there, a beautiful thing for everyone to see and to remember Madeleine by.'

'Please?' said Louise. 'You do such lovely draw-ings. Please, Gracie, please do it.' There she was again, her eyes brimming until they overflowed. Madeleine watched her with silent curiosity. How could one person shed so many tears, she wondered. Jenny hugged her youngest daughter closely, tight, tight until their shared spasm of quiet grief was over and they could both smile weakly at the vicar again. Madeleine turned her head away from them and stared into the fire, finding strange comfort in the random dance and the purring voices of the flames and, deep inside them, the sound of her sister's voice.

Later, in her room, she took out Grace's sketchpad and leafed through it. Though Grace had always tried to hide it, she was slightly the better of the two at art. Sometimes at school or when they were painting with Aunt Susan they would swap their work round and each would finish off the other's. It was not intended to confuse anyone; it just seemed the best thing to do. But there was one painting that Grace had completed on her own. It was her picture of the stepping stones, with the river bubbling and shining over them, and a girl with yellow hair sitting by them. She could have been Madeleine. She could have been Grace. It was the best picture Grace had ever done, and it was the one that had made Aunt Susan say, 'You have a talent, Grace Barnes. It is Grace, isn't it? Why don't you always draw like this for me?'

Grace had looked quickly at her sister, and Madeleine had smiled at her, reassuring her, enjoying the reflected glory of Aunt Susan's praise.

It has to be this one. It is that place, your place. That's where you are.

Madeleine edged the drawing away from the pad and stowed it in a bag. Next morning she took it to the vicar's house. The door was open, but there was no answer to her knock. She slipped inside and put the sketch on his kitchen table.

10

Colin watched Madeleine from his upstairs window. It was the first time he had seen her since the day of the funeral; as far as he knew it was the first time she had left her house. He stood with his hands clenched in his pockets, unable to run downstairs and speak to her, unable to open his window and call out to her. How pale Grace looks, he thought. *How slowly she walks, like someone in a dream. I should go to her, we should share this grief together, but my words are locked inside me.*

He went to his desk, to his pile of Latin and Greek books, and sat down wearily. He folded his arms across the books and put his head down on them. *Madeleine, Madeleine, I want you back.*

Elspeth was just crossing over to Ben's farm when she saw her cousin. With a cry of pleasure she ran to her and put her arms round her.

'Grace, I'm so pleased to see you out and about!'

Madeleine allowed herself to be hugged, then made to turn away towards her cottage, but Elspeth clung on to her hand.

'No, I won't let you go home, not yet! It's such a lovely day – don't you love November when it's like this, when it's so cold and blue! Come and walk with me a bit. Come and see Ben with me. He'll be that pleased to see you, I know he will.'

Madeleine allowed herself to be led away from the vicarage to the big farm. Elspeth's bright chatter bubbled round her, shimmering and meaningless, and underneath it flowed like a deep, slow river, her own measureless conversation with her sister. The pigs squealed as Elspeth opened the farm gate. Ben's mother came out of the farmhouse door and stood with her hands on her hips, watching the two girls.

'Is Ben about?' Elspeth asked her brightly.

'No,' Joan Glossop said. She turned to go back into the house. Elspeth smiled at Madeleine and squeezed her hand. 'See, I've brought Grace with me.'

Joan turned back. 'What a lovely day for you to be out walking,' she said warmly. She looked at

Elspeth and shook her head. 'Ben left the house at the crack of dawn, and I don't know where he's gone, and he didn't take it into his head to tell me. He took all his savings with him, that I do know.' She folded her arms as if she was expecting an explanation from Elspeth.

Elspeth faltered. 'He's not told me nothing,' she said. She felt her cousin's hand slipping out of her own, heard her walk away back to her own cottage, and still she stood, biting her lip helplessly while the pigs screamed for food in their sties.

Very early that morning, when the early sun was sparkling on the frost, Ben set off to walk the twenty miles to town. He climbed up the steep lane out of the valley and came out on to the road that ran to Hallam, the nearest big town. He passed the outlying straggle of Dyson's Fields and was surprised to see a line of trucks pulled in against a hedge, and men with picks clambering out into one of the large fields.

'You digging for gold?' he asked them, high-spirited with the thought of what he planned to do when he reached town. The foreman wiped his nose on the back of his hand, and instantly another dewdrop dangled in its place.

'New houses,' he said. 'Room for fifty or sixty in this field.'

'Oh aye?' Ben asked, frowning. 'I've heard nought about that. And who's going to live in 'em, right up here?'

'Not a clue,' said the foreman. He struck the hard earth with his pick, and again, hardly dinting it. 'Not me, anyroad. Beyond the back of beyond, this place is. What's a man to do, living here?'

Ben laughed and went on his way, and soon forgot about the new houses. There was no traffic, and he walked in the middle of the road singing at the top of his voice. Around him the hills looked fine with their sprinkling of frost. When he'd covered about ten miles a farm horse and dray pulled up next to him.

'I'll give thee a ride to town if tha promises not to sing,' the farmer shouted, and Ben pulled himself up next to him.

'I see they're putting new houses up back there,' the farmer grunted.

'Can't imagine why anyone'd want to be stuck up there,' Ben said. 'Know ought about them, Marty?'

'Nought,' said the farmer. He clicked the horse on. 'Heard watter board bought the field off old

Dyson some time back. Sell anything, he would. Sell his mother's grave if it'd put money under mattress.'

Ben chuckled and closed his eyes. He imagined Elspeth, fresh with morning, bringing in water from the windy yard at the back of her cottage, shooing the hens away from under her feet. He imagined her breaking the skim of ice on the water bucket, tipping it out so it clinked on the stones. She would be singing maybe, nice and loud the way she did, nice and full and lovely. And then shouting to young Mike to get a move on, he'd be late for school at this rate. 'You're the lass for me,' he mumbled, and Marty looked at him in surprise.

'Tha's in a sprightly mood today, young Ben. Got business to do in town?'

'Could have,' Ben grinned.

'Important, is it?'

'Happen,' was all Ben gave him. 'Set us down at Townend, Marty. This'll do fine.'

Ben sprang down from the dray and patted the horse on the rump, so the cart trundled briskly away from him.

'If tha's on road again in a couple of hours I'll tek thee back,' Marty called.

'Ta,' Ben shouted. 'But I don't know as when I'll be finished here. Might take us two minutes, it might take us two days.' He walked away briskly, taking the sharp morning in his stride, singing lustily again.

The main street was already bustling with shoppers and coffee stalls. Ben pushed past them all until he came to a jeweller's shop. He looked with wonder at the rings on display in the window. They were all so fragile, with their tiny brilliant stones. They were like bands of stars. He pushed open the door, and his courage failed him. Here he was in his mucky boots and the baggy jacket and trousers that served as his best, and there in front of him was a carpeted floor such as he'd never seen in his life, and a staring girl as pretty as a doll. He tiptoed to the counter and dumped his bag of coins on the glass top. He took a short piece of dirty string out of his pocket.

'I want a wedding ring,' he announced, scarlet with pride and embarrassment. 'I want it to cost no more than what's in here,' he tapped the bag, 'and it's to be no bigger nor smaller than this,' and he held up the piece of string, which he had secretly measured round the fourth finger of Elspeth's glove after church last Sunday. He was aware of the grime under his nails and in the lines of his palm. He stuck his fists in his pockets, but when the assistant stooped down and brought two rings out of the cabinet under the counter and slid them on a red velvet cushion towards him, he couldn't resist touching them.

'Eh,' he breathed. 'She'll look lovely in this one. This one, an' all. Which one would you have?'

The assistant smiled at him. He tried to imagine Elspeth with her hair combed back shiny and neat like this shop girl, and powder and stuff on her face, and her hands so white they seemed to be made of china. The girl slipped one of the rings on to her finger and turned it slowly round and daydreamed for a second or two about the young man in the solicitor's office over the road.

'I like this one,' she said. *I wish, I wish*, she thought to herself, twisting the ring once more for luck, and when she opened her eyes again she was shocked to be looking into Ben's red-faced stare.

So it was bought in two minutes after all, and Ben walked the twenty miles back home with it, grinning widely, and pausing every few miles to open up the little velvet box and huff into it as if he was blowing kisses at the wedding ring.

When he got home he showed it to his mother, who pursed her lips and sniffed it as if it was a delicacy to be eaten. 'How much did you pay for this?' she demanded.

'I've been saving up,' Ben muttered, ducking his head.

'Well, it was too much.'

But Ben's heart was singing, and nothing his mother said could make any difference now. The fact was, she knew it too. He had done his duty. He was only a baby when his father left home and remarried, but as soon as he was old enough to run about he'd been given jobs to do to help her. He left school on his thirteenth birthday and worked the farm like a grown man. Now he was twenty years old and ready for a wife, and in his mind he had always wanted that wife to be Elspeth. It didn't occur to him to wonder how his mother would feel about sharing her house with another woman. He felt she must surely love Elspeth as much as he did.

'Some men come knocking at the door today, wanting lodgings,' his mother said, dismissing the ring. 'Said could I take some of 'em in the house and some in the barns. Scotch men they were. Funny sort of English they talked. Couldn't understand half what they were saying.'

'What they want lodgings for?' Ben asked, twisting the ring to make it flash in the firelight.

'Say they're working for Water Board or summat.'

'It's them new houses,' Ben told her. 'Up on top, at Dyson's.'

'Oh aye? Said there'd be a lot more looking for lodgings. Could be working here for years.'

Ben looked at her, alarmed. 'You said no, Mum?'

'I said nought of the kind. I said I'd think.'

'I'm wanting them barns for saddlebacks, you know that. I've plans for more sties.'

'Oh, pigs, pigs, pigs!' his mother snapped. 'Those squealers will be the death of me.'

Ben said nothing. If he could have his way, he'd sell off the sheep and cows and just breed pigs. He'd have them roaming free, too, not cooped up in sties.

'Why would folks want to live up there, anyroad, up at Dyson's?' his mother asked.

'Dunno. There's nought to do, if they han't got farms. And there's no room up there for farms, they're going to be that tight together. Fifty, sixty houses, the bloke said. Like a little town. Funny business, to me.' Ben put the ring back into its box, gently, as if it was as fragile as an egg. 'I'll just slip out to see Elspeth,' he said, and paused for a moment as if he was waiting for his mother's blessing.

'Go on then,' she said, glancing up at him, annoyed. 'If you have to, get on with it.'

He felt foolish and nervous when he knocked on Elspeth's door. Normally he'd push it open and just call her name or walk in. Her little brother Mike leaned out of a bedroom window, staring at him as if he'd never seen him before. Ben stood with his head bowed, scraping muck off his boots, and when Elspeth came out, unfastening her pinafore, more faces appeared at the windows. She laughed up at them, shaking her fist, loosening her hair, and it was all Ben could do not to gather her in his arms in front of them all.

'Well?' she asked. 'What do you want with me? I'm peeling spuds.'

He turned her away from the prying eyes at the windows. The words that he had been forming in his head fell over like a row of dominoes. He fumbled in his pocket and brought out the little velvet box. His fingers were trembling and Elspeth looked at him with wonder, watching the big pink hands, scrubbed clean now, a tiny crescent of grime under the thumbnail. He opened the box and put the whole thing into her hands, unable at the last minute to take out the ring and slip it on to her finger as he had imagined himself doing. And when she gasped, and lifted out the ring herself, and slid it on to her finger, and held it out to the low sun to catch its sparkle, he still couldn't find the words he meant to say.

'Ben, is this an engagement ring?'

He shook his head. 'It's a wedding ring. If you'll have it, I thought, just the one would do.'

'So I can't wear it.' She slipped it off her finger and back into the box, teasing him, putting it back into his hand and closing his big fingers up around it, turning half away from him with her hair clouding her eyes.

He stared at her hopelessly, digging his hands into his pocket. 'Not yet, like,' he gulped, miserable to his boots.

'It's lovely, Ben,' she said, solemn at last, turning her face up to him.

'It's yes then?' His throat was as dry as paper.

'It's yes.'

And he wanted to tell her that he adored her, that she was the best thing in his life. Instead he grinned at her, just grinned.

'I would like a bit of velvet in my wedding dress,' Elspeth told her mother that night. 'Velvet purrs like a cat. And I would like velvet curtains in my room. Our room,' she added, blushing and laughing, her hand to her mouth.

'I'd see what his mother has to say about that,' Madge said. 'She won't be easy to live with, you know that, don't you?'

'I won't be marrying her,' said Elspeth.

'That's what you think.' Madge twitched her lips. 'And Ellie, my love, don't think of marrying yet, with your cousin so soon dead. Wait till the summer, when the twins' birthday is over. Can you wait that long?'

'Course, Mum.' Elspeth coloured up. She hadn't even thought about that. How could there be a wedding, with all Birchen in mourning? How could she have run in laughing and smiling to show her mother the ring?

'It's not wrong to be happy, my love,' her mother said. 'Don't be ashamed, child.'

Elspeth turned away, too full now to trust herself to speak. At one time she would have run to the twins to show them the ring. They would have teased her again about Ben, like they always did. They would have drawn pictures of the wedding dress and of the bridesmaids' dresses that they themselves would have planned to make and to wear.

'I miss her, Mum,' she whispered, and Madge put her arms round her and rocked her.

'I know, my love, I know. You make your wedding plans. Be happy, Ellie, for all of us.'

It was not an easy thing to do, but Elspeth decided to show the ring to her cousin. For the first time in her life she felt shy. Madeleine was sitting in her usual seat by the fire when Elspeth went in.

'I found out where Ben was off to yesterday,' Elspeth said, trying to keep her voice normal and steady. *It's like Grace is in a deep, dark cave, she said to herself I want to draw her out of it, into the sunshine again.* She kneeled down on the hearth rug, shifting Louise's cat Pudding out of the way, and opened up the box. 'Look. It's for our wedding.'

Jenny Barnes and Louise came over to her and admired the ring. Madeleine watched them all, saying nothing.

'I wanted you to see it,' Elspeth said. She took the ring from the box's velvet grasp and held it out, and Madeleine at last lifted her hand and took it from her. She turned it round and round, transfixed by the sparkle of the diamond, catching its reflection, making its rainbow light dance like water over pebbles. Round and round she turned it, till Elspeth put her hand over it and took it away from her.

'Don't!' she laughed. 'I've heard you can hypnotise yourself with such things!' She put the ring away, snapping the box shut, and stood up quickly.

She looked down at her cousin, her heart filling up again with grief for her. 'When the time comes, in the summer, I want you to be my bridesmaid.' She blurted it out, unable to restrain herself. 'We could make the frocks together.' She held her breath. Surely this was what her cousin needed; to be busy, to have tomorrow to think about instead of yesterday. But Madeleine was silent, and when Elspeth looked at Jenny, her aunt just shook her head, sad in her smile; old and pale and sad.

11

That Christmas the Barnes house remained undecorated. It had always been the twins who brought the bunches of holly down from the tree at Marty's farm, their cheeks as bright as the berries. No one had the heart to do it this year. The Christmas presents were left unopened for days, till Tommy's curiosity got the better of him. He unwrapped the whole pile in one go and delivered each of the presents personally. They were all simple things.

'You've got a book from Aunt Susan,' he told Louise. 'Only it's locked. That's daft.'

Louise took the little red book and turned the key in the clasp.

'There's no words in it!' Tommy laughed. 'What good's that?'

'It's a notebook,' Louise said. 'I've got to put the words in myself.'

Tommy huffed and ran outside to kick his Christmas ball round the yard. Louise stroked the smooth pages of the book. She wrote her name and age in it, and the date, and locked it again. She couldn't imagine having anything else to write in it, ever. Her mother gave her a ribbon for the key and tied it round her neck. 'Now you can have secrets,' she smiled.

'I've got them already,' Louise assured her. 'Mum, shall I tell you one?'

'Ssh! You're not supposed to tell secrets.'

'But you'll have to know some time. Ben and Colin were putting a window in the church this morning.' She took her mother's hand. 'We'll go and see it, will we?'

'Call your father,' said Jenny. Her voice was suddenly ragged. 'We must all go. Together.'

When they arrived, Ben and Colin had just finished putting the window in place, one standing on a tall ladder inside the church and one outside.

'In memory of Madeleine Barnes,' Colin read the little plaque out loud, his voice shaking. 'Died, 20th August, 1946, in her sixteenth year.' Well, now he had said it, and the saying made it real. 'You know why she died, don't you, Ben?' he said roughly. 'She died because I was chasing her. I killed her.'

Ben gazed at him helplessly, unable to say anything that might comfort him, not even knowing the words that might help. *If it was Elspeth who had died that day, he thought, I would have laid myself down on the cold ground and not got up again, never.*

The vicar held a special service to dedicate the window. Miss Skinner played an anthem on the organ, as sweet and quiet as she could make it. The winter sun was low and found the coloured panes easily. The light fell through on to the benches where the Barnes family were sitting, and Louise held her arms out so they were bathed in the splashes of blues and greens and golds. She turned to her mother, her eyes were shining, spreading her hands out so Jenny would see how she was jewelled with the colours of the window. It seemed to her to be a kind of miracle, and maybe it was, because from that day the deep loss began to heal, and she was able to think of her sister without crying.

Madeleine stayed in the church after the rest of the family had gone home. She stared up at the window for so long that the colours began to tumble together, like a kaleidoscope, spinning and fusing together, drawing her into the vortex of light. *I am you, and you are me. I have lost my self forever now. You have taken the spirit part of me with you, where it belongs. Everything on earth that means anything is trapped inside the little panes of this window. I can hear the river whispering outside, as if it is the only thing left alive. Your river, Grace. I can hear your voice in the river.*

She was roused by the sound of someone coming into the church and she hunched herself forwards as if she was praying, so she wouldn't be disturbed by having to acknowledge the presence of another person. She didn't want anyone to sever this moment between herself and her sister; she wanted to keep looking at the jewel lights of colour that represented them both: to spin with them, to be broken into those pieces of painted glass, to become coloured air. But then she recognised the slightly hesitant step of the young blind man, Seth. She raised her eyes and watched as he made his way slowly along the wall, feeling it, his hands sliding from stone to pane to stone, and she knew that he was looking for the window. She was glad it was high up under the church spire. She didn't want him to touch it or to learn its patterns in his own unfathomable way. She could hardly bear to watch him inching his way along the stones, his fingers spread out like spiders. At last he reached the brass dedication plate, and she could hear him whispering the words to himself as he traced the letters. Then his shoulders stiffened, and he turned slightly, listening.

'Are you there?' he asked out loud.

Madeleine held her breath and stood up slowly, and then sidled out of the bench and tiptoed out of the church. She leaned her back against the wall, breathing deeply. Her heart was lurching as if there was a wild bird in her chest, frantic for freedom.

Now she was aware of another sound, carried from the top slope of the hill by the wind. It was the sound of men's voices. She shielded her eyes and gazed into the sun, and could make out the silhouettes of men hauling machinery of some sort up to the Ghost Woods. Strangers were coming to the valley, had been coming and going for weeks like an army taking possession by stealth. She had heard drifts of gossip about them and now she could see them for herself. She was shocked by their loud, sure voices, by the arrogance of their laughter. They were not any local farmers, she knew that.

A cab trundled over the bridge and stopped in front of the Hall. Lord Henry climbed out, arched his back to stretch himself, and then lifted his hand to wave to her. Instead of returning his wave as she would have done once, she went slowly back to her cottage. Her mother was standing by the window, her arms folded, staring out at the figures on the hillside.

'It's queer how strangers keep coming to Birchen these days,' she said.

Sim Barnes joined her. 'Happen they're summat to do with those new houses up at Dyson's.'

'Who's going to live up there, that's what I'd like to know. Who'd want to?'

'His Lordship's home,' Madeleine said dully. Her mother and father exchanged glances.

'Never!' Jenny said crossly. 'Without any warning? How does he think I'm going to find food for him?'

Madeleine ignored her and went up to her room. She went over to the window and looked out across the yard. The sun had gone, and the sky was pale yellow. There would be no light in the church now. The window and its plaque would have lost their glow of life.

I cannot read all these letters, said Seth to himself. But the word is long, and I know it says Madeleine. And yet Madeleine lives. The girl who died was surely Grace. If I had called out, Grace, Grace, take care of the stones, I could have saved her. Madeleine danced with me, and Grace died. Why does Madeleine keep that locked up in her heart? I should tell someone, and yet she of all people has the right to choose, to slip into her twin, to lose her real self: it is what they did in life. Who am I to make her tell her secret? One day she will tell, and on that day I will stand by her. And on that day, if I am brave enough, I will tell her the secret of my heart.

When Jenny Barnes and Louise, who never left her side these days, arrived at the Hall, Lord Henry was already having a go at lighting the fire in the main room. It fluttered miserably, and Jenny crouched down to it, easing the pile of logs aside to let air in for the flames to move.

'Why didn't you send us word, sir? We could have had the place warmed up for you, and good food ready, and the beds done.'

'There's no need for any of that,' Lord Henry said. 'I'm only here for one night. I was going to camp down in here, you know.'

'You can't do that,' said Jenny, shocked. 'I'll make up a bed in your room and light a fire up there for you.'

'As you wish.' He lifted his hands in a submissive, weary gesture. 'There'll be a visitor tomorrow.'

'A visitor? Is he to stay, sir?'

'Certainly not,' said Lord Henry. 'There is only one thing I want you to do, Jenny. If you would be so good as to send your boy up and down the valley and tell everyone to come here at ten tomorrow morning, I would be most grateful. That's all I want you to do.' He sat down in his favourite chair, which looked down the lawns of his garden and across the valley. Jenny saw in him a tired old man, the life gone out of him. 'It is very important that they all come. It is very bad news for the valley, I'm afraid.'

Jenny Barnes crouched back on her heels, watching the fire's glow. There could be no worse event in the valley than the death of her child, but she did not mention that to Lord Henry. The words were too raw in her throat to be spoken.

'You rest yourself, sir,' she said. 'I've a ham in the larder that'll make something for the gentleman tomorrow, and we've a good soup on the go at home. I'll send Louise over later with some for you, and we'll get Tommy and Mike out with that message. Don't you worry about a thing.' The fire was blazing well by now. She piled logs on it. 'Shall I do the lamps, sir?'

He raised his head. 'No, indeed, I like to sit in the firelight and watch the darkness filling outside. In my London house we have electric light, but I don't take to it.'

Jenny and Louise let themselves out of the room. 'What does he want everyone here for?' Louise whispered. 'A party?'

'I would say that man's in no mood for a party,' her mother said. 'It's bad news for the valley, he said. But why he should expect everyone to come traipsing up to the Hall on a working day, I have no idea. Run and tell the boys, Louise.'

'It's bad news for the valley!' Tommy and Mike gasped out the message at the threshold of every farm and cottage, and then galloped up to the S and D stone in the Ghost Woods. 'Bad news! Bad news!' they sang out under the silent trees, and the black crows flapped wearily up from the branches.

'What d'you think it is?' Mike asked.

'It's the bloomin' Germans again,' Tommy assured him. He picked up a fallen branch and pointed it at the sky like a rifle.

'Don't be daft. War's over. It must be summat even worse.'

Next day Birchen was rich with rumour and gossip, and by ten in the morning every farmer had left his field and come down to the Hall. They stood their muddy boots at the door and came through in their socks, and their feet made wet marks like fishes on the tiles and floorboards. Miss Skinner led the children smartly out of school, and they came in a whispering trail, wondering if they were going to have the Christmas party late, and whether there would be presents. Behind them walked Madeleine, head down, lost in her own thoughts. And after her came Seth.

He hesitated in the doorway, sensing a strangeness in the Hall. He knew his way round it better than anyone; he knew the individual smells and the sounds of nearly every room. From time to time he did odd jobs of carpentry and joinery for Lord Henry, mending drawers and chairs with as much care as if he owned them himself. He was only twenty-five, but he was as skilled in carpentry as a man twice his age. He had a feel for wood that sighted men lacked, his Lordship always said, a love of the touch and smell of it.

He was very familiar with the servants' hall downstairs, where his Lordship and Lady Charlotte held the Christmas party for the village. He knew the steamy kitchen where he used to go to warm himself when he was little, when his grandmother was the cook there. She had brought him up after his parents died, and it had always seemed to him that he had two homes then: the little cottage on the hill, and the kitchens of the Hall where she spent her days. He used to listen to the servants' stories about the old man, Lord Henry's father. Him and his blessed shooting parties, Grandmother used to say, plumping dough in her floury hands, squeaking the air out of its blisters. Couldn't shoot a haystack. Blind as a bat. Well, so am I, little Seth would say, but I reckon a haystack would be a fair target for me to have a go at, if anyone would let me. Wonderful smelly spiky stacks of hay, as big as mountains when he used to scramble up them with Ben and the other children of the valley.

There was one upstairs room in the Hall that he had always loved, and that was the library. He knew as a child how to creep down the long slippery corridor that led to it, where his feet made whispering echoes. It was the oak door itself that he loved the most, not the people behind it, rumbling on over their sherries and cigars. The door was carved with all kinds of animals, and what he loved most as a little boy was to run his fingers over the raised images. The first time Lord Henry found him there Seth was seven years old, and he lifted the child up and helped him to trace all the shapes and name all the creatures, the squirrels and foxes and badgers and mice, the owls and rabbits and curlews, weasel and stoat. Seth knew them all by the sounds they made up in the Ghost Woods and the meadows and up on the heather-covered moors. He knew them by their voices and by the thud and scamper and rustle they made. He learned their names from his grandmother, and from his Lordship he learned their shapes. He used to crouch down to the bottom of the door and feel the letters of the clever man who carved them, years ago. J.Sorrel. Jacob Sorrel. Seth's ancestral grandfather.

But today Seth didn't stop to touch the creature door. There was too much tension in the air. He could hear it in Lord Henry's voice as he greeted them all. He wasn't smiling, that was what it was. His voice was strained and old. *Her Ladyship isn't here, Seth thought to himself. She hasn't been here for months, not even over Christmas. She loves the valley. She talks to me about the scents of the flowers and the murmuring of the river, and how peaceful it all is compared with her London home. And yet she hasn't been all autumn, her favourite season, and isn't here now, when his Lordship has called his 'important meeting'. It makes me uneasy.*

Seth walked on past the library, following the sound of footsteps to where the corridor widened out and the echoes changed. They were in the big drawing room. He made for the dim glow of light that told him where the window was, and turned his chair sideways, liking to feel the comforting winter sun on his face. He sat listening to the voices in the room, registering in his head the presence of the various families. Sim and Jenny Barnes. Tommy. Louise. *The twin will be here*, he thought, *but she sits in her own grieving silence. How I would love to bring comfort to her.*

I can hear Colin, with his light voice. So he's talking again, after his weeks of mourning. I hear he's good-looking, like his father, the vicar. Now there's a fine man. Poet, and a good one at that. Walks heavy on his stick now. His hip must be bad. Mrs Vicar is here too. And the farmers are all in a bunch, ruminating in a huddle by the door. I can hear Ben and his bride-to-be, Elspeth. Ben's mother, jealous, proud, sad Joan. Elspeth's brothers. Madge, her mother. Warm as toast, that woman. Warm as toast and butter. Miss Skinner the teacher. Lovely voice, she has. Fine touch on the piano. Dora Proctor from the post office shop; gossip, midwife, layer-out, baker of the finest bread in the valley, sets my stomach growling as soon as I smell it. And the three cottage families with all their noisy children. The lads from the sawmill. Gamekeeper. Ted Gilbert, the smith and gravedigger, smelling of horses and snorting like a stallion into his handkerchief. Old Susan Sorrel, my grandfather's sister. Now there's another one with secrets.

Yes, we're all here. You can start now, Lord Henry. And he does. As soon as he speaks, I can hear the strain in his voice. The old man is afraid.

12

'I'll come straight to the point,' Lord Henry said. He cleared his throat miserably. 'The Water Board has obtained permission from the government to purchase this valley.'

Behind the puzzled faces of the villagers was the great latticed window where Seth was sitting, facing sideways as if he could see out of it. The tiny diamond panes were bent with age so that the green and dun slopes of the hills beyond came through in fractured sections, like the pictures in a stained-glass window.

'What would they want to buy the valley for? There's nobbut a trickle of watter running through it.' That was Marty, the tenant of Lord Henry's biggest hill farm, brusque as ever. Enough water for a child to drown herself in, were the wounded words that hung in the air and were spoken by no one. And the thought distracted the villagers, so they did not pick up the clue that Lord Henry had dangled for them.

I must go on, Lord Henry thought to himself. *I must spell it out for them, as the church clock spells out the hour with its chimes.* 'We are within reach of four major cities. Great industrial centres, between them housing several million people. The current water supplies are inadequate.'

'So they want our piddling little river?' Marty again, red-faced. A ripple of uncertain laughter tittered round the room. 'And what about them big resivoys over the hill? Han't they took enough water already?'

'Even the great reservoirs already in existence fail to meet the demands of industry. The Water Board,' Lord Henry cleared his throat again, 'the Water Board has made a compulsory purchase of this valley.'

Silence again. A great thinking silence, into which the old grandfather clock ticked like a beating heart.

'What for?' Dora Proctor stood up, the ends of her shawl clutched tight in her fists.

You have to say it, Lord Henry thought to himself. His lips were dry, his throat ached with tightness. *You have to say the exact words, even though they know and understand, so there is no doubt and no mistake in anyone's mind. You may have to say it several times.* That was what his wife had told him before he left their London house. Even so, the words lay like dry crumbs of bread in the back of his throat. 'The intention of the Water Board is to build a reservoir here.' He clasped and unclasped his damp fingers behind his back. *My beautiful home. This paradise.* The green diamonds blurred.

'But where would they put it?' Dora demanded. Her voice was sharp and raven-harsh.

Lord Henry nodded and swallowed. Of course she understood. She was simply making it possible for him to use the right words. 'They are going to flood the whole of our valley.'

At that moment the door opened and a thin man entered. As if they were the audience of a play, still trying to understand its plot, the villagers turned to look at him, a new character, the star part, maybe. Louise started sobbing, recognising him as the man who had come in his dusty car to talk to his Lordship, whose leftover lunch she had rejoiced over so long ago. Her father took one of her hands in both of his. Someone started shouting, Dora it was, in her coarse, sharp voice. The room rumbled with the sounds of alarm, and then the sounds all fell away into a watchful, hurt silence.

'Ah,' the thin man said. 'Ah,' moving his head from side to side, his glasses flashing cold in the frosty sunlight.

'I don't trust him,' muttered Sim to his wife. Between them Louise chewed the end of her plait.

'Believe me, I have made every effort to stop this happening,' Lord Henry continued. He seemed to be pleading with them, but they were beyond listening to him. He was no longer the principal actor in the play. 'I have attended meetings with the Water Board, I have written to the Prime Minister, I have spoken to our Member of Parliament. There is no stopping it. So I have invited Mr Major from the Water Board to – to speak to you.' Lord Henry raised a limp hand by way of welcoming the visitor, then turned away as if he could no longer face the people of Birchen.

'Trust me,' the skinny visitor said. *They're a simple lot*, he thought, gazing round. *Rustics. But they'll understand*. 'I speak for every man, woman and child in this country when I say that we must have water. For our industry, for our hospitals, for our cities, for our families. We cannot survive without water. We must have it, winter and summer, in times of drought as in times of flood.'

'The spring in our back field has never let me down yet,' Marty shouted.

Mr Major ignored him. 'We need a massive container of water to feed our major northern cities. Lord Henry has made the situation quite clear to you. We have been given permission by an Act of Parliament to purchase this entire estate – the Hall, the farms and cottages that go with it.'

'You've got resivoys already, not more'n a mile from here.' Marty, red-faced, massive, rose out of his chair, big fists hanging clenched at his side. 'I were five year old when watter board started them, and what did they do? Chucked us out of our farm to mek way for them.' He stood swaying like a boulder about to topple. His wife put out a restraining hand. 'Nay, leave off,' he told her. He never took his eyes off the man from the Water Board. 'Tha can't keep doing this. Tha can't keep shifting us from our homes like tha was pushing a bunch of stock about.'

'This reservoir will be linked to the others,' Mr Major continued. 'It will be a different type, with an earthwork embankment. Not masonry, ladies and gentlemen, but soil.'

From the back of the room came a cry of anguish. Everyone turned to watch old Susan as she pushed her way out of her seat, her trembling hands gripping the chair in front.

'Remember Elder Dyke! That was an earth dam. My dad worked on that.' Her voice was hoarse and harsh with emotion. The words came through in shreds. 'Whole thing collapsed. Remember? Washed away. Everyone. Whole village. Washed away. Don't you remember? You do. You must.' She turned her head to look at the other villagers. Her face was mad with grief; she was seventeen again, a girl who had lost the man she loved; she could hardly stand up for grief and pain; her whole body was racked with that memory of grief, and all anyone could do was watch her in numbed silence, till old Jacob Proctor grunted and stuck up his hand like a child in a schoolroom. Some of the village grandparents nodded to each other and bowed their heads, at the memory of the disaster over the hill that had happened in their childhood. 'We want no more of your earth dams round here,' Susan shouted. 'You'll destroy our homes, you'll destroy our lives! You're taking everything away from us!'

Elspeth jumped up and ran to Susan and tried to coax her back into her seat, but Susan was having none of it. She pushed the girl away and hurried out, leaving her words hanging in the silence of the room like fluttering flags.

'Birchenwater will be magnificent,' said the man, as though Susan had never spoken. 'It will be an engineering triumph. Totally safe. You have my assurance that the security of the structure will be of prime importance. The core – ah, but you don't want the technical details – you have my word for it, it will be as strong as a mountain. The biggest earth dam in the British Isles. It is a great achievement. A masterpiece. After the devastations of war, we will have a symbol of rebirth.'

'But what about us?' Dora screeched.

What an unpleasant voice that woman has, Mr Major thought. *Like a cat whose tail's been trodden on.*

'What about our homes?'

'You will have new houses.' *That's stopped her squawking.* 'New houses, specially built, already under construction just two miles away, in Mr Dyson's fields.' Ben started, remembering the builders up in Dyson's rough field on the road to Hallam, remembering their scorn at the idea of living in that wild and windy place beyond the back of beyond. Nought for folks to do there if they haven't got farms. And where would the farms be? Under the water, that's where they would be. A wild terror rose up in him; he gasped aloud for breath. He clenched his fists tight in his lap, making the knuckles creak. Elspeth stole her hand across his.

The man from the Water Board boomed on. 'Houses specially built for this community, at a good rent. No more leaking roofs and damp walls. No more stink of paraffin lamps. No more outside closets and unhealthy spring water. You will have electric lights, running water on tap, and,' he paused for greater effect, 'indoor lavatories.' He let that bit sink in. 'You will have private gardens, public transport, warm, modern houses. And for the first year – they will be rent-free. The Water Board has already purchased this Hall and the cottages and lands that go with it. You have hereby received notice to quit, ladies and gentlemen.'

A startled gasp of comprehension went round the room. Mr Major continued to speak briskly over it. 'Written notice will come by letter to every household, but at his Lordship's request I made the journey from London to tell you in person. But the message is the same. Work has already begun on the Dyson site, as some of you will have noticed. Within the next eighteen months all the new houses will be completed, and you will have the opportunity to move into them. The work on the dam will be finished within five years from now, and the flooding of the valley will commence immediately on completion. And on that note, ladies and gentlemen, I declare this meeting – closed. Thank you.'

13

Susan Sorrel was sitting by the bridge when the villagers left the Hall. They gathered round her, as if by protecting its oldest inhabitant they would be able to protect the village itself. She was idly watching the troutish colours of the stream, assembling in her head the greens and white she would use if she were to paint it, the touch of red, the swish of blue. A deep nameless sense of tragedy and loss clouded her thoughts; in her mind she could not separate the idea of the two floodings that were nearly seventy years apart. Yet, watching the water, she felt strangely calm, as if she had come through a deep sleep. 'Look at the colours,' she murmured. 'The colours make the water lovely.'

Elspeth came over to her, clinging on to Ben's arm. 'You all right, Aunt Susan?' she asked. Her voice snapped the old woman home to the present, to her confused emotions. Susan glared at her.

'No, I'm not all right, and never will be.'

'We don't have to go. They can't force us,' Elspeth told her.

'They can. They'll let the water in and drown us,' muttered old Jacob Proctor. He fumbled in his pocket and brought out his pipe, still warm from before the meeting.

'Better drowned than left to grieve,' muttered Susan. She closed her eyes. She felt familiar dread washing over her like rain, her hair and her eyes and her limbs were heavy with it. 'Can't make me move, ruddy watter board. Never been a time when Sorrels haven't lived here, farmed here. Built the dry-stone walls, carved out the fields, drove sheep across the mountains. All our bones lie in the graveyard over there,' turning her white face up to Elspeth. 'Even Twinny. She's one of us. We're all related, one way or another, back in time. Inside the graveyard and outside the grave-yard lie the bones of the Sorrel family,' rocking herself as she crooned the words like a familiar childhood song. 'Lie still, lie still.'

'I wish you'd be quiet, Susan.' Dora Proctor joined her father and stood with her arms akimbo, staring down at Susan, scolding her.

'No need to look queer at me, Dora.' Susan scrambled to her feet, roughly brushing away the twigs and grasses that clung to her skirt. 'What's to be quiet about?'

'We're wanting to think about this,' Dora told her. 'You're barging into our heads like a carthorse, with your wild talk about bones. We need time and quiet to think.'

'Don't think. Don't let it happen.' Susan heard her voice catching with sobs, and put her hands over her mouth as a child might. Her nightmare was made real again, brought back into harsh daylight. She shook her head, covering her face completely now. She could almost hear the voice of the young man who had told her he loved her, long ago and as clear as yesterday. Elspeth put her arms round her, her own eyes sore with tears. Aunt Susan was strong and wise; Elspeth had never known her to break down before. She crooned gently, like a mother to a heartbroken child.

'She's very disturbed. It's only natural. I'll talk to her,' the vicar said.

'You will not talk to me. You're only an incomer. Forty years here? You know nought.' Susan whimpered into her hands.

'We'll fight it,' the vicar promised her. He spread out his hands the way he did in church, like Jesus the shepherd. But his words fell into a silence and his hands were open and empty. He let them drop limply to his sides.

'His Lordship says there's no fighting it,' said Ben, pink with sorrow. *My farm is not my own. I've no money. When it's gone, I'll have nothing. Nothing. I'll never, never be able to buy another.* 'No fighting it.' His words pittered like the beat of a toy drum, every syllable separate, falling into their thoughts. *My farm does not belong to me.*

'Then we'll speak to the King himself,' the vicar promised.

Susan laughed, strong again. 'The King himself.' She spat on the grass, and Tommy and Mike squirmed round to grin at each other. 'As if the King himself cared two hoots about old Susan Sorrel and her bones! King of England's putting his country together again.'

'That's right,' said Dora. 'Where do they think they'll get the men from, to build this thing? There's hardly any fit men left after the war.'

'They'll find 'em,' rumbled Jacob Proctor through the blue haze of his pipe smoke. 'Where there's work to be had, men'll come, fit or not.'

Elspeth looked towards the old farmhouse that was to have been her home. 'I don't understand,' she said. 'I can't take it in. What's going to happen to us?' Ben shook his head, his eyes blinking fast, holding back tears. *My big man, soft as a baby*, she thought. 'What's going to happen to our wedding now?' She thought of the white dress she was making with her mother, draped over the chairback like a cloud of lace. 'And our room, Ben, our lovely room, that will be blue like the sea. Our wedding, and our home, and our being together forever?'

He clenched her hand tightly, saying nothing. *Our farm*, he thought, desperate. *My animals. My pigs.*

If anything irritated Elspeth about Ben, it was this silence that he loved to sink into. She liked to have her questions answered instead of hanging in the air like the scraps of dusting rags that stayed out on the washing line in the rain, as if they didn't really matter. *I know what he's thinking about*, she said to herself. *He's worrying about what's going to happen to his blessed pigs, that's what.* She squeezed his hand. 'I do love you, Ben,' she said.

'Aye,' he said, his cheeks bunching up with embarrassed smiles. 'I reckon.'

'What about those new houses, up there?' Dora Proctor asked Jacob. 'Indoor lavatories, did he say?'

'Tha can keep indoor lavvies,' her father snorted. 'Who wants lavvy germs in the house?'

'Take me home, Colin. I'm weary,' said Susan suddenly. Over the past year Colin had become her favourite, since he had grown tall and good-looking. He reminded her of David, the sweetheart that she had lost. Colin took her arm and led her back to her cottage, walking in silence next to her. As they reached the gate Madeleine passed them on her own, her head bowed, and he turned to watch her.

'I'm all right now,' Susan said. She glanced at him and saw the sorrow in his young, tense face. 'Go and talk to Twinny, I can see you want to.'

'I don't know what to say,' he said helplessly.

'Go on. The longer you leave it, the harder it gets.'

Impulsively Colin left her and ran after Madeleine. She looked up at him, surprised, and then away again, hugging her arms around herself, and he walked wretchedly by her side, words flitting like birds around his thoughts. It used to be so easy, when there were three of them;

talking and laughing, joking and teasing, three best friends. Now one of his best friends was dead and the other couldn't bear even to look at him, afraid of what he might be wanting to say, afraid of crying. As soon as she reached the house she ran inside without looking back at him.

'I want to say I'm sorry,' he said aloud, when she had gone. He watched how his breath ghosted the words in the frosty air. 'It was my fault. It was all my fault. I want us to be friends again, like we used to be.' He turned away, cold and lost. 'But nothing can ever be like it used to. I can't ever be forgiven.'

Up on the hillside he could hear the rumble of digging machinery, the thud of hard earth, and the sound of it reminded him of the morning in August when he had watched Ted Gilbert turning soil in the graveyard.

14

A busload of workmen arrived from Hallam the next morning. The men were loud and eager, marching over the bridge and through the village as if it was their own. Miss Skinner paused in her dictation while they tramped through. Her face was white and tense, the skin stretched tight over the bones of her cheeks, and the children stared at her, their excitement draining away. The farmers straightened up as they carried food to their sheep in the fields; the women froze at their wells and their sinks. Louise crept her hand to the key dangling from its ribbon round her neck.

Jacob Proctor ran out of his cottage when the second busload arrived. He waved his rabbiting shotgun in the air and hurled abuse at the men, his frail voice wavering over their surprised laughter as they marched past him. Dora brought him a mug of tea and swapped his shotgun for his shepherd's crook. 'You're an old fool, Dad,' she told him. 'You've been told, there's no fighting it.'

But by the time the third bus arrived Jacob had been joined by Marty and Ted and the other farmers. They blocked the narrow bridge, and when the men took their chance on the slippery stepping stones the farmers linked arms and stood like a layered hedge on the bank. The shouting on both sides was fierce and angry but the workmen splashed their way upstream and carried on. More lorries came, and this time the workmen were deployed to build a ford to take heavy vehicles and equipment across the river. As fast as they worked, Jacob Proctor and his growing army pulled away the stones that had been dropped in to dam the water upstream. After school the children watched, jeering. Some of the wives came to help their husbands. No progress was made that day, or the next, and by the third day tempers were frayed on both sides. The farmers flung stones into the water to keep the men back.

One of the older workmen began to wade across and Jacob lifted up a stone, ready to fling it at him if he came any further. The man took no notice.

'Come back, Ely,' his mates shouted, but he waded on. He reached the village side of the river unharmed and thrust his whiskery face at Jacob.

'You're a game old bugger,' the workman said, 'but I wouldn't want to see you hurt.'

Jacob raised his arm again, brave, faltering.

'Remember me?' the workman said. 'I came to you as a homeless labourer looking for work – twenty years since now. You set me on wall-mending, remember?'

'Aye, I do,' Jacob grunted. 'Ely summat.'

'Aye, Ely summat,' the man grinned. 'I'm still a homeless labourer, just looking for a bit of work to keep me flesh on me bones. It's all I ask.'

Jacob grunted again, peering at him, raising the past out of the ageing man's features.

'You used to read the Bible every morning before we worked, remember that? Sin and hell, you used to preach at us. Sin and hell. I've never forgotten. I'm not thy friend, but I'm not thy enemy, Jacob Proctor. I'm a jobbing worker, that's all. I own the clothes I stand up in, and that's all I need in life. And my pride. There's nought sinful in that. But if you hurt any of us with your stone-throwing, or any of us hurts any of you, I'm

106

telling you, it'll be your fault, and you'll burn in hell for evermore.'

Jacob let the stone slide out of his hand. All his courage failed him at the thought of meeting the Devil himself. He turned away, flapping his hands at his sides, and the other farmers watched him, curious, uncertain what to do. The workers moved across and silently carried on with their job.

'Come on,' Marty said. 'Reckon some of 'em have got real jobs to do.'

Before the month was over, Marty left the valley to take on his sick brother's farm up at Crook Hill, some ten miles away from Lord Henry's estate. He drove his sheep over the tops and came back to load up the farm carts with beds, tables, chairs and children. They trundled away without saying goodbye to anyone.

'Rats deserting a sinking ship,' Jacob Proctor growled. He and Lord Henry's gamekeeper were sitting on the bench outside Dora's post office shop.

'Don't blame Marty,' said the gamekeeper. 'I don't blame him one bit. He's the lucky one. He'll have a farm of his own now. It won't be easy, but he'll still be doing what he knows best. I love my life here. All I ever want is to be up on the moors, just me and my dog. It's all I ask, and I reckon Marty's made the same way. I'd die before they turn me into a townie, Jacob.'

'If we stick together we can still fight it.'

'There's no fighting it, you old fool. What you going to do, line 'em up and shoot 'em with your airgun?'

And burn in hell for it. Jacob blurred his lips and sank into silence.

By nightfall a dozen navvies had moved into Marty's farmhouse. Huts were put up in the fields where his sheep used to graze the hillside, for more workers. All day long, lorries clattered over the new ford and through the village. Next morning the gamekeeper was seen striding up to the tops with his dog at his heels and a knapsack on his back containing his grandfather's sheep shears, off to try his luck as a farmhand in some other valley, or to join a shearing gang next summer, working its way round the country. His cottage was taken over immediately.

A spur of rail track was run from the main line over at Joansford to carry stones from the local quarries, and clay from the moors around Joansford. The trucks clattered backwards and forwards, backwards and forwards, and the hills echoed with the noise of it all. Soon work began on a six-foot-wide trench like an open wound that was being dug right across the valley, and the children of the village watched it happen, full of excitement and curiosity. Most of the older villagers kept away. It was as if, by ignoring the progress of the destruction of their valley, they were telling themselves that it wasn't really happening. In the same way, the navvies kept away from the village. They had their own supplies brought in on the buses with the men from Hallam; they went home at night on the bus or up to their huts and barns. They were a separate community, and to the villagers it was an enemy camp.

But old Susan Sorrel took herself off to the site every day, shouting at the workmen to go away, to leave the valley in peace. Sometimes they laughed at her. Sometimes one of the younger men, the dark-haired boy from the little caravan, would come over and offer to take her back to her cottage.

'You don't want to stand out here,' he would say to her. 'It's no place for a lady to be.'

Then her anger would melt and she would make her voice weak and helpless, pleading with the workmen to be quiet. 'Don't wake the baby,' she would beg, wringing her hands together. 'Let the little one sleep.'

The village children turned their wondering faces up to her, not knowing her in her strange new madness. And sometimes she told the men to be careful, to be very careful, they would be the first to drown when the waters came. And then, just as suddenly, she was herself again, marvelling at the rich colours of the deep-turned earth, and at the lines of hefty men working together, their cheeks bright with effort and laughter; at the primitive shape of bony gantries with their long, awkward necks. She would hurry home for her pencils and paper and get Colin to carry her stool down so she could perch close by and draw. And Colin would stand by her, narrowing his eyes, watching the men keenly. The boy from the caravan smiled and waved to him once, and instinctively Colin lifted his hand to return the greeting, then turned sharply away and went back to his lonely studies.

Every week Jenny and Madge let themselves into the Hall and walked round the rooms, checking things out of habit. There was little dust to flick away, and the tapestries and curtains remained just so, the plates stacked in the kitchens, the linen stored in the cupboards. The pink-and-rose counterpane on Lady Charlotte's four-poster bed was turned back, ready for her to slip into at any minute. Then one day, Jenny, Sim, Madge and several more who had been employed by Lord Henry received letters to say that the Hall was being closed down. A removal firm would be arriving, and they were asked to supervise the removal of the curtains, carpets, paintings, ornaments and furniture. They would be paid well for this task and, after that, their salaries would cease. Lord Henry's secretary said he was very sorry.

Madge wept as she folded the fine curtains and bed linen for the last time. 'I'll never have the chance to touch anything so beautiful again,' she said. She looked round at the carved oak panels on the walls. 'I love this place, I do. I love every room like as if it was my own. I can't believe it's all to go under the water,' she sighed. 'It's a sin, it is that.'

'And that lovely library door, with all the animals carved on it,' Jenny Barnes said. 'They can't just let that rot.'

'Seth should have it. He loved it so much. Remember how he used to creep up here and stroke it, when he was a child? It's his by rights. It's a Sorrel door.'

'And where would he keep it, in that little house up on Dyson's Fields?' Sim Barnes laughed when they told him. 'It'd never even pass through one of those doorways.'

When the removal men had finished their job and all the fine furniture and carpets and curtains had been removed, the carved door creaked on its hinges and dust settled on the reliefs. The rooms stood bare. The voices of the women swirled round the corridors and up the wide staircase as if the building had become a cathedral. Louise went with her mother round the Hall, her footsteps echoing as she tiptoed from room to room, touching the marble fireplaces, the panelled walls, the crazed windows. She named them all in her red notebook, as if that would keep them safe, like a spell. And at last there came the sound of the key turning in the lock of the studded front door and then, silence.

15

At the end of February, the snows came in a swirling blizzard, as if someone was pulling a curtain across the valley.

It's snowing, Grace. From her window Madeleine watched the first fall of the year. She breathed on the glass and rubbed away a patch with her sleeve, and the snow huffed against it like white moths searching for a way in. She watched their slow and steady dancing, mesmerised, entranced. She eased up her window and held out her hands, watching how for a second the crystals kept their exquisite shape before they dissolved, and more came, and still more.

How beautiful it is. Look how the snowflakes fall and fall. Usually I know when it's going to snow, when the sky goes as yellow as old cream, or I can smell it, like Mum can. Or shiver like Aunt Madge and say it's too cold yet. Too cold for snow. But this time the snow just sneaked up on us. And I knew, as soon as I woke up. I could hear the silence, as if the world had stopped breathing. And now look, look at the new white world. Everything is different. Our beautiful tree is cast in a shroud, as if one of the monks' ghosts has walked down from the woods and frozen in the night. And the lawn is like a calm, white cloud. No one's been out on it yet. We could be the first, like we always used to be. Come with me, Grace. Touch the ghost tree.

She turned, and there was her sister standing next to her, as clear as life. Yes. Yes. And Madeleine laughed with joy.

She opened the window fully and slid out on to the shed roof. Her bare feet plunged into the soft chill of the snow, and she gasped with the shock and pain of it. She jumped down and landed knee deep where it had drifted against the wall. *Run with me. Run with me.* She saw herself skimming across the snow like a bird skimming across a frozen pond, her sister laughing beside her, the two of them turned to white geese with their wings outstretched, lifting up, soaring into the grey sky towards the sun that was as pale as lemons. *Fly, Grace. Fly with me!* She spread out her arms and lunged clumsily from side to side, dragging her numb feet, her nightdress clinging damply round her knees, hauling her down. The flakes of snow drifted into her mouth and her hair and the neck of her gown, into her eyes, blinding her, piercing her like shards of glass. *Cold, cold, we're so cold.* But they must reach the tree. *I'm here with you. Stay with me. Stay close.* She fell forwards, and the soft down of snowflakes covered her. *Touch the tree. Touch the tree. Yes, yes, touch the tree.*

'I've not lost one child. I've lost two,' Jenny Barnes said, when Sim carried Madeleine into the house later that morning. The girl's lips were blue, her cheeks as white as wax. Sim rolled Madeleine in a blanket and laid her on the patched settee in front of the fire. Jenny rubbed her daughter's hands and feet, chafing life back into them while Sim built up the fire, his fingers trembling, his mouth open wide with soundless sobs. Louise and Tommy watched, solemn and afraid. At last Madeleine opened her eyes and stared round the room as if she couldn't believe where she was.

'You've not lost her, Mum,' Louise told her. 'She's woken up.'

'It's not what I mean,' Jenny sobbed, all her strength gone from her now. 'Oh, don't stand there. Fetch your Auntie Madge.'

Louise put on her boots and ran round to Elspeth's house. Madge came immediately, full of bustle and comfort. She coaxed Madeleine to sit up, talking to her all the time, rubbing her cheeks to bring back the colour, enveloping her in her own warmth.

'You daft little sparrow, we nearly lost you then,' Madge said, kissing her. She ladled porridge out of the porringer over the fire and handed the bowl to her sister.

'Feed her,' she said. 'She's your child, Jenny.'

Jenny spooned porridge little by little into her daughter's mouth as if she was a baby. And when she had eaten, Madeleine lay back and fell into a natural sleep. Jenny tucked the blankets round her and smoothed the damp hair away from her face.

'I don't know what to do with her,' she said. 'We're just about getting on with things, me and Sim. We have to, for Louise and Tommy. Keep busy, we tell ourselves. Keep going. But this one's closed herself up completely, and there's no getting back to her.'

'It's natural, her grief,' said Madge. 'We can't ever understand how close they was, those two. It's like they were one person. When they were little they had a language of their own, do you remember that? It made no sense to anyone else, but they talked to each other for hours.'

'Or sometimes they didn't even need to talk, not with words. A look would say everything. They just understood each other. They were like reflections; what one did, the other did.'

'How can we even begin to imagine what it was like to be them, and what it's like for her, now? They've never been apart. I remember them in their cot, Jen. Just lying there, looking at each other, knowing each other like no one else knew them. They belonged to each other.'

Jenny stroked Madeleine's hand. 'Before they were born they warred in my belly like a couple of armies. I didn't know I was having twins, but I might have guessed. But soon as they come out, they was all to each other, like they were one child. One child with two bodies. It was all I could do to tell them apart, and I still look at her sometimes and think, no, this one's Madeleine, not Grace. And then I think, don't be daft, course it's Grace! How can a mother not know her own daughter! And at least I have one of them. At least I have Grace, that's what everyone says to me. But I haven't, Madge. I've lost them both.'

'Give her time,' Madge said. 'She'll come back to you.'

'I don't believe that. I believe I've lost her forever. She's a stranger in my house. Maddy's still with me I can sit by her grave, I can put flowers there, I can talk to her.' And then she stopped. 'Oh, Madge. And what will happen to the grave, when they flood the valley? Will I lose that too?'

She went over to the window. Through the ceaseless dance of the blizzard she could see the churchyard. *My child is asleep under the snow*, she thought. *But the other one – this other one walks the frozen earth like a restless ghost.*

16

Soon the great new scar in the earth was covered over as if it had never been. The men retreated to their homes in Hallam and further afield. There could be no more work done until the snows had gone. Up on the hillside only the little caravan remained. Day after day the feathers of snow drifted down and down, and then froze hard. Sheep, rabbits, hares all lay dead in the snow. The warmest place around was the sawmill, heated by coal, but soon supplies ran out, and even the mill fell into silence. There could be no more deliveries to the valley; the snow was too deep. A supply of coal was tipped up on the steep hill before the descent from Manchester, miles away. The farmers set off at three in the morning, slithering on the packed ice of the moon-white tracks, and fetched the coal down in a convoy of horses and carts. They had Jacob Proctor's chain horse tied behind to pull the load up the steeper hills. They dumped the coal on the packhorse bridge and the villagers came out with buckets to carry their own supplies to the cottages. It was broad daylight by then, one of those brilliant blue days when the hills were dazzling with snow. Weary, the men trudged back to their cottages, the sun bright in their eyes.

Jacob led his chain horse back to the barn and rubbed liniment on its strained tendons, then on his own rheumaticky shins.

'It'll be better for you, up in those houses at Dyson's Fields,' Dora told him. 'You're not a young man, Dad.'

'Bah!' her father snorted. 'Tha's turned traitor, Dora Proctor, and all for the promise of an indoor lavvy.' He stomped back into the snow to help Colin with the last of the shovelling.

The boy from the caravan was coming down the track, head bowed against the brilliance of the sunlight. He had long, wavy black hair tied back with a piece of string, and under his old army jacket he wore a brightly coloured shirt which was open at the neck. The villagers watched him through their windows as he trudged towards the cottages. Ben's mother made the excuse to go outside and stoke up the fire against the wall, where she had a plum pudding boiling in its big pan for the coal shifters. She stood warming herself by the welcome heat, watching the coming of the stranger.

Colin and Jacob were standing together by the bridge, shovelling up the last of the coal to carry over to Susan's cottage. Jacob squinted across at the approaching figure. 'One of them bloody navvies,' he muttered. 'He's having none of this coal, mind. It's spoken for.' He kept his face turned away as the young man approached him. Colin stayed where he was, his eyes cast down, shifting a wedge of snow with his boot, one way, back again.

'Any shops here?' the youth shouted.

'No,' Jacob answered, without turning.

'There's the post office,' Colin said to Jacob.

'That's for villagers,' said Jacob. 'Not strangers.' He trudged away, head down, into his cottage, and closed the door.

'So where's the nearest shop?' the youth asked. 'There's no food for me and Ely now the bus has stopped running. We're the only ones left up there. We've nowhere else to go, neither of us.'

Colin paused. He was conscious of the watching eyes through the windows, and knew

121

how far his voice and the stranger's would carry. There was no other sound in the valley; even the stream was hushed into frozen silence. 'You'll have to go to Hallam, if you can get through. There'll be no fresh supplies here till the snow's gone.' He knew him from the team working on the trench, the only one that Aunt Susan would speak to. The boy was a couple of years older than Colin was, perhaps nineteen or twenty, but he had the build of a strong man. He smiled at Colin now, expecting friendship.

'You farmers must have stuff tucked away. We can pay for it.'

'I'm not a farmer. I'm Colin Hemsley, the vicar's son.'

'Oh aye?' The young man hugged up the collar of his coat. 'All right, vicar's son. Thanks for your holy charity. If you find a spare meatloaf in your larder I'll pay you well for it. Oliver, my name is. I reckon you know where to find me.'

Colin watched him as he trudged away again. He should call him back and invite him to the vicarage, he knew that. His mother would ask him in, stranger or not, invader or not, and send him back with something from the larder. He had only to shout 'Oliver', and the youth would turn back.

Even now he could follow him and bring him down to the vicarage. He wanted to speak to him again, perhaps even to get to know him. He was fascinated by his manner, his strong good looks, his confidence with strangers. He had never met anyone quite like him. The nearest to his age in the valley was Ben, and he was a grown man now, about to be married. And then there was Seth, locked into his dark, strange world, needing nobody, it seemed. He was seven years older than Colin anyway. And three young men from Birchen sawmill who had been killed in the war.

Colin had never really befriended any of them. He had only ever joined the village children for church services. His only real friends had always been Grace and Madeleine. He felt drawn towards Oliver, wanting to know more about him, about the odd way of life that would bring him to an unknown place to work for a while and, when the work was done, to leave. *How much of the country does he know?* he wondered. *How much of life?*

I'd like to step up the hill and sit with him when the men hunker down outside their shacks of a night, he thought. *I'd like to share a drink and listen to their tales. I'd like to be doing what they're doing, a heap of men and lads all together, all working on this massive job. And when the great machinery rumbles in, like the tanks of war, what a thing that'll be! When they've built the dam walls and the water gushes in and fills the whole of this valley; what a pride they'll have! And when they pack up their bags and turn their backs on the valley, I'd like to go with them. What's to keep me here, with Madeleine dead and Grace closed up like a fist against me?*

But these were secret, traitor thoughts, and Colin shared them with no one. His destiny was mapped out; as soon as he was old enough he would be sent to theological college. His father had decided that for him before he was born. He would never be free, like Oliver. He would never get the chance to know any other kind of life. Yet here was his opportunity to talk to Oliver at least, to talk to someone from outside the valley, from outside his own life. He could take something up there tonight. A couple of loaves, some cheese and stuff. No one need know.

Then he noticed Madeleine coming down across the fields, stumbling on the fresh snow. He was surprised to see her away from her house after her accident in the snow. He watched as she passed close to the stranger, hardly aware of him. She walked with her hands deep in her pockets, head down. On the packhorse bridge Oliver stopped. 'Hey, Beauty!' he called, a smile of recognition on his face. For a brief moment Madeleine paused and looked across at him.

The words chimed, bringing unwonted to Colin the memory of the chase, the laughing rush down the mountainside, the tricks and teasing of the girls' laughter, the way one of the girls had danced around Seth, the way the other had careered down to the river, and faltered, arms flung out for balance, on the brink of the stepping stones. He shook his head and, like a flake of snow, the memory skittered away.

Oliver and Madeleine looked at each other as if they were about to speak, and then she bowed her head again and went on her way. But for a time Oliver stood with his hands in his pockets, watching her, smiling, until she reached her cottage door. Colin felt a rush of anger and something else that he couldn't quite understand, an emotion that he had never known before. He realised then that it was jealousy.

17

At last the thaw came, and with it the navvies began to return to their huts and barns. Rapidly the temperature changed, and overnight the melted snows cascaded in streams down to the river, waking everyone in the village, so still had the silence been for weeks. Madeleine opened her eyes and smiled at the sound of the water. She could hear Grace's voice in it, singing. In her creaking bed, Elspeth woke up, briefly alarmed. 'It's happening!' Then she pulled her bedcovers round herself. 'Not yet,' she murmured. 'Quite safe.'

Old Aunt Susan lay listening to the gush of water, half awake and half asleep, imagining a great tide surging down the hills and swamping the valley; and the river rising like a beast, shouldering its way through the cottages, bursting through the doors and windows, bringing the thick stone walls crashing down with its unbearable strength. In terror she leaped from her bed and looked out of the window. The sound of the water's rush was everywhere. She pulled on her coat and boots and stumbled up the slippery hillside to Marty's old farm.

'I'm not leaving here,' Susan shrieked to the dark, sleeping barns. 'You've come to do your filthy work, but you'll not shift me.' *Trying to drown us all, that's what they've come for.* 'Get off with you, all of you.' *And they jeer at me. They laugh at my bones. They laugh at my voice gone weak with the years. What do they care! It's work for them.* 'There's a baby sleeping!' she shouted. 'Don't you care about that?'

She scrabbled in the watery snow and picked up a handful of wet pebbles, flinging them feebly against the wall of one of the barns.

'Once upon a time I was a lovely young girl, able and strong,' she crooned, scraping up more pebbles. *Ah, you would have taken notice of me then, when the world was as young as I was. But you just laugh at me. Go home, old woman, you say. Go back to your bed and keep yourself warm. All you do is laugh and turn your broad backs on me. I would burn your huts if I could. I would*

*fling stones on your roofs to deafen your dreams,
but I've no more strength than a child. My stones
drop short, while you snore in your beds.*

Oliver came out of his caravan, yawning,
scratching his head. 'Is that Susan again?' he
called. It wasn't the first time Susan had broken
his sleep like this. He pulled on his old army jacket
and boots and trudged towards her. She stared at
him, bewildered now, not knowing any more why
she was standing outside Marty's barns with the
cold night winds whipping round her, up to her
ankles in slushy snow.

'Are you David?' she whispered, memory
starting up in her like a startled bird.

'Not David. Oliver.'

'I am alone with the wild dark hills around me,
until the white ghosts come and lead me to my
bed,' she sang, making a lullaby of it, her voice
sweet as a child's.

A head poked out of the window of the van. 'Is
it that old witch again?'

'I'll see to her,' Oliver called. 'Get back to sleep,
Ely. It's thawing fast; we might be back on the job
today.' He turned back to Susan and took her
arm. 'Come on, gently does it. It's slippier than
ever, now it's thawing.'

She leaned against him, all her wrath spent, old and tired and bewildered. She could see now that this young man wasn't David. David was a long time ago.

Oliver took a stone from her fist and dropped it on the ground. 'It's no good shouting at us. I keep telling you that.'

'They don't care,' she muttered.

'No, they don't care. Why should they? It's a job of work to us. When this job's done we'll pack our bags and load up our vans and donkeys and be off somewhere else, building roads and bridges and the like.'

'Your donkeys screech too much. Know how to stop that, don't you?' She lowered her voice, like a child whispering a secret. 'Tie stones to their tails, that'll stop 'em. You know nought, you men.'

They trudged on in silence until they came to the barns of the village farms.

'They'll be lambing soon. The year won't stop while there's this carry-on,' she muttered. 'Wet weather like this can kill newborn lambs within minutes.'

Oliver took her right to the door of her cottage. 'Will you be all right now?'

'It's the baby I worry about.' She turned her white face up to him. 'Who's to see to it?'

'Don't you worry. It'll all be taken care of.' Oliver pushed open the door for her and went back up to his caravan. A grey dawn was just beginning to break.

Susan stood listening to the hiss and drip of the thaw outside her window, and at last she knew it for what it was. Gradually the pounding of her heart slowed down and her fuzzy senses began to clear. She made herself some tea and sat nursing the hot cup in her hands, warming herself. 'They'll be laughing at you, Susan,' she chuckled. 'Keep your head screwed on, girl, or they'll be locking you up. "All she can talk about is bones and babies," they'll be saying. I heard you, Susan Sorrel. Keep your trap shut, girl.'

She looked round her room. It seemed to belong to somebody else these days. It was messy and dirty; her nightclothes were in a heap by the dead fire where she had stepped out of them, her dishes unwashed on the table. All her sketches had been shoved together in an untidy pile. A paint-brush lay next to the tin plate she used as a palette, little dried-up patches of paint crunchy round the rim, and the bristles of the brush gone hard and useless. 'Somebody else lives here now,' she said. She looked down at her scrawny arms with their dry, hanging skin. She shook her head. 'Somebody else lives here, girl. Not you.'

18

Work on the reservoir intensified after the thaw. Soon new workers were swarming over the valley, knocking on doors to ask for lodgings. They were met with blank hostility. Dora Proctor was the first to offer to take them in. She told the foreman that she would open up the barns for a dozen men, once the lambing was done.

'You'll do no such thing!' her father shouted, his weak voice shaking with anger. 'You're a traitor in our midst, Dora Proctor. I'll sleep in the barn myself before I'd let them in. Besides, I'll need the sheds for hay next summer.'

'What's the point of making hay?' she asked him. 'We'll have no beasts by the time we move up to Dyson's Fields. Use your sense, Dad. This is good money. We'll need carpets and such when we move up there. I'm not taking any of this old stuff with me. It can drown with the house.'

'I'm not giving up so fast.'

'You and your pride. Don't be so stubborn. There's no giving up to do. It's done.'

Another farmer, Gilbert the valley butcher, decided to move to another valley, where his sheep had overwintered on a cousin's farm. As soon as he moved out, his house, his barns, his sheds, were all taken over by workmen.

Madge brought two workmen into her disused cowshed. 'You could have a mattress on the floor,' she told them, sorrowing for them. 'We need the money,' she said defensively, as Elspeth stared at her. 'What do you think we're living on, now my job at the Hall's gone? Jenny and Sim will have to do the same, if there's any sense in them. Besides,' she risked a smile, 'it's a bit of life, isn't it? A bit of the outside world.'

A van trundled over from Joansford every week with supplies of fresh meat and vegetables, and Madge and the smith's wife took to waving it down when it reached the packhorse bridge and taking their pick of the goods before the workmen's cook came down. Dora made an arrangement with the van to bring her fresh stuff for the post office shop. It saved her the weekly visit in her father's trap to Hallam market. She thought it was a wonderful thing. Jenny refused to visit the van herself, but sent Louise to buy fresh greens. After all, there would be nothing more coming from the kitchen garden at the Hall. Louise stood on tiptoe, peering in at the display of brightly coloured fruits and vegetables, cheeses and meats at the back of the van, marvelling that there could be so much to choose from. The van driver gave her an orange and she clutched it in both hands, wondering whether she was supposed to bite into the shiny, pocked skin.

'Traitors!' Susan shouted at them from her window.

'Traitors or not,' replied Madge, 'you tucked into that steak and kidney pie Elspeth brought round for you. Where d'you think I bought the meat from, now our butcher's gone?'

'There's nought to be done about it,' said Dora. 'We might as well accept it now and make our plans. Actually, if you ask me, it's for the good.' She had already been up to the Dyson's Fields site to watch the progress of the building there, and had picked the bungalow she would be moving into. 'Dad thinks it's the end of the world, but look at him. His farming days are over, and he's got to admit it. He's too stiff to climb the knoll now, nearly too stiff to climb his own stairs. It's a blessing, this.'

'The enemy is in our midst,' hissed Susan, but Dora laughed and phoned an order to Joansford for more supplies to be sent to her shop.

'Wait till you see those houses up there,' she said to Madge. 'I can't believe you haven't been up to have a look yet. Lovely big windows they've got, to let in the light and the sunshine. I'll be happy to go. I'm sick of this dark little hole now.'

'It'll be nice to be near the station,' Madge agreed. 'I like the idea of being able to pop into town when I feel like it.'

'Dora's going to live in a buggaline,' Tommy told his parents that evening. His chin was red and sore from sucking the half-orange that his mother had cut for him. Louise was still eating her half, tipping her head back and squeezing the juice into her mouth.

'Bungalow,' she corrected him. 'It's a house without an upstairs.'

Tommy stared at her in disbelief, juice dribbling down his neck.

'I can't wait to go up there,' her father said unexpectedly. He looked defiantly at his wife, expecting her to protest. She said nothing. Her thoughts went to the grave in the churchyard, golden now with wild primroses. What was to hold her here, when there was no grave to visit, when the church itself was at the bottom of a lake?

'There's transport to Eccles and Hallam from up there,' Sim went on. 'It's only a couple of miles down to the railway station at Joansford. I can find work again. I can't wait to go, Jenny. We're in limbo here. What am I doing, planning on feeding the rose bushes up at the Hall, mowing and rolling the lawns like carpets, when they'll soon be under the water? What's the point of it all?'

'I've never loved this house since Maddy died,' Jenny Barnes said at last. 'I hear her and see her in every room. The house will never be right for me.' Her eyes brimmed with grief. 'I think you're right, Sim. We need to start again.'

Madeleine held herself so silent on the stairs that neither of her parents knew she was there until they heard her running back to her bedroom. There was her sister sitting on the bed, smiling just so, just right; and in the same second she was gone. Madeleine closed the door and stood with her back pressed against it, refusing to let her mother in. 'I won't go!' she shouted. 'You can't make me go!'

I won't go, Grace. How can I leave you here, cold and alone and drifting and wandering? We belong together. I promise you. I won't go.

19

In late spring a man from the Hallam newspaper came to the village. It was a hot day but he was wearing a tight suit and tie, and a bowler hat. He parked his car at the end of the lane and stood on the packhorse bridge, watched furtively by every child in the school. He gazed round, taking in the Hall, which was reflected in a perfect image of itself in the little lake in front of it. He fished in his pocket and brought out a pad and pencil, and looked thoughtfully at the post office shop. Its porch was heavy already with clematis. Dora's bike was leaning against the wall, and all the windows were open to let in the sweet air. He turned from side to side, noting the bridge, the church, the vicarage, the mill, farmhouses and cottages. And then, beyond them, the stretch of the green valley, and the lambs springing and racing together in the fields. His eyes followed the line of the hills as they swept round to embrace the whole valley. He turned back to the Hall again, noting every mullioned window, every stone and lintel, as carefully as if he was drawing it. The children and teacher watched him in silent fascination. When at last he came towards the school and knocked at the door there was a thrill of excitement. Miss Skinner nodded at Louise to let him in.

'I'm from the *Hallam Gazette*. I'd like to talk to your teacher,' the man said, lifting his hat to her like a real gentleman would to a lady. 'And some of you children as well, if I may.'

The children bobbed their hands in the air, full of importance. 'First, first, baggy be first!' Tommy begged.

'You don't even know what the gentleman wants to ask you,' Miss Skinner said. 'But I expect it's about the reservoir.'

'It is,' the reporter said. He brought his notebook out again, and at that moment Louise decided that she was going to be a reporter when she grew up. She pulled her red notebook out of her pocket and unlocked it and smoothed it open. Report on the resevoy, she wrote. Tommy tried to see what she was writing and she cupped her hand round the page.

'What do you think about it, Miss Skinner?' she scribbled, copying the words of the reporter.

'It will not affect the children,' Miss Skinner said. 'Their education will not suffer in any way.'

Louise stopped writing and stared at the teacher. She hadn't thought about what would happen to the school before. What would they all do? She closed her eyes and tried to imagine the water rising over the desktops, papers bobbing like the white ducks on the Hall pond, books reduced to pulp, children clutching their pencils and floating, brown water swilling round them; and Miss Skinner swimming up and down, chanting tables, reciting the alphabet, telling from memory their favourite story of the Pied Piper of Hamelin. Her black gown would billow round her, her hair would drift like river weeds.

'It has been arranged that the children will go to the school in Joansford,' Miss Skinner said. 'And I,' she turned her head away, gazing out of the window, 'I will retire.'

'I see.' The newspaperman nodded, frowning as if this was the wrong answer to a test. 'But how do you *feel* about it, Miss Skinner?'

The teacher didn't answer.

'I see,' he said again. He tapped his pencil on his notebook, and Louise did the same. 'So what are your feelings,' he went on, 'about the plans for that magnificent Hall?'

'Perhaps you would care to tell us what the plans are.' Miss Skinner smiled a strange, cold smile at him. 'You're the newsman.'

He cleared his throat. 'I thought you would know. When Lord Henry sold the Hall to the Water Board—'

'Excuse me, Lord Henry never agreed to sell the Hall. It was a compulsory purchase,' Miss Skinner interrupted him. 'It broke the poor man's heart.'

The children exchanged glances. Tommy pulled a face at Louise and she whispered to him, 'His Lordship was forced to sell the Hall, along with all the farms and cottages belonging to his estate. Everybody knows that! He even appealed to Parliament.'

The reporter bowed his head to Miss Skinner, just slightly. 'Of course.'

'It might have helped if your newspaper had taken up the matter at the time. It's rather late now.' Miss Skinner's voice was tight and strained. The children looked at each other anxiously. Was their teacher going to cry?

141

'The purchase of the valley is not news, I'm afraid. The news is that the Water Board is now selling the Hall to a wealthy American. He is planning to have it taken down, stone by stone, and to rebuild it elsewhere.'

IMPORTANT NEWS! Louise wrote into the amazed silence. Her hand was shaking. The Hall is to be saved.

After the man from the newspaper had gone, his car backfiring like a gun all the way up the hill, Miss Skinner let the children go home early, which was something that had never happened before in anyone's lifetime. 'I have a headache,' she told them. She went back to her cottage up the track from the school and drew her curtains, so she could not see the children clambering over the gates of the Hall, swarming up the steps, dancing a wild and freakish jig across the lawns, skimming stones across the lake.

Jenny Barnes was sowing beans in her garden, and looked up, frowning, when she heard the shrieking voices of the children. She and Sim ran up the track at once to see why they had been let out of school early and allowed to run wild round the gardens of the Hall. When Louise ran to them and told them the news they turned away, amazed, lost in thought.

'The Hall is to be saved!' Jenny shook her head in disbelief.

'The whole thing's mad, but this is the maddest part of it,' said Sim.

'I don't know what to think, Sim. Excited, like the children? Moving the Hall! What an idea! It's a wonderful thought, really. That old Hall is so lovely, it's so special. I've worked there all my life, since I was no older than Louise. Yes, it's right it should be saved.'

She folded her arms and looked away from the Hall to the houses on the other side of the bridge. 'But I feel angry that someone with money can just pluck it away, just like that, like it was a rosy apple on a tree. It's our Hall, Sim. And I'm sad too. It makes it all real somehow. We're going to lose our valley. We're going to lose our homes. But if they can move the Hall, why can't they move the houses too? The whole village could be saved!' She felt slightly hysterical. She wanted to run like the children, scampering over the mossy stones, screaming and laughing, trying to make sense of it all.

'That Hall belongs here. It won't be Birchen Hall anywhere else. It can't ever be the same, no matter where they put it. And if they moved every stone of every house and built it all up again, they couldn't give us back what we're losing. This!' Sim dug his heel into the ground. 'This soil. This valley. We can live anywhere and make our home, Jenny. Stones don't make a home. But if we can't have this valley, we have to let go and start again. And you've said yourself, it's better for us to move away from it.' He moved over to his wife, wanting then to put his arms round her and hold her to him; too shy, here in this public place. 'We can't drag the past with us.'

'I suppose you're right,' she agreed. 'I know you're right.'

'It'll be better for Grace, too, when we go.'

'It'll tear her in half.'

'There's time. By the time the houses up there are ready for us to move into, she'll be ready to come with us. Be patient.'

20

When the children ran screaming out of the school, Madeleine was climbing up the steep bank towards the Ghost Woods. Today was her sixteenth birthday. It was the most painful of all days. That morning she had looked in the mirror and seen Grace, surely Grace. 'Happy Birthday,' she whispered, 'my other self.' *I knew you before you were born, when we swam together in the darkness. I'm still with you.*

Downstairs her father was raking the ashes in the hearth. Dusty as his hands were, he had cupped them round her face and searched her eyes for some glimmer of light. 'After today, things will get better,' he said, and she had held her face still, like a doll, till he dropped his hands away and went back to his task.

After today there is another today, and another, and another. What does he mean, things will get better? You'll still be gone.

Already the outer trees of the Ghost Woods had been torn down by the navvies, leaving ugly gashes in the earth. In no time at all they would all be gone, but just now the ground between the old silver birch trees was a purple mist of bluebells. The woods seemed fuller than they had ever been, as if they knew they were maybe putting on their final show. Madeleine kneeled down among them, breathing in the sweet, fragile scent, cupping them to her face so her hair fell forwards like a veil. After a time she sat back on her heels, and knew that someone was watching her. She sensed who it was. He had watched her before, many times. Usually she ignored him, but not in the hostile, silent way the other villagers ignored the workmen. It was simply that most of the time she didn't take in his presence, any more than she took in the presence of people who were close to her. Figures were ghosts around her, and some were meaningful because she had known them all her life, and others were strangers. They floated in and out of her days, all of them, interfering with her conversations with her sister.

He was leaning against one of the birch trees behind her, his hand pressed against the bark. Without looking up, she said, 'I know you're watching me.' It was the first time for months that she had spoken directly to anyone, instead of keeping silent or simply answering their questions. She had no idea why she spoke then, and involuntarily she began to lift her hand, as if she had betrayed herself into an act of disloyalty.

He ducked his head, smiling. She was like a timid squirrel or hare; a sharp movement would startle her away. 'Hey, Beauty. Just wondered what your name is.'

She lowered her hand, still not looking at him; staring in front of her, wondering. 'Why?'

'So I can give you a name when I think about you.'

She drew in her breath. 'Why should you think about me?'

'I think about you all the time.' He put his hands in his pockets, scuffing the leaves under his boots. It's true, he thought. Even though I've never seen her close to before, I've been thinking about her all the time, since that first day I came to the valley and saw her by the stepping stones. He would like to reel in that moment and take the chance that he had not taken then. Instead of calling to her and going on his way as he had done then, he wished he had gone over to her, held out his hand to help her across the stones. She had been running and laughing, chased by someone. A village boy, perhaps? Had the boy caught her and held her in his arms?

Oliver cleared his throat, conscious that he was probably making a fool of himself. 'Don't you ever think about people who aren't here?'

'Yes, I do.'

He waited for her to say more. She bent down again, plucking bluebells, studying each flower before she pulled it.

'They don't like being picked. They'll die soon,' he told her.

'I know that. I want them just for a while.'

'Will you come up again tomorrow to pick more?'

She said nothing. He walked round to her and she stood up immediately and began to walk away.

'You didn't tell me your name,' he called. 'I'm Oliver.'

She didn't look back.

She's a strange one, he thought. *A beautiful strange one*.

He shrugged and went back to his work. The men who had been working near him thought he had gone into the woods to relieve himself, but

Ely, whose job was to fill the donkey cart with stones, nudged him and winked. 'Don't do to be friendly with the natives,' he warned. His breath was hot and stank of tea. 'They don't like us, Ollie. They'd do us harm if they could, most of 'em.'

Oliver laughed. Old Ely treated him like he was his own son since he had moved into the tiny caravan with him. 'Keep yourself to yourself, that's the only way to manage when you live the way we do, jobbing. Never give up your independence, not for no one.'

But Ely was an old man and had been a loner all his life. That was the way Oliver wanted to be, before he met the strange, sad girl from the valley.

'What's her name?' Ely asked, opening his spiky teeth to grin at him.

'Beauty,' Oliver grinned back.

Madeleine walked slowly down the hill. Oliver. Why had she let him talk to her? 'Will you come again tomorrow?' he had asked. Maybe she would. Maybe she wouldn't. The scent of the flowers in her arms was rich and almost unbearably sweet. She breathed it in deeply. She saw Elspeth coming towards her and closed her eyes.

She would have turned back to the woods if it hadn't been for Oliver. She didn't want him to think she wanted to see him again, or to follow her there. And she wanted to be alone in the woods if she went back there. He had no right to intrude like that, as if the woods belonged to him now. *But he can't take them away from me*, she thought. *They're my woods. Our woods, Grace.*

'The children are running wild,' Elspeth called out, full of excitement. 'Did you hear the news? The Hall is to be moved.'

Madeleine frowned. For a moment she imagined the Hall lifting up and sailing over the valley. She imagined herself and Grace wandering through its rooms in the blue dresses they had worn to the last party there. 'It's your colour,' Elspeth had said to them at the party, stroking the soft material, lifting it against Grace's cheek. 'Just the bluebell colour of your eyes.' She stared at the flowers in her hands, wondering why she had wanted to pick them.

Elspeth clapped her hands together. 'Think, Grace! If they can move the Hall, they can move Ben's farm. Think of it!'

'But why?'

'Why? Lord knows! An American has bought it. Well, he can buy the farm too. Pick it up and pop it next to the Hall, wherever that's going. Might be America! And we'd rent it off him, same as off his Lordship. I don't see why not. I'm going to write to the newspaper and see if I can find out who this American is. Grace, don't you think it would be good?' She panted up to her cousin. 'I can't go and live in one of those little houses up there when I'm married. Nor can Ben. Nor can his pigs. Eh, but imagine Ben's pigs travelling to America!'

Madeleine let Elspeth's excited chatter and laughter wash over her. Her thoughts were drifting back to the woods, and the purple-blue mist under the trees, and the young man who watched her everywhere. *He only knows me. He only knows half of me. He's the only person in the world who doesn't know that I'm half a twin.* Oliver. It was a nice name.

Elspeth hugged her suddenly, fracturing her thoughts, and Madeleine turned away.

'You'd better not crush these bluebells.'

'Are they for Maddy's grave? I'll come with you. And then Mum wants you to come round and try on your bridesmaid's dress.'

Madeleine shook her head. It was unthinkable, to walk alone behind the bride in church.

Elspeth paused. 'I haven't forgotten, you know. It's your birthday. Mum says it's better not to mention it, but it's not right, I think.' She kissed her cousin impulsively. 'I want you to be happy. We all do. And you will be, one day. You'll be happy again and we'll be friends like we used to be.'

So many people said it to her, as if they meant it, as if they really thought it was true; as if for their sakes Madeleine had to say, yes, I'm happy. How easy it must seem to them, to be happy.

'And I've told you,' said Elspeth firmly. 'I'm not getting married unless you're my bridesmaid. We always promised each other, didn't we? The three of us. It mustn't make any difference now, even without Maddy. She wouldn't want you to break your promise.' Her fingers pressed Madeleine's hand. 'I won't be happy. I won't marry Ben if you won't be my maid. There. I mean it. Oh, Grace.' She hugged her cousin, who stood impassively clutching the bluebells, retreating already into the quiet part of her mind. 'Please.'

Next day Madeleine saw Oliver again. He and some of the other men were shifting a delivery of stones on to carts. As she walked past him she could feel his eyes on her. She was intensely aware of him, but she wouldn't let herself look at him. Instead of going up to the Ghost Woods as she had intended she went home and straight up to her room. She sat on her bed, hugging her pillow, rocking herself backwards and forwards.

21

A month before Elspeth and Ben's wedding, the single men of the village organised the annual Bachelors' tea. It had happened every May for as long as anyone in the village could remember, and had been rehearsed covertly in cowsheds and barns for weeks. This year Ben presided, pink and proud and nervous, never to be a bachelor again, and teasingly reminded of it every five minutes by one or other of the villagers. The tea was held in the school, with flowers in vases, and sandwiches and cakes set out neatly on the little desks where almost every one of the villagers had sat in their own schooldays. The guests wore their best clothes, and the ladies were competitive about their hats. Dora's had magpie feathers in this year.

'She's got the right voice for it, anyway,' Elspeth said privately to her mother, and they exchanged wicked glances.

After the meal, Ben, Colin, the three young brothers at the Canons' farm, proud young Tommy, and the older farmers who had stubbornly refused to take wives, dressed up in the pageant clothes and performed a show. It was the same show every year, with added topical references, all sung in dreadful rhyme. Madeleine listened impassively to the howls of laughter around her; she watched her father, red-faced with pleasure, and her mother dabbing tears of mirth from her eyes, and wondered where they could have found the instinct to laugh again.

At the end of the performance the vicar climbed up the three steps to the infants' class. *He's a different man*, his wife thought, watching him. *He's grown old now*.

'This will probably be the last Bachelors' tea party to be held in this village,' he said. 'But when you have moved up to Dyson's Fields, I beg you not to let these customs go. The village community is a family.'

Tommy yawned aloud, thinking they were in for a Sunday sermon, and then clapped his hand over his mouth, his shoulders shaking with suppressed giggles. Mike snorted next to him.

155

'I've nothing more to say,' said the vicar abruptly. 'Except that this is the last time that I will be able to ask Ben to sing for us, because soon he will be a bachelor no more. Ben—'

He held out his arm towards Ben, and the villagers roared their approval.

Ben ducked his head, almost purple with embarrassment. 'Sing, lad!' The farmers banged their fists on the tables. 'Ben, Ben, Ben,' they shouted, ready for laughter and mockery, ready to be lifted out of the shadow that the vicar had cast over them. Ben looked as if he would weep with shyness, but he caught Elspeth's eye and told himself that it was something he must do, must do without shame for her. He had only ever been heard singing hymns to his pigs as he cleaned out the sties, and when at last he stood up, his hands thrust in his pockets, his back pressed against the wall for support, everybody waited for his favourite, 'We sow good seeds and scatter'. But as he stood there in a paralysis of terror, with his eyes closed and his heart thumping and twisting in his breast pocket like a newborn piglet, he remembered a song his grandfather used to play on the wind-up gramophone. Word for word and note for note it came back to him, and he sang it as sweetly and reverently as the long-forgotten tenor on the record had sung it.

'"All in the April evening, April airs were abroad",' he sang, '"the sheep with their little lambs passed me by on the road—"' and the grinning children and the winking farmers were hushed and attentive, heads bowed, thinking of the April light that flooded the rugged slopes of Black Tor with loveliness at the end of every winter, and the miracle of birth and new life that they themselves helped to bring about.

Madeleine looked across at Elspeth's rapt and loving face, and remembered how she and Grace had shrieked with teasing laughter at the thought of her marrying Ben the pigman. *She loves him,* she thought. *She loves him with every bit of her, and if he was handsome and clever and rich she couldn't love him more than she does now. Will it ever be possible for me to love someone in the same way? We said we wouldn't, didn't we, Grace? We won't marry anyone, ever. No one will come between us. What will I do? What's going to happen to me?* The thought of her future without her sister frightened her beyond measure – it would be like wandering alone and afraid up there on the black moors, without paths or boulders to mark the way, without any companion to share with or be guided by. Terror made her cold.

Elspeth met her eyes and smiled at her, and Madeleine's loneliness welled up again. She looked round for a way of escaping, but the farmers were standing in a bunch in the doorway, whistling and shouting now as Ben brought his song to an end, stamping their heels to make the floorboards jump.

'Eh, give over that,' Ben said, grinning. 'Let's dance, shall us?'

Seth brought out his tin whistle, blowing down it with his hand cupped over the airhole to warm it up. Ted squatted down with his concertina, making it sigh as if it were a living creature. Jacob lifted his fiddle from the shabby old case. The children nudged each other, waiting, fascinated to watch the way he could extend his chin to twice its length before he tucked it on to the chin rest. He winked at them, knowing nothing. The chairs and desks were pushed back, and the dancing started on the floor that was buckled with years. Ben and Elspeth were the first up to dance, warm with tenderness, locked away from every other person in the room, special. Ben's mother watched them, her lips puckered, and refused the smith's invitation to make up the set together.

As soon as the music started, Madeleine went outside and leaned against the gate at the end of the little schoolyard. The stars were just coming out, the moon was full and huge. She could see the lights of Marty's old farm up on the hillside, and wondered whether Oliver was outside his caravan, listening to the distant strains of the village music, picturing her. She was confused. Why did he keep coming into her mind like this?

Grace, I have to tell you about Oliver. I know he looks at me. He watches me in a special way and I can feel myself going dizzy with his watching. I keep thinking about him. I've never felt like this before. I've never felt like this about Colin. All the time I thought I was in love with Colin, I never felt like this. Did you? Is this how you felt for Colin? And if you did, you must have hated me for the way I flirted with him and teased him, but it was only because he was coming between us. I wasn't trying to take him away from you. I just didn't want him to take you away from me. Did you understand that? I thought I wouldn't be able to bear it, if he took you away from me. I couldn't imagine being without you, ever. I'll never be without you. I won't let Oliver come between us. I won't look at him. I won't speak to him again. I won't even let on that I know he's there. But Grace – my head is singing with thoughts of him. What can I do?

Colin had noticed her leaving the schoolroom and after a time he came outside, looking for her. *How lonely she looks*, he thought, *like a ghost-figure, silver in the moonlight. When the moon ducks behind the trees she could just fade away with it and disappear forever, she looks so fragile.* He watched her for a little while then forced himself to go over and stand by her. 'Come and dance?' he asked, awkward. He wanted to reach out and touch her, put his arms round her. Never in his life had he felt so tender for her. And yet she was locked away from him, an ice-maiden, and he had no idea how to reach her. At one time he would have just grabbed her hand and dragged her inside the school, hoping she was Madeleine, and she would have laughed and protested and run willingly with him. But at that time both the sisters would have been there, signalling to each other to swap hands, so that after a while he would never know which of the two he was dancing with, and which of the teasing faces he

160

could kiss at the end of the evening. And maybe he had been wrong all the time. Maybe this was the sister he had loved the most. 'Please dance.'

Madeleine shook her head, saying nothing. He went back to the schoolroom and stood in the doorway, watching her, how the moon lit her face and gleamed in her eyes, and he followed her gaze up past the dark woods to the straggled line of huts and vans by Marty's farm. He scuffed his foot on the step, startling her deliberately, and went quickly back into the school.

22

Sheep shearing began the next day and would carry on through to July, from farm to farm. The farmers helped each other, gathering the sheep down from the hills and driving them to the river, where they'd made a dam of stones to create a sheepwash under the bridge. The older boys were let off school to help, and came home proud and exhausted, eating a man's supper. Tommy helped for the first time, dressed in his dad's oilskins, scrubbing the oil and dirt off the fleece, wrestling with the sheep that wriggled like live sacks of potatoes between his knees.

'I want to be a farmer, Dad,' he told Sim, his eyes shining.

Sim nodded, proud of him. 'It's not a bad job, growing things,' he agreed.

Tommy stinks of sheep tonight, Louise wrote in her notebook. He ate two meals in one, and fell

162

asleep with his nose in his pudding.

The shepherds who gathered sheep off the moors didn't go in the river with the sheep; even in high summer the wind could be biting cold on the tops, and they needed to keep themselves dry and warm. They trudged up and down the valley sides with their dogs, their voices and whistles echoing. The sheep ran along the tracks that had been used for hundreds of years, their feet skittering the loose stones as they jostled and bossed each other. The navvies stopped their work and watched, amazed, as hundreds of sheep scrambled past them, the dogs racing round them, the old shepherds striding behind.

'You wouldn't think they'd bother, eh?' laughed Ely, always glad of a chance to rest, flexing his shoulders to ease the ache of work. 'All that carry-on, and they'll be out of here before they can even eat the things!'

The shearing finished at Ben's farm. He had his own way of working, which he'd learned from his grandfather. He preferred not to wash his sheep but to wait for a warm day and watch the yellow line of grease rising as the ewes sweated.

'Makes 'em easier to shear,' he told Elspeth. 'That's my way of doing it, anyroad.'

'My way now,' she said.

Elspeth knew as well as any of the men how to work with the sheep, though she couldn't shear as fast as Ben. He showed her how to dig a hollow and light a small fire there to keep her pot of ruddle warm. She loved the smell of the sheep as they rumbled past her, loved the clamour of their voices. Deftly she ruddled a spot on the middle of each sheep's back to show they were Ben's. *My sheep*, she thought, *when we're married. But they'll probably be sold off by autumn. Maybe I'll never even see next year's lambs.*

After the shearing, all the farmers were called to a feast at Ben's farm. It had always been this way, since long before living memory; the shearing feast was at the big farm, just as harvest was in old Jacob Proctor's barns. Ben's mother prepared joints of mutton, bowls of mint sauce and Yorkshire pudding. This was her day of days. Ruddy from cooking, she beamed round at the men and poured homemade ale for them from an old earthenware jug.

'By, she's a looker, Joan Glossop, and always has been,' Jacob muttered. 'Pity life turned her face sour.' He stood up and raised his mug to her. 'Reckon this'll be last feast, Joan.'

For a moment she paused, her hands clasped round the brown pot jug which her own mother had used, her grandmother before her. She set it carefully on the scrubbed table and stood, her hands still round it, gazing down into the winking froth of the ale.

Elspeth watched her. One day it should have been hers, this rite. One day she should have been at the head of the table, laughing and proud with the farmers, hot-cheeked from cooking, tipping ale so it frothed in the mugs; the queen of the valley. As if he could read her thoughts, Ben came and stood behind her, his hand on her shoulder, claiming her, his breath warm on her cheek.

While the feasting was on, Tommy squirmed out of the kitchen and ran out to play. His cousins and the three mill cottage boys were waiting for him, kicking a dented ball backwards and forwards. As soon as they saw him they ran hollering to the great trench which gaped like a massive quarry from one end of the valley to the other. They were not allowed near it, yet it fascinated them. It seemed to the children, when they looked down on it from the hills above the valley, that it reached right into the centre of the earth. The ground around it had been cleared and flattened, making it a fine playing field. They dared each other to approach the gaping trench, deliberately kicking the ball wide so it rolled close to it. Just beyond the boulders that served for goalposts, the workmen were shovelling up heaps of sand and gravel, dim figures inside dusty clouds. Ely whistled to the boys and shouted to them to clear off and play somewhere else.

'Leave them be,' said Oliver. 'They're only playing.'

'They get harmed, we get blamed,' Ely grunted. 'I'll scare 'em off,' he grinned.

'You will if you smile like that at 'em,' the foreman agreed.

'How deep's that hole, mister?' Tommy shouted.

Ely scrambled down the gravel-heap and sauntered over to them, baring his six spindly teeth in a ghastly smile. 'More'n two hundred and fifty feet,' he told them. The stubble on his chin and his eyebrows were white with dust. 'Can't fathom that, can you? You could put three of them Halls standing on top of each other in that trench, and still be room on top. You could fall down it, one of you, and never be seen again. And d'you know what lives down there? Snakes!'

'Cor!' The boys peered down the steep sides, clutching each other's elbows.

'What's it for, mister?' Mike asked.

'We'll fill it with concrete. Tons and tons of concrete, to make it rock solid. Want to be a builder, do you?'

'Yes, mister,' said Mike.

'I'll be a farmer,' said Tommy. 'I can do shearing already.'

Ely laughed. 'Not much chance of farming, not when this lot's done.' He swung his shovel across his shoulder and sauntered back to the worksite, conscious that the boys were watching him.

'Clear off,' the foreman shouted. 'Brats,' he muttered, turning his back to them.

'They're just kids,' said Oliver.

'We should never have started this job till the village was evacuated. Someone'll get hurt.' The foreman cleared his throat and spat into the dust. 'Come on, Ely, put your back to it. We've another load to shift today, man.'

The boys cheered as Ely ran like a young man up the side of the sand pile, oaring his shovel at his side as if he was paddling a boat.

Half a mile away, their echoing voices could be heard in the village. Madeleine stood up in the kitchen of her house and went to the door. She stood, hands on her hips, staring across towards the cloudy worksite. She was intensely aware of her sister standing at her side. The air between them throbbed like a drum, and it was the throb of fear.

A new load of sand was just being tipped, the noise of it clattering round the hills. Limestone lay in massive piles ready for use, brought in every day by train on the little track running in a spur off the main line, and sand was brought in by the slow lorries that made their way through the Joansford pass. As the lorry was tipping, the men were below it shovelling it into barrows, to be made into tons of puddled clay. The thick dust rose in clouds around Ely as he joined them, swallowing him up; a ghost figure.

The boys had run back to their pitch, passing their ball from one to other. Oliver, at the top of the pile, shielded his eyes for a moment against the low sun, watching them. A girl was running towards the pitch from the village, her hair streaming behind her as yellow as sunlight. *But she never runs*, he thought. Whenever he watched her she drifted, slowly, like someone in a dream. And when the dust haze cleared the girl had gone, and he turned away, smiling to himself. There was no girl there, and never had been. She was nothing more than a trick of the sunlight.

As he turned, the lorry finished tipping and began to move away. Its wheels locked on a bed of gravel, and it backed quickly, thudding up against the pile. Oliver was knocked off balance. He struggled to find his feet and the pile began to crumble like the scree of stones on a mountainside.

'Watch out!' he shouted. He threw down his shovel and tried to scramble back, then flung up his arms and half rolled, half jumped away from the avalanche of sand.

'Ely!' he yelled, but the old man was singing to himself, nine years old again and wanting to kick a ball around rather than shift gravel and sand. He didn't hear his shout, nor did he hear the thunder of the cascading pile until it was too late. With a terrible cry Ely went under, and the sand continued to flow down on to him.

Out on their rubbly pitch the boys cheered; Tommy had just kicked the ball into the trench.

'Ely, Ely!' Oliver shouted. He struggled back on to his feet and ran into the clouds of the sandfall. The foreman loped across and pulled him back, coughing and choking in the white plumes of dust. As soon as the sliding stopped, the men ran forwards again, scrabbling sand away by the fistful, frantic. The lorry driver set off, unaware that anything had happened on the other side of the pile. At last Ely was pulled out.

'He's still warm,' Oliver panted. 'He's all right.' He leaned back on his hands. 'Let him be all right.'

But the foreman was on his knees, his head pressed against the old man's chest. The boys came galloping up from the side of the trench, wild with fright.

'Get someone,' Oliver shouted over his shoulder to Tommy, and then straightened up, because there she was again, running towards them, her golden hair streaming. She stopped near the pile, her face white and cold and staring. The boys ran on past her and hollered to the houses. Elspeth was the first to come, sobbing with the horror of it as she ran, and behind her came Madge clutching blankets. They stood in aghast silence, villagers and workmen as still as clumps of trees. Ely was dead.

'Two in less than a year, two terrible accidents,' Dora Proctor wailed. 'We're a blighted valley.'

'Shut up,' her father growled, and she bowed her head and ran home, howling like a child.

Ely had no family that anyone knew of, and nobody had any idea where he had come from. Like many of the men, he had sniffed the work from miles away and had arrived with nothing more than an old army knapsack with the basics of clothes inside. He had shacked up in Oliver's little caravan and had told him that he couldn't ever remember living in such luxury before, and they had lived there like father and son since. It was decided that he should be buried in the village graveyard. For the first time since the work had begun, workmen and villagers stood side by side in the church. Oliver was grim and silent, taking on the role of chief mourner. At the back of the church the blacksmith's little daughter held out her arms to catch the lights from Grace's stained-glass window.

After the burial, Colin stood watching Oliver. He was standing on his own by the newly turned grave, head bowed, and Colin had a powerful sense of the young man's loneliness. At last he made up his mind about him. He walked up to him, preparing his words, awkward. 'I'm sorry about Ely. Was he a friend of yours?'

'I knew nothing about him.' Oliver half turned his head, narrowing his eyes to look away towards the worksite, and Colin stiffened, hurt at what seemed like a rejection.

'Anyway, I just thought I'd say...'

Oliver looked back and nodded his head. 'But I thank you for your kind words,' he said, stiffly formal. Clumsily they shook hands and then looked away again, uncertain as to what to say next. The foreman jerked his head and the navvies began to move away from the churchyard. Work was to start again immediately. Colin and Oliver walked out of the yard together and paused by the vicarage.

'That your bike?' Oliver nodded towards an old motorbike at the side of the house.

Colin laughed. 'It's pretty old. It was my father's, in his younger days. He said I can have it if I can get it to work.'

'Lucky chap.'

'Well, Mum's dead against it. You know what mothers are like!'

Oliver narrowed his eyes. 'Can't say I do. Always wanted one.'

He walked away and Colin gazed after him, grinning. 'Mother or bike?' he called.

'Brrm brmm.' Oliver didn't turn round. 'Brrrm rrrrowww.'

23

Everybody brought flowers from their gardens for the church, strewing a path of petals for the bride to walk on. The farmers bound flowers round their rakes and hoes and made an arched tunnel with them along the church pathway. The church had never been dressed so richly before. Nobody stayed away from the wedding, not even if they were unwell, or had quarrelled with Joan Glossop, or had pressing work to do. Nobody stayed away that day. They were united in showing that the church was theirs, that the couple was theirs, that nothing would spoil the happiness of the day.

But there was nothing Elspeth had been able to do to persuade Madeleine to be her bridesmaid. She took the dress that she had made, sure that when her cousin saw how fine it was and how lovely she would look in it, then she would say yes. But Madeleine's eyes went wide with horror at the thought of walking down the aisle behind the bride, with everyone's eyes on her, without Grace. She held Elspeth's hands in both her own.

'Please, please don't want me to do it so much,' she begged. 'Because I can't; not even for you.'

Elspeth cried when she got back home again.

'Don't you worry. We can alter it for Louise, easy,' her mother consoled her.

'It's not that, Mum. It's always Grace and Madeleine, Madeleine and Grace; they always put each other first. There's no room for anyone else, even now.'

'You've got Ben,' Madge reminded her.

'I know, Mum. And I'm lucky. But she's got no one. That's why I'm crying, see.'

Madge said nothing. *That poor child Grace is letting her dead sister control her life*, she thought, but she did not say the words out loud. The idea chilled her to the bone.

On the wedding day Miss Skinner played the motet that she had tried to teach every schoolchild in the valley and that nobody had ever got right apart from one of the twins, Grace or Madeleine, she had never known which. She would have invited Ben to sing it if he hadn't been the groom himself, so the rest of the choir made the best of it, Dora Proctor lunging mercilessly at the high notes. Louise walked behind the bride, demure and lovely in the dress Elspeth had altered for her. Jenny's hand crept towards Sim's.

'Everybody's crying, except us. What's the point of getting married if it's just going to make people sad?' Louise whispered aloud, her plaits swinging smartly.

Elspeth laughed. She never stopped smiling throughout the whole ceremony, as if she had never known what happiness was until that day, as if she was the queen of happiness. When she came out of the church, a married woman now, she looked as if her face would split in half with smiling. Ben's cheeks shone as if he had polished them up for market. Madeleine closed her eyes against the unbearable joy. How could her mother smile? How could Louise skip on the toes of her satin shoes and twirl and pirouette? How could her father laugh out loud like that?

Jenny Barnes clutched Madeleine's hand. 'Things are getting better now, my love,' she said, pleading. She touched her daughter's still face and tried to urge her forwards to look at the bride and groom. 'Look how happy they are! Isn't that a lovely thing, Grace? Be happy! For Elspeth's sake, be happy!'

Madeleine let her mother lead her by the hand to stand and be photographed with the bride and groom. She stood slightly apart from them, aware of Colin close by her. When the photographs had been taken the guests surged forwards to shower the bride and groom with petals and kisses. 'Mine, mine!' the girls shrieked as Elspeth held her bouquet up. She caught her cousin's eye.

'Catch, Grace!' she called, and tossed the bouquet into the air. The little girls rushed forwards, hands held high, pushing Madeleine aside in their excitement.

She stared round, bewildered and utterly lost. 'Mine!' she heard Grace shout, surely it was Grace's voice. 'Mine!' she said, and involuntarily she held out her arms and caught the bouquet. She pressed her face into the sweetness of the flowers, and they were cool and soft as kisses against her cheek.

'Marriage isn't all it's trumped up to be,' said Ben's mother to Elspeth during the wedding feast out on the village green, and Elspeth gazed at her, still smiling. 'Remember that, my girl.'

Elspeth laughed. Ben was dancing on his own, a little drunk with happiness, a mug of Joan's homemade ale slopping in his fist. Someone threw him his shepherd's crook and he used it like a walking stick, trying to do a comic swagger like Charlie Chaplin in the old films, tripping over his feet to make the little ones laugh. The older children were showering the track between the church and the farmhouse with flowers from the wedding, making a path home for her and Ben to walk on. Nobody had ever done it before, and no one had suggested it. It suddenly seemed the right thing to do, in defiance of the workmen digging and shovelling and shouting to each other out on the great rising bank of the dam. Joan craned her neck, watching the children, her lips pursed.

'I can't imagine how our Elspeth's going to get on with Joan,' Madge muttered to her sister.

'Joan was never like that as a girl,' Jenny said. 'She should have moved out to Laurie's pig farm when she had the chance. She'd have been a fulfilled woman, instead of the cold fish she turned out to be.'

'Who's Laurie?' Louise asked, round-eyed.

'None of your business!' her Aunt Madge smiled. 'It's a wonder you don't trip over your own ears, they flap about so much.'

In the big, lofty farmhouse that night, Elspeth went shyly up to the room she was to share with Ben. The walls had been washed in a deep blue, the colour that she had wanted, the colour she imagined the sea to be. She hung Aunt Susan's wedding present on a nail over the iron bedhead. 'It's perfect!' She turned round to Ben, laughing. 'She painted it just for us, Ben. Our farm.'

A wave of panic came over him then. *Not our farm*, he thought. *Not his Lordship's, not anybody's. The bloomin' Water Board's.* And there was Elspeth, lovely and shy at his side, his wife, turning her face to him, to the picture and back to him, blushing with happiness.

'Looks a bit lopsided to me,' he said, as nervous as she was.

'That's what I love about it. I don't like things to be too straight and neat, I don't.'

Ben smiled. 'Come here to me.'

She giggled, remembering what Louise had said the day he proposed to her.

'What's my little hen chuckling at?' he whispered, finding out with his fingers how her dress would unfasten and fall away from her. He was tender for her, shy and gentle and longing.

''Cause you don't smell of pigs, not one bit today!' she murmured. He stopped her mouth with kisses and lifted her on to the bed.

She woke up during the night and snuggled herself into his warm back. She could hear the wind breathing through the roof-stones, mice scuttling above her in the loft space. She could hear Joan snoring along the corridor, and the creaking of furniture stretching itself after the fire had sunk to ashes in the grate.

'It's a noisy old house,' she whispered.

Ben strained to listen, hearing nothing unfamiliar.

'You not scared, Elspeth?'

'Course I'm not. It just wants babies, that's all,' she said dreamily. 'Babies in every room, then we wouldn't hear anything else.' She lay awake for a bit, watching the branches swaying outside the window. 'This is where our first baby should be born,' she said. 'Don't you think, Ben?'

Ben was silent, struggling with his fears. *What's going to happen to me and Ellie, and the babies*

180

that's to come, and the pigs and all? What's going to happen?

Ben's mother watched Elspeth at her work around the farm and in the house, and had to admit grudgingly that the girl was quick and thorough, never shirking at any task she gave her and ready to move on to the next. 'There, that's done,' she would say, giving a little quick pleased clap with her hands. 'Now, what's next?' Or she would lift a heavy scuttle of coals or logs out of Joan's hands. 'Oh, I'll do that, Mam,' she would say. 'Give it here.'

Joan said nothing welcoming or encouraging to her, still begrudging the fact that she had to share the house with another woman. She especially hated the way Elspeth toyed with the ring that Ben had given her, twisting it round on her finger to make the star catch the firelight.

'You'll twist it off,' she snapped one night, unable to hold back her irritation. 'You'll lose it.'

'No, I'll never lose it,' Elspeth gasped, her cheeks flushing deeply. 'I love this ring more than anything in the world.'

Joan tutted, nagged by the fond look that passed then between her son and Elspeth, excluding her completely.

'I think this house needs brightening up,' said Elspeth, jumping up. 'It's really dark and old-fashioned.'

'It's the way I like it,' Joan said, poking the fire viciously.

'I could make some lovely yellow curtains for here. The sun would pour in through them in the mornings – just imagine how pretty it would be.'

'No,' said Joan. 'I can't imagine.'

Elspeth looked over to Ben for support, but he just gazed at her, his eyes blue with wondering how she could have said such a thing to his mother.

'Besides,' said Joan tightly, 'it won't be anything soon. It won't be anything at all.' The house ticked back into uncomfortable silence.

'How I miss our Ellie,' Madge confessed to Jenny. They were doing their monthly tour of the Hall, out of habit. They liked to open up the doors and let air in, hating the musty smell of closed houses.

'How can you miss her? She bobs in every day!' said Jenny Barnes, her heart suddenly gripped at the thought of her own, irreplaceable loss.

Madge heard the cold edge in her sister's voice and could have cursed herself for speaking carelessly. But still, the words had been said and there was no unsaying them. She tried to laugh it off. 'She's such a noisy one! Singing in every room of our house, morning to night. I don't get that now.'

Jenny thought of the twins singing in their room together, making up harmonies, their voices perfectly matched. She let the memory linger, savouring it. 'I don't expect she does much singing where she is.'

Madge pulled a face. 'She says nothing about it, and silence speaks volumes. But her Ben adores her, that's plain to see.' She stopped suddenly, listening with her head to one side, frowning. 'Someone's in the Hall.'

'Can't be. Children are all at school,' said Jenny, but then she heard it too, a slight scuffle of shoe on wood, a whispered breath.

They stepped out of the drawing room and looked down the corridor, and there was Seth, running his hands across the library door, enjoying the shapes of the birds and animals that his ancestral grandfather had carved. The women watched him, breath held so as not to disturb him.

'Like he's praying,' Madge whispered. 'Like he's in a living dream.'

After a while she went to him and touched his arm. 'Closing up now,' she said.

'That's all right.' Seth let his arms fall to his sides.

They walked together down the corridor and he waited while Jenny turned the key in the front door.

'What d'you think about, Seth, when you touch the door?' Madge asked, curious. 'Do you see anything, in your mind, I mean?'

'I don't really think anything. I just do it. Just touch them all, one by one, that's all I want to do. Tell you something, if I were rich, I'd buy that door!' He laughed at the idea. 'Wouldn't fit in any house though, would it?'

'Not those houses up there,' Madge agreed. 'You'd need a mansion.'

He made his way surely across the track and over the stepping stones. School had just finished and the children were coming out. Louise saw her mother at the Hall gates and came running to her, clutching her red notebook in her folded arms. Seth called out her name as she passed him, touching her hair lightly, and then turned to laugh and joke with the boys. Oliver had given them a ball to replace the one they'd kicked into the trench. He had left it on the porch of the school, whistling jauntily as he walked away. Tommy kicked the ball straight to Seth. He sensed it by the sound it made and fielded it neatly, edging it away from Mike's tackle, and sent it cleanly away from the cottages towards the open fields.

'He knows his way round this valley better than any of us,' Jenny said. 'What's it going to be like for him, up there at Dyson's Fields?'

They watched him as he made his steady way up towards the cottage where he had lived on his own for ten years now, since he was sixteen years old. Louise unlocked her notebook and wrote, Seth's footprints.

'What's that supposed to mean?' her mother laughed, screwing up her eyes to read it.

'I'm writing a list of all the things that belong to the valley,' Louise said. 'All the things that belong here and can't be taken away when we move. Like the S and D stone in the Ghost Woods.' She ran off, her plaits thumping her back, her pencil tucked behind her ear, and then paused to walk daintily past a team of workmen.

'And Louise's childhood,' Jenny said softly. 'That belongs to this valley. This will be her last summer as a little girl.'

24

The great chestnut tree in the churchyard was the first in the village to blaze its autumn colours. The golden leaves drifted down piece by piece, random and casual, and it was as if the unleaving would never end.

Aunt Susan knocked at the door of Madeleine's cottage and asked her to come with her and paint the tree. 'Ochre, russet, burnt umber, vermilion,' she chanted. 'The names are as rich as the colours themselves. Come with me, Twinny. Come on.' She held out her hand and led Madeleine out to the churchyard and into the spin of leaves. Susan painted while Madeleine sat with her paints and paper at her feet, untouched. She was passive and completely at ease. In the distance she could hear the drone of machinery; steady and slow like the hum of insects. Her thoughts turned to Oliver and the special smile he gave her whenever she passed him. *He only knows me*, she thought, and wondered that she could find the idea so comforting. She forced it away, ashamed.

Colin could see her from the desk in his bedroom. *She's turned beautiful*, he thought to himself, then slammed his books open savagely. *It'll be better when I've left. Better for all of us.*

He had a Latin exam to work for as part of his university entrance. There was no doubt in his mind, or his father's, that he would pass. There was no doubt in his father's mind that Colin would enter the Church. It was what he had always wanted for his son. So Colin spent most of his time studying, and when he needed a break he usually walked up to Oliver's caravan, though both his parents disapproved of the friendship. There was still a great deal of animosity among the villagers towards the 'navvies', as they called them.

'I don't like you going up there,' Colin's mother said. 'Leave them to themselves, it's best.'

'Why?' Colin asked, and she looked to her husband for support.

'I don't think you could possibly have anything in common,' the vicar said.

But Colin and Oliver felt completely at ease with each other. Even at school Colin had never felt he had a friend of his own, as close as this. They could talk about anything together; yet deliberately, Colin never mentioned Grace and Madeleine. All that was too raw, too private. But he did confide his doubts about his future career.

'Don't do it, then,' Oliver had said, shrugging his shoulders. 'Come travelling with me, hey? Easy.'

'You don't understand,' Colin had told him. 'It's actually easier to do what my father wants.' One evening he had taken his Latin books up to the caravan to show to Oliver. He felt a little proud when Oliver frowned into the mystery of the strange words.

'This is the world you belong to,' Oliver had said, fingering the books with a kind of reverence.

Colin shrugged. 'It's the only world I know. But I sometimes think yours is better.'

'Better!' Oliver laughed, astonished.

'Truer, more real. More important. I don't know why.'

I still don't know, he thought, remembering the conversation. He watched Madeleine sitting quietly in the churchyard, watched the leaves with their slow, glorious, effortless dance.

One day when the sun was as low and full as a ripe fruit, and the air hummed with the song of insects, Joan Glossop and Elspeth were gathering apples in the orchard. The bruised ones were left for the orchard pig, but the sound ones were brought in for sorting and storing, some to be cooked straight away and made into jams and apple cheeses, some to be stored in trays in the dark apple loft. The sharp, sweet scent of the apples filled every room of the house.

'How I do love the smell of apples!' Elspeth laughed, breathing in deeply. 'And the taste of them. I never knew I loved the taste of them so much!' She ate one, closing her eyes to enjoy its crisp bite and burst of sap, and then ate another straight away. Her lips and chin and hands were dribbling with juice. She reached out for a third. 'Can't stop eating them, Mam,' she giggled.

Joan frowned and stood back, hands on hips. 'Are you pregnant?' she asked.

Elspeth stopped scrunching the apple and stared at her. 'What makes you say that?'

'When women starts fancying things, it's a sure sign. Besides, you've got that damp look round your eyes.'

Elspeth felt stifled by her, by her womanly knowingness. She went out of the kitchen, idly plucking another apple from the bowl as she passed it. She wandered round the house, brimming with wonder and thrill. She gazed at herself in the spotted mirror over the sink. *Could it be true?* She touched the mirror eyes, wondering. Beyond the mirror she could see Ben out in the yard, leaning over the wall of the pigsty. 'How he loves those pigs!' she smiled.

She went out to join him, still scrunching the apple. 'Admiring your babies?' she teased. She allowed her hand to slide down to her stomach, wondering again whether Joan could be right. Could another woman know before she did whether or not she was pregnant? Ben stretched forwards to tickle his favourite pig, a great black sow that had just littered five piglets.

'These ones are such a queer colour, Ben. I think a pink pig is more natural. And look at their great flappy ears.'

'That's to keep the flies and the sun out their eyes. Don't you love their little curly tails?'

'They're like little rings. I could pick them up and hang them on those hooks by the barn door, easy,' Elspeth laughed. She twirled away from him, wanting him to notice her in her favourite mint-green gingham dress, stained as it was now with juice, wanting him to see how wet her eyes were and how much she loved apples today. She tossed the core into the sty and the piglets rushed for it, squabbling in little greedy grunts.

'Listen to them talking,' Ben chuckled. 'Just like kids. Squealing and whimpering, telling each other, they are. That's mine, that apple. I saw it first. No, it in't, it's mine. Just like children.'

He understood his pigs better than anybody, better than he understood his mother, better than he understood Elspeth, though he worshipped her. He sat on the wall watching them while Elspeth waltzed away and thought dreamily about litters of babies, cosy as apples in their tray. Ben swung his legs over and sat on the sty wall, enjoying the dozy heat of the late afternoon. The piglets ran squealing to him, expecting more food, nudging his boots and raising themselves on their back trotters to nuzzle round the knees of his trousers. He chanted the wonderful names of breeds of pigs, as if he was singing a song to them. Curly-side, Saddleback, Middle White, Tamworth. If he could ever have dared to tell anyone his dream, it would be that he would be a breeder of pigs, and famous for it. He couldn't imagine doing anything else, couldn't even contemplate it. But he didn't mention his despair to anyone. He could find no words to express it. He drove it deep, deep inside himself, and doggedly kept his head down, working each day as it came, working it to its fullness. One more litter of pigs – then what?

That night Elspeth dreamt that the farmhouse was sailing on water like an ark, all the villagers swimming up to it and climbing in, piling into it, all the cattle and sheep safe on floating rafts of fields, all Ben's pigs towed behind in their bobbing sties. 'Leave room for the babies!' she shouted out loud, and Ben woke up with a start and rocked her till she was sleeping quietly again.

25

There were still days when Sim Barnes's grief for his daughter welled up like a dark sea inside him, and he had to go away, out of the cottage, and find physical work to do. On these days he went to the gardens of the Hall. Louise always knew where to find him. He was raking piles of leaves to make into a bonfire when she came running to him.

'Dad.' Her arms were folded tight across her notebook. 'Have you heard the awful news?'

Her father groaned and straightened up. 'What awful news now?'

Louise took a deep breath and opened up the book. She held it out to him. American offer falls through. 'That's what.'

Sim shook his head, unable to read it without his glasses.

'The American has changed his mind. It's true

because Dora Proctor told me. The Hall isn't going to be moved after all. Isn't it terrible!'

Relief warmed her father's face. 'It's good news, that. Best news this year!'

'How can it be?' Louise stamped her foot in despair. She had cherished the thought of the Hall flying away, like the golden palace in the story of Aladdin, to a distant, blue-skied land. Sometimes in her thoughts she would be in it, alone, and sometimes all the family, all her favourite people. And at other times, the whole village, not a soul left behind. But whoever was in it, the Hall was safe in her dreams. The Hall would live forever.

'It belongs here,' Sim told her. 'Wouldn't be right to take it away. Would never be the same in another place, any more than the trees and plants and flowers could just be dug up like some folks is planning, and stuck in those bald patches they want to call gardens up at Dyson's Fields. Leave the plants to drown where they've always seeded, and buy fresh, that's what we must do. They belong here. Put them all in your list, Louise. Put everything in your list.' He crouched down and shook dead flower heads into the palm of his hand as he did at the end of every summer, gathering in the seed to be sown next spring. He did it slowly; his hands were trembling. 'These seeds now. They'll go into the soil here when it's had a winter's sleep, and we might be gone by the time they've flowered. But they belong here.'

Louise trailed after him back to the cottage. Sim poured the seeds from his cupped fist into brown envelopes and licked down the flaps, pulling a face at the sour taste of the gum.

'I don't want the flowers to drown, as if nobody loves them,' Louise said mournfully.

'They won't be alone in the earth. The soil will be full of seeds and roots and nuts.'

Louise gasped, overwhelmed by the dark horror of it all. 'And what will the squirrels do, when they look for the nuts they've buried? And all the animals that live in the earth and in the grasses and in the trees; what will happen to them?' Her voice rose to a wail. Her mother, preparing the night's meal with Madeleine, looked up sharply and shook her head at her husband. 'The rabbit warrens and the foxes' lairs, the badger setts, the mouse holes and the little weasel runs, all filling up with water – and then the birds' nests in the trees, all filling up with water like bowls of soup.' Louise's face was red and scorched with tears; she was unstoppable now.

'The parent birds will fly away, and the little ones will drown because they can't fly yet. And when the summer birds come back, the swallows and the martins – what will they do when they find that their nesting barns have gone?'

'Louise, Louise, you can't take all their worries on your shoulders.' Jenny rocked her in her floury arms.

'But I do worry about them. We can't even explain anything to them. They won't even know what's happening when the valley fills up with water.'

'Bless your tender heart,' Jenny smiled. 'I think if you could you'd be picking the worms up and bringing them to your new home with you.'

'The new house will have Pudding and the kittens, won't it?'

'No,' said her father. 'There'll be no room for the cats up there. There's hardly room for us in that scrap of a house. It's no place for cats and kittens. They'll have to stay.'

'Stay here?' Louise's eyes widened in horror. 'But they'll DROWN.'

'They'll save themselves,' her father said. He had never spoken so harshly to her before. Her hysteria scared him. He couldn't hug her, the way

196

Jenny did. He wanted to hurt someone now, to find a way of releasing the months of suppressed anger and grief and helplessness. He was glad Louise was crying; she was crying his tears. 'They'll run up to the moors and fend for themselves.'

'But they won't UNDERSTAND.'

Madeleine let it all wash over her. She went to the window. Up on the hillside, the workmen had lit oil lamps inside the barns. She imagined Oliver sitting outside his caravan watching the sunset. She could hardly remember the valley as it had been before Oliver came, before the men created the slowly growing dam sides and the great scar across the green fields, before the spoil heaps rose up like giant molehills.

Her breath steamed the cold glass of the window, and she leaned forwards and wrote 'Oliver' into it, and breathed on it again. Oliver. She couldn't get him out of her mind. Every day she passed near him and refused to look at him, and every day she felt his eyes on her. She imagined herself going to see him, up in what was left of the ravaged Ghost Woods where he had spoken to her in spring. She could slip out of the house later, when everyone was asleep. She could steal through the moon's shadows like one of the farm cats, right up to the barns, and she would call out his name and wait for him to come out to her. Her blood sang for him. The image of Grace slid into her thoughts and she forced it away. *Grace would say no. Grace would say, we promised each other. No one will ever come between us, she would say.* But Grace was dead. Dead. *You left me. You left me on my own. Oh, Grace.* Madeleine rubbed away the letters with her wrist.

'There's another bit of news,' Louise said. Her sobs had shaken away now; her voice was tired and babyish. She giggled as she opened up her notebook and showed her mother what she had written.

Shock news. Today it was disclosed in the post office that Ben is to become a proud father next spring.

'Elspeth's going to have a baby,' she whispered. 'Isn't that fabulous!'

Later that evening Madeleine went to the stepping stones at the bottom of the village. From there she could see the men, who had finished work, walking over the packhorse bridge to their various sheds and barns, or climbing into lorries and buses to be taken back to Hallam for the night. Some would be calling at the new public house that had opened at Dyson's Fields. Their tired voices echoed off the hills. A harvest moon was just rising, massive against the skyline, golden as a ripe marrow, and she held up her face to it. It was a year since Grace had died, almost to the day. She listened to the whisper of water around the stones. She could still hear her sister's voice in it.

She heard the last of the men coming down from the far site, making their way up the steep road to the pub. One of them broke away from the others and came towards the village, and she realised with a slow beat of her heart that it was Oliver. He came steadily towards her and she half lifted her hand, smiling involuntarily, ready to walk towards him. But he veered away, not even seeing her, and went to the vicarage. Still hoping he might turn round and see her, she followed him, and paused by the gate. He tapped on the door and stood leaning against the wall, whistling. Colin came out, pulling on his jacket. Madeleine was surprised. She hadn't been aware of the growing friendship between the two young men.

'I've fixed that part for your bike,' Oliver said.

'Good man! Ah, that's grand, that is.'

'It was easy. We've got all the tools up there. Glad to do it.' They walked together to the back of the house, where Colin's battered motorbike crouched under its green oilskin. Madeleine could hear the tinkle of tools as they worked on the bike; their sudden shouts of laughter. She walked down slowly, pretending to herself that she was going to call on Aunt Susan. She would have to walk behind the vicarage to get to her cottage. Now she could see Colin and Oliver bending together over the bike; Colin's blond hair, Oliver's dark.

'I'd love a bike like this,' Oliver said.

'Why don't you get one then?'

Oliver laughed. 'On a navvy's wage? Fat chance!'

'I'll take you out on it, when we get it fixed. Teach you to ride it, if you like, before I leave.'

'Where are you going?'

Colin laughed. 'Got my results today. I've got in to St John's. It's a theological college, up in Durham. I start in a couple of weeks.'

Oliver straightened up, tapping his fist with his spanner. 'Going to be a vicar, then.'

'Looks like it.'

'Do you believe in God?'

'What?'

'It's a fair question,' Oliver laughed.

'Ask me again in three years' time.'

'Are you pleased about college?'

'The old man is.'

'What about you?'

'Can't say.' Colin paused, seeing Madeleine, only a few paces away now. Oliver followed his glance and smiled at her, his face warm with recognition.

'I'll be glad to get away,' Colin said.

Madeleine walked on quickly.

Colin followed Oliver's gaze as she crossed the lane to Susan's cottage.

'She's a strange one,' said Oliver. 'A beautiful strange one. A lost soul.'

Jealousy flickered like a dangerous flame. Colin looked away, saying nothing. He never spoke about the twins to Oliver; didn't want him to know anything about them. It was too painful, still; and besides, they were nothing to do with Oliver. He was an outsider.

Madeleine knocked on Susan's door. She could hardly control the turmoil of emotions that she felt. She realised that she was jealous because Colin hadn't told her about his entrance exam and

201

his results. At one time she, she and Grace, would have known before anyone else in the valley. She would have known the results were due. She would have known that he had applied to go to university. So much had happened, and she knew nothing about any of it.

And she was excited, too, because she had seen Oliver again, and he had smiled at her. But he was Colin's friend now. How could they have become friends, without her even knowing? She heard the sputter of the motorbike engine starting up, dying away again, more laughter. She paused, and then walked into Susan's cottage. She put her arms round her old great-aunt as if it was months since she had last seen her. It might as well have been. She had not noticed how frail the old lady had become, like a bird in her arms. She hadn't realised how querulous her voice was now, and how her bright mind had grown fogged with worry and confusion. She had aged ten years in the last twelve months, and Madeleine had never even noticed.

'You've come back!' laughed Susan, quick to know her, and forgetting again in the instant. 'Where's the other one?'

The bike roared past, like a beast woken from its slumber.

'Where've you been?' Colin's mother asked when he came home much later, oil-stained and wind-swept, his cheeks red with cold air.

'Out on the bike. We got it started.'

'I don't like you going out on the bike. You're not to go to Hallam on it, do you hear me?'

'Mother!' Colin turned his back on her, exasperated. He cut himself a huge wedge of bread and plastered it with butter and jam.

'Who's we, anyway?'

'Me and Oliver.'

'I don't know any Oliver.'

'He's working on the site. You do know him.' He sat down next to her. 'What do you think about St John's?'

She touched her cheek, a nervous gesture that made her look suddenly young and fragile. It was her chance to say, 'Is this what you really want to do?' and she let the chance go. It was her husband's dream that his son would follow him to the same college. 'Your father's proud of you. We both are.'

He stood up and cut himself another wedge of bread. 'They're doing a concert up at Marty's barns next week.'

'Who are?' His mother was labelling jars of pickles, admiring the way the little onions snuggled together in their brown sea of vinegar. She reached up and placed the jars on the pantry shelf.

'Oliver's doing a dance at the concert! That should be a laugh,' Colin said, his mouth full of bread. 'I'd like to go, but I won't. It's their do.'

'I should think you won't,' his mother said. She heard her husband scraping his chair back in the study, and she poured milk into the pan to heat for his cocoa, as she did every night at this time. 'I don't want you mixing with the workers.'

'Fraternising with the enemy.'

'You know what I mean.'

'No, I don't. Not really.'

'They're not welcome here, that's what I mean.'

'Well, he's my friend.'

'I wish you wouldn't say that. He's not your type, this Oliver.'

Roused to sudden anger, Colin threw his bread knife down. 'What is my type? You've never given me a chance to find out!'

His mother said nothing. She bent down and picked up the knife from the floor, and Colin walked out of the house, hands in his pockets. He was embarrassed and confused; he had never raised his voice in anger before. He saw Madeleine coming out of Susan Sorrel's cottage, and turned away, back into the vicarage. He was trapped between his mother and his dearest friend. He no longer knew how to speak to either of them.

He ran up to his room and stood with his hands in his pockets, staring out of the window. He could still see her walking slowly back to her own cottage. Her hair was silver in the moonlight.

'You're beautiful, Grace,' he whispered. 'I wish I could tell you.' Then he noticed Oliver step out of the shadows of the yew in the churchyard. 'Hey, Beauty!' he heard him say, and saw her look round, her face lit up and pleased. Oliver sauntered across and spoke to her. Colin could not hear his words then, or her shy response, but he watched them walking slowly away, side by side, in the moonlit lane.

26

When the afternoon of the concert came, the strains of music from the workmen's shacks floated across the valley. It was bright, outrageous music, the music of brass and strings and accordions, the music of singing and dancing and of laughter. Where the Ghost Woods had been there was now a kind of amphitheatre dug back into the hillside. People were sitting round it on boulders, and a large flattened area had become a stage.

'They're having a show! See?' Louise's eyes were shining. 'Come on up with me, Grace. I want to write a review of it for my notebook.'

She pulled her sister's hand, and Madeleine went, reluctantly at first and then with a growing curiosity and a mixture of excitement and strange dread at possibly seeing Oliver again. She held his name in her thoughts as she was tugged along by Louise; she held the memory of the warm touch of his hand against her own as they walked together in the starlight.

The girls skirted the old woods so they wouldn't be seen, heading for the shadows of the few remaining trees. They ran along the top track, breathless and exhilarated by the scramble, and then edged themselves along the slope until they were looking down on the makeshift theatre.

The actors were all men in costumes, some dressed comically as women, with long wigs made out of mop heads, speaking in loud, coarse voices or simpering falsettos. Madeleine glanced along the row, searching for Oliver. At last he joined the waiting actors. He was dressed in an old-fashioned suit that was too big for him.

'There's that man.' Louise followed her glance. 'You like him, don't you?'

Madeleine said nothing.

'They're all talking about you, you know,'

'What do you mean?'

'They say you're making a fool of yourself. Mum says she doesn't like it. They shouldn't be here at all, these men. Nobody wants them here.'

Guffaws of laughter buffeted up to them as Oliver stepped forwards and did a comic dance routine, pretending to be drunk, teetering and regaining his balance just when it seemed he would fall. He carried a bottle in one hand and a shepherd's stick and mug in the other, and with every swaying step he tried to fill the mug, missed, tried again, missed, and ended up tilting the bottle and pouring it over his face.

Louise shrieked with laughter. 'He's being Ben!' she howled. 'Ben at the wedding party! Oh, he's so good.'

Madeleine stared at her. 'Surely not!' she said. But it was true. He was dressed exactly as Ben had been dressed at the wedding: the long black coat, the pressed grey trousers that he had borrowed from her father; his hair floppy with washing. And incongruously he was carrying the hazel stick that Ben used to poke the pigs with. He must have stolen it from Ben's yard. Someone threw him a stuffed toy shaped like a piglet and he hoinked across the stage area with it, tripping over his feet like a drunken fool. How did he know about this, if he hadn't been spying on the wedding?

She pulled Louise up sharply. 'Come on.'

'Ah, but he's good. It's only a bit of fun, Grace.'

Oliver was singing now, full-throated as Ben did in church, floating Ben's favourite hymn across the early evening. *Oliver has a beautiful voice*, thought Madeleine angrily. *He would have. He just would have.* She felt herself trembling at the lovely sound of his voice. She paused and looked back at him, and Louise gazed up at her sister, smiling knowingly.

'Couldn't we stay a bit longer?' she pleaded. Oliver had stopped singing now, bowing to the riot of applause and whistles from the audience.

Madeleine stood there, torn between anger and curiosity, and realised that she could be seen from the stage. She broke away quickly, running to find the shelter of the trees.

'Come on,' she hissed to Louise. 'We don't want them to know we've been watching.'

But Louise decided to pretend she hadn't heard her and bowed her head, scribbling intently in her notebook. Madeleine ran back down to the farm, confused by her mixed emotions of anger and betrayal, and with the memory of Oliver's full, strong voice ringing in her ears.

Outside the vicarage Colin was crouching by his motorbike as though he was praying to it. His tools were spread round him on the ground. She ran straight to him.

'D'you know what they're doing up there?' she demanded and he looked up at her, surprised. She hadn't spoken directly to him for months. 'Up at Marty's?'

'I do know, as a matter of fact. They're having a show. Ollie told me.'

'Ollie!' she said in disgust. She was breathless, and her hair was loose and windswept, lovely around her flushed cheeks.

Colin smiled. He felt warm to her in spite of everything. 'Oliver, then.'

'They're making fun of us, that's what they're doing. They come and take over our village and then they have the cheek to ridicule us.'

Colin rubbed his cheek, leaving a black smear of oil across it. 'We do the same. Remember the Bachelors' tea party. No one's safe there.'

'That's different. We live here. They've no right to make fun of us, to lie about us. Oliver pretended Ben's a drunkard, and he isn't, he just isn't like that. He must have spied on the wedding. He had no right!'

'You're keen on him, aren't you?' Colin spoke slowly, looking down at his oily hands. 'Oliver, I mean.' *She's changed*, he thought. *She's getting her old spark back, but, all the same, she's changed.* He was pleased about her anger. He wanted to put his arms round her to calm her down. He had never felt such tenderness for her. Desperately he wanted her to deny what he had just said, to say that Oliver meant nothing to her.

'I hate him!' she said and turned away, more confused than ever. So Louise had noticed and Colin had noticed and the villagers were talking about her, and all she had done was to walk down the lane with Oliver a few times and to let him hold her hand by the bridge. She hadn't even told him her name, though he had asked her over and over again. Her name was her secret, and he teased her to know it, and called her Beauty instead.

She watched Colin as he worked on his bike, intent now on his task. She felt closer to him than she had done for a long time. He was acutely aware of her. He was tongue-tied now, searching for something to say that would keep her there by his side.

'Are you definitely going to be a vicar, Colin?' she asked him.

Colin gave a scornful laugh, surprising her. All her life she had known that he was going to follow in his father's footsteps; it had never occurred to her till now that he might want to do anything else.

'Thing is, the old man expects me to do it, and I don't really know what else I'd do,' he said, shrugging. 'What about you?' He glanced up at her, meeting her eyes at last.

'I've got to get a job, Mum says. Or go to secretarial college in Hallam. Once we leave here—' She looked away from him, overwhelmed. It was impossible to imagine leaving. The conversation ended there; she could think of nothing else to say. She walked away, wrapped up in herself again.

That night, and the next, she heard someone whistling outside her house after she had gone to bed. She knew it was Oliver. She lay in bed, trembling, until the whistling stopped and a light scuff of footsteps told her he had gone. The third night came and she sat reading at her window, still in her day clothes, glancing out into the darkness every half-minute, and Oliver didn't come.

27

'I hear you went up to the navvies' concert the other day,' Jenny Barnes said. 'It won't do.'

Madeleine glanced at Louise, but her sister kept her head down.

'There's a lot of bad feeling against those workmen.'

'They're only doing their job,' said Sim. 'I'd ask them for a job myself if I was a fitter man. You get good money on a site like this.'

His wife ignored him. 'You've been seen walking out at night with one of them. Keep away from him, Grace. Keep away from them all. And that goes for you too,' she said to Tommy.

Madeleine sat in silence.

'You can finish the baking for me, and take a loaf to Aunt Susan,' Jenny said. 'Your father and I are going to take a stroll up to Dyson's Fields. It's time we chose our new house.'

'Can we come?' Louise and Tommy begged, and their mother nodded to them absently.

'You do understand what I'm saying, don't you, Grace? I don't want you to walk with him again. We don't like them. We don't want them here.' She sat down by Madeleine. 'We want the best for you. We want you to be happy again. But don't mix with those people. That's not the way.'

Later, Madeleine called in on Aunt Susan with some new-baked bread. Susan was bewildered when she saw her, trapped for the moment in the game her memory was playing with her. She was tricked into thinking she was seven years old again and that Madeleine was the schoolteacher. She folded her hands demurely and hung her head low.

'I've lost my slate, miss,' she said in a little-girl voice. Madeleine was still not used to these strange changes of identity in her great-aunt. She never knew what to expect. Sometimes Susan was tormented and grief-stricken and that was impossible to cope with, as nobody knew what she was trying to say or what she was remembering. But sometimes she seemed to become a child again, and Madeleine could even imagine her as she might have been eighty years ago, so well did she recall the events of her childhood and act them out. The problem was knowing how to respond to her. 'She's like in a dream,' Jenny had told her, 'and you don't wake sleepwalkers up, do you? Let her stay in her dream, if she's happy there. Just act along with her, that's what I do.' So Madeleine told Susan that she didn't need her slate that day, as they were going to be doing some painting instead. Susan clapped her hands, her eyes lighting up with pleasure, and spread her paper and paints on the table while Madeleine cleared out the grate and got a good fire going.

'Paint with me, miss,' Susan asked her, and Madeleine sat by her old aunt and patiently explained to her the things that Susan herself had taught her; how she must use her colours sparingly and keep her brushes clean. She showed her how to mix colours, and Susan watched, breathless with the magic of it.

'What shall we paint?' Madeleine asked.

'A fishy in the water,' Susan giggled, slapping paint on the page. She looked up sharply, the childish look gone from her face; the voice deepening to an old lady's again. 'They say a child drowned in the river, did you know? Knocked her head and drowned, just out here.'

'I do know,' Madeleine said quietly.

'She was just like you,' Susan whispered. 'Oh, I do miss her.' She reached out and touched Madeleine's face with her dry fingers, so tenderly that Madeleine could hardly bear it. She pushed her chair away and stood up abruptly to tend to the fire.

When she left Susan's she went up the track, over the stepping stones, up to where the Ghost Woods used to be, and beyond them to the ridge and the moors. Dead heather snagged at her skirts. She walked on blindly, past the scattered boulders with their fantastic, contorted animal shapes. Up here the wind was fierce, rain came in squalls with hail like gravel. She didn't care. She walked on, fast, her boots and her legs spattered with the mud of the dark peat. Grouse rose up around her with their heckling cry, Go back! Go back! and the black raven croaked on the wind.

At last she turned round. She felt calmer now. Sunlight burst through the slate clouds, spot-lighting the farmhouses in the valley. Soon it would be dusk. She was cold, her clothes were wet through. She began to run to keep warm, and as she came to the track that would take her off the ridge and down to the lower slopes she saw a man coming up towards her. At first she thought it was one of the hill farmers, and then she realised that it was Oliver. She hesitated and he looked up, hands on his hips, catching his breath back. 'Hey there, Beauty,' he called.

'Hello.' Madeleine stopped running and came slowly towards him. She was smiling. She couldn't help it. She was bright with smiles and so was he.

'You're wet through,' he said, when they reached each other.

She glanced down. 'I know. I got caught in a hailstorm up there.'

He took his jacket off and placed it over her shoulders and she tucked her fists inside the collar, pulling it close. She smiled up at him. 'Why aren't you working?'

'I am. I'm not on site today. There's a load more navvies coming and the foreman's set some of us on to putting up tin shacks for 'em.'

'Not up here?' she laughed. 'They'd get blown away.'

'No. Over where the woods used to be.'

'The Ghost Woods? They're haunted, you know. There used to be an abbey there, oh, hundreds of years ago, and we see the white monks sometimes.' She chattered carelessly, high with pleasure and excitement, and when he laughed and caught her hand in his she pretended not to notice.

'No, it's true,' she said. 'We've all seen them.'

'Aye, I believe you.' He lifted her hand to his lips and kissed it. 'I used to think you were a ghost. I used to think I'd never see a smile on you.'

She looked away, letting her hand slide out of his. 'Won't you get told off?'

'I'll go back in a minute. I just wanted to speak to you. I saw you running down from the ridge and I thought you might be in trouble or something.'

'What did you want to speak to me about?' she asked archly.

He took her hand again. 'I want to know your name.'

She was silent. *Mum doesn't understand*, she thought. *Everybody else in the world sees me as half a twin, except for Oliver*. He pressed her hand to his lips again and then bent down and kissed her on the mouth. It was a long, sweet kiss. She was dizzy with it, her first kiss.

'Why won't you tell me?'

'I can't.'

'You always say that! I can easily find out. You're a funny girl. A funny, lovely, sad, beautiful girl. I can ask anyone, but I want you to tell me.'

They started to walk down the slope together.

'Come on,' he teased. 'You must have a name. What can I call you, when I think of you every day? I see your face, but I have no name to put to it. You know mine. Do you think of me sometimes? Do you say my name? Oliver. Do you say that sometimes?'

'Will you promise not to tell anyone?' she asked, husky with emotion for him.

He laughed. 'If you want.'

'You won't tell anyone that you've talked to me? You won't speak about me to anyone?'

He kissed her again for her earnestness. 'I promise, I promise. What's your name, shy little Beauty?'

And for the first time since her sister had died, she spoke her own name out loud, giving it life, giving it birth. 'It's Madeleine.'

'Madeleine,' he said softly. 'A beautiful name. My beautiful Madeleine.' He put his arms round her and she felt herself soft and warm against him, dizzy again for him. They walked along the path, his arm still round her, her head leaning against his shoulder. There was a sudden riot of hammers on metal, and they saw that the navvies were watching them and thundering out a mocking hullabaloo on the sides of the shacks they were constructing; 'Ollie! Ollie!' they were shouting. She pulled herself away, alarmed and ashamed. The men whistled and jeered, 'Ollie, Ollie! Caught a pretty bird, have you?'

He laughed and waved to them. It was a boastful gesture, and in that moment she hated him again.

'What's her name?' one of the men called.

'It's Maid Madeleine!' he called back.

She pressed her hands to her face, hiding herself from him, from the cheering men.

'I lied,' she stammered. 'About my name. I lied.'

She started to run, not using the track that would have taken her towards the chanting navvies, but plunging straight down the hummocky slope, skidding and slithering, arms flailing, her breath jerking from her. It wasn't until she reached her cottage that she realised that she still had his jacket round her shoulders.

28

Colin had just returned from a visit to Durham, where he had met his tutor and been given a reading list. He was committed now. He liked his tutor, he liked the college. It would do, after all. His father would have his way and he knew it would please his mother if he could just tell her that he liked St John's. He could picture her waiting eagerly for him, preparing his favourite meal, wanting him to tell her every detail of the two days he had spent away from home. As he jumped down from the navvies' bus he saw Madeleine running down to the cottages, her skirt damp and muddy. His first thought was to run to her, to show her his book list, to tell her about the beautiful castle in Durham, the fine cathedral, the ancient colleges. He waved to her eagerly.

'Grace!' he shouted.

She stopped at once, panting for breath, staring

at him as if she had been pulled out of a trance. She was obviously distressed. Even from a distance he could tell that.

'Are you all right?' he called out.

She was too upset to answer. She shook the jacket off her shoulders and let it slide to the ground, and she ran into her house.

Colin crossed over the bridge and picked up the jacket. He recognised it at once for Oliver's. Jealousy reared like a horse inside him. What an intimate thing it was, to wear someone else's clothing. He shook it angrily, as though he was shaking her away from it. His first thought was to toss the jacket over the bridge and let the river do what it wanted with it. Then he considered just leaving it there on the parapet where Oliver might see it when he walked down one day. 'Damn him!' Colin said out loud. 'Damn you, Oliver!' After a moment's hesitation he stowed the jacket in his rucksack and strode home.

'How was Durham?' his mother asked as soon as he went in. She had been watching out for him all afternoon.

'Fine.' He bent down and kissed her. 'It's a beautiful town, Mum.'

'Good. Good. Tell me all about it!'

But he couldn't get the thought of Oliver's jacket out of his mind. The memory of it draped around Grace's shoulders, the distress in her eyes when she had let it slide down to the ground, haunted him and challenged him. He couldn't ignore it, yet he didn't know what to do about it. He sat in silence during mealtime, while his father tried to quiz him about Durham and St John's College. 'Fine,' was all he could say. 'It was fine.'

As soon as the meal was over he stood up and went out of the room. He pulled the jacket out of the rucksack and left the house, slamming the door after him. His father shrugged and went into his study. His mother cleared the plates from the table. The special meal had been barely touched. 'I will be glad to move from this valley,' she said, loudly, hoping her husband would hear and come and sit by her and ask her what was the matter. 'There's poison in this place now.'

Colin went straight to Marty's farm. Some of the men were coming out of the main farmhouse where they had been eating together. Some were already in their huts and barns, their lamps lit for the night. Without any real sense of what he was going to do or say, he thumped on the door of the caravan. Oliver opened it at once, surprised and pleased to see him. He was buoyant still from his meeting with Madeleine, and had taken her flight for sudden embarrassment at the men's behaviour. He hadn't given it any more thought. She was a strange girl. That was what fascinated him about her.

'Come in,' he said to Colin cheerfully. 'I've got some tea brewing.'

Colin hesitated in the doorway. He could see the mattress on the bare floorboards, the covers crumpled and roughly thrown back. He was wild with suspicion and jealousy.

'No, I won't come in,' he said. He pulled the damp jacket out of his rucksack and held it out. 'Yours, I believe.'

Oliver rolled up the jacket and put it across his shoulder, tucking his head against it as if it was a pillow. 'It should still be warm,' he said dramatically. 'It should still smell of her.'

'Come on out.' Colin could hardly suppress his anger now. 'I want a word with you.'

Oliver put the jacket on and stepped outside, smiling questions. 'What's up?'

Colin walked on quickly, his hands fisted in his pockets. Oliver paced beside him, plying him with questions about the visit to Durham, which Colin answered in monosyllables. They dropped down to the worksite at the valley bottom, where a muddy spoil heap towered next to a newly excavated valve shaft.

'Careful,' Oliver said. 'You don't want to be walking here in the dark. Go down two hundred feet and more, these shafts. Know what they're for?'

Colin shook his head. He didn't care. He had nothing to say, and Oliver, puzzled at his silence, was filling up the uncomfortable space with words.

'They'll take the overflow into tunnels. Wish I was clever, like you. I'd like to be one of those engineer chaps, working all this out. It's brainy stuff; even I can tell that.'

Colin swung round, his rage boiling and unsuppressed now. 'Don't you want to know where I found your jacket?' His voice was strangled in his throat.

'Where I left it, I should think. Only between you and me, it's a secret. She's a secret.'

'I challenge you to say who you're talking about.' Colin tried to speak with dignity, aware that his old-fashioned words made him sound ridiculous, furious with himself.

Oliver laughed. 'I made a promise. Can't break a promise to a lady.' He walked away, silent for a moment, and then swung round and flung his arms wide. 'Colin, I'm in love with her!' he shouted. His voice echoed round the valley. 'I'm in love with Madeleine!'

Colin closed his eyes. He was sick with shock. 'Madeleine is dead.'

'What? What do you mean? Dead?'

'Dead and buried in the churchyard for over a year now. How dare you mock her family like this? It was Grace you gave it to. You say you love her, and you don't even know her name! And do you know what she did with your jacket? She threw it down in the mud outside her house. That's how much she loves you.'

Wild anger flared in Colin. It was greater than him, an unknown beast that was beyond his control. He had never known anything like it before; he didn't even recognise it for what it was. He lunged out at Oliver, punched him so he sprawled backwards, and as he fell he threw himself on top of him, pummelling wildly, savagely. They grappled with each other, rolling over and over in the darkness. Colin was strong with rage, out of his mind. He didn't care what happened. Oliver rolled away, hauling Colin with him, staggering to stand them both up, and Colin dragged him back down again, knowing nothing but grief and anger and jealousy.

'For God's sake, for God's sake, stop!' Oliver gasped, trying to fend off his blows, trying to anchor them both down as they rolled closer to the edge of the shaft hole. 'Keep clear of the hole, for God's sake.'

'No one will ever know,' Colin said aloud, his voice strange and animal. 'You're only a navvy. You're only a scum. No one will ever miss you.' He felt the edge of the pit under his leg and with a massive pitch of strength heaved himself away, rolling Oliver round towards the hole. Oliver kicked desperately against his side to free himself, and Colin felt his own legs going over, felt the weight of his own body pulling him down, sliding him inexorably over the rim of the hole. Cold terror washed over him.

29

Colin's mother lit a fire in the living room, ready for when her husband had finished writing his sermon and would come out for his cocoa. She was distracted. She should have spoken to her husband about Colin's university place, and she hadn't. She had let the boy down, and he would go on with the course, hating every moment of it. It was not what he wanted to do. It had never been what he wanted to do, and his father had been blind to it. Colin had looked to her to speak to his father on his behalf, and she had ignored him. She took a handful of cherry tree twigs from the basket by the porch. The coils of bark slid away as she snapped them and laid them over the crumpled newspaper in the grate. *It is not what he wants to do with his life. Have I done what I wanted with my life?* she asked herself and the answering thought came back to her, *Yes, you had a child, but you let him down.*

She struck a match and held it away from herself, watching the little yellow-blue spurt of flame. She held it to the paper and it began to burn, turning brown. Bluey-grey smoke spiralled from it, then a flame leapt up and wrapped itself round the twigs, like a greedy tongue. It licked higher and higher and soon the twigs began to glow red and they too started burning. She placed little pieces of coal round the twigs, careful to put them over the brightest flames. Here and there the flames dodged about for air, and now there were only tiny spaces between the coals, with smoke pouring through them. The black holes began to gleam like golden eyes, and at last the flames discovered air. They danced out of the holes like leaping yellow devils, twisting this way and that, greedy and wild. She sat back on her heels, watching them, fascinated. She heard the bang of the kitchen door, and knew that Colin had come home. She placed a log on the top of the fire. The flames curled round it as if they were embracing it.

She didn't turn round, but stayed kneeling on the rug. He was exhausted, she could tell by his movements. *I won't ask him*, she thought. *He'll tell me in his own good time*. She pressed her hands together, waiting for him to speak to her.

'Mum.'

He was sobbing. She turned round quickly. He had blood on his face. He'd lost a shoe, and his shirt was ripped. He was covered in mud.

'I want to talk to you.' He sat down heavily, like an old man.

'What have you done?' She came over to him now and stood looking down at him, not touching him, her arms straight at her sides. She knew everything and she knew nothing.

'I tried to kill someone.'

'What? What are you talking about?'

He put his hands over his face. 'I tried to throw him down a pit.'

She laughed, shocked and relieved. 'Fighting!' She tried to make light of it. She was shaking.

'He saved my life. I nearly went down, and he pulled me . . . he pulled me, he hung on.' He broke down. 'I don't know how he managed it. I could have died.'

His mother watched him, cold with fright herself. 'I think you need to get yourself washed,' she said. She tried to keep her voice calm. 'I'll run a bath for you. Tell me about it later.'

'I'll never be the same again,' he said savagely.

She stared at him. She did not know her son. Shock made her angry. 'I suppose it was those hooligans up there got you into this.'

'I don't know what came over me. I wanted to kill him. I tried to kill him.'

She was helpless to touch him or comfort him. 'You'd better talk to your father about this. I'll go and boil up some water for you. Get yourself cleaned up, and when he comes through, talk to him.' She went out quickly into the kitchen. She pulled the door to behind her and stood with her back against it. She put her hands to her face and sobbed. *This is my son, speaking wild impossible words to me. I don't know what to do. I don't know how to help him.*

When she went back, Colin had gone. There was a scrawled note on the table: 'I'm sorry. I'm not fit to be your son. I can't stay. Colin.'

30

'He'll come back,' the vicar had said to his wife on the morning after the fight. 'Where would he go, after all? He's no money, no spare clothes. He's taken nothing with him. He hasn't even gone on his bike.'

'That's a blessing, at least. I'd hate to think of him charging round the countryside on that thing. In the state he was in, anything could happen. Anything.' Instinctively she looked towards the dresser. She stood up from the table, her hand to her mouth. 'But the keys have gone.'

Her husband followed her gaze. 'Then he's coming back,' he promised her. 'That's what it means. He's coming back.'

But the days passed, weeks passed and there was no word from Colin.

It was a dark winter, shrill with icy winds. The vicar toured the barns and huts of the workmen, searching for his son, and came home with sparks of ice on his coat and in his hair. Nobody knew anything. Nobody knew where Oliver was either. The farmers scoured the hedges as they dragged feed up to their stock. The villagers waited in horror, but no news came. The police were called and went away with a photograph of Colin, taken at the time of Ben's wedding; and still no news came. The valley was trapped in a hiatus of ice; waiting, watching, listening for the missing Colin. Nothing moved in the white sky or the white earth.

vicar's son reported mising, Louise wrote in her book. She sat staring at the letters. 'I don't think we'll ever see him again,' she sobbed.

'He'll be all right. He can look after himself.' Madeleine's voice was sharp with anxiety. She leaned over Louise's shoulder and fitted in the 's'. 'If you're going to be a reporter, you'll have to learn to spell,' she said.

'Don't you care?' Louise shouted. 'Don't you care about anything?'

Madeleine huffed and turned away, her fists tight at her side. She thought back to the last time she had seen Colin, how he had come running eagerly towards her from the navvies' bus, how she had spurned him. She had always spurned him, since Grace died, and now she had driven him away. She was quite sure it was her fault, whatever had happened. She had driven away her best friend, and she had never made up the broken friendship. Now it was too late. She ached for him to come home again.

'I don't think he's far away,' she said gently. But the thought was brutal in her, knocking inside her ribs, that Louise was right, that they would never see him again. She sat in the church in breathless silence with the other parishioners every Sunday, while the grey-faced vicar asked them to pray with him for his son's safe return.

'We just want news of him,' he said, and his voice was trembling. 'His mother said he was unwell the night he left. Anything might have happened to him.'

And cement lorries tipped load after load down the west shaft hole. The children stood watching in silent awe. The hole was like a greedy mouth swallowing up the liquid, gaping open for more and more. It would take days to fill it, so deep it went, and so far into the hillside the rivulets of cement trickled.

31

On the last day of February the skies cleared into a brilliant cold blue. The huge cranes were set in motion; sounds of clanking and shouting echoed from one end to the other. Elspeth was feeling restless all day. She had been ironing, nursing her aching back with one hand. She finished her work and paced round the house, too fidgety to sit down, too tired to walk up the lane to see her mother. She went to the kitchen door and leaned on the jamb, watching the way the evening sun made the frosty fields smoke. From way up in Marty's barns she could hear the noise of the workers, their voices ringing in the clear air. Their clamour could be heard in every room of the house.

'I wish they'd go!' she said suddenly. 'Can't they give us a minute's peace! Must they always be here?'

She went out into the yard. She could feel the baby tugging inside her and instinctively laced her fingers across her belly, cradling it, soothing it. She tipped her head back and followed the line of the huge cable that was slung high above their farm from one side of the valley to the other, marking the line of the dam wall. Her mouth was dry. Her throat was dry, so were her eyes. She looked at the cable, high, high up, hundreds of feet up. *That's how high the water is going to be, and my home will look like a toy beneath it. I wanted to spend the rest of my life in this house and, when we were married last year, it still seemed possible, when we danced round it spreading Mum's flowers round it, it was like a ring of enchantment, holding it safe. But nothing is safe. It's going to happen.*

'Come and see what they've done, Ben. The cable's up,' she called, her voice cracking on her parched tongue.

Ben trudged out of the kitchen and stood with his mouth open and his head twisted round, gawping up at the sky and the silver band that was strung across it, and said nothing. The agony that was inside him was unspeakable, least of all to Elspeth. He walked past her into the milking parlour. She could hear him shifting pails. She could have been helping, but she had no heart to go to him. *A sad heart turns the milk sour*, she said to herself. *I wouldn't touch the beasts tonight.* She followed him into the shed and stood in the doorway, one hand lifted against the post, her other hand flat against her belly where their baby swam, just willing Ben to look up and take notice of her.

He did at last. 'What?'

'Don't you mind?'

'What for?'

'About that damned cable. Over our house. Like a bad dream, right across the valley, right over our house, Ben. Don't you mind?'

He finished with the brown cow and patted her rump to shift her, edging the pail carefully out of the way.

'Never mind the bloomin' milk.' Elspeth felt like kicking the pail over.

Ben grunted and lifted his stool over into the next stall. 'What good will it do, minding about it?' He whistled behind his teeth for Toppy to come over to him.

'That whistle, that damned whistle!' Elspeth lunged forwards, and this time she did kick over the pail, sending its creaming froth fountaining over her skirt.

'Steady on, girl,' Ben said, slow and sweet as if one of the cows had gone clumsy. 'Give it to the pigs rather than waste it on your frock.'

But Elspeth had run back into the yard, sobbing and wretched. 'I want us to start all over again,' she shouted, her voice jerking and angry. She didn't care who heard her now, or whether Joan was standing gleefully at the window with her eyes lit up like lamps. *I want to go back to before Maddy died, before we were called to that meeting in the Hall, before Ben asked me to marry him. I want to be a girl again, running out of school with the others. I want to be a little child, and my mum looking after me, and everything safe and known and unchanging. I don't want this! None of this!*

Ben came out of the barn, a pail of pig swill in his hand.

'You think nothing of me, or your mum, or the house!' she shrieked, anger and pain making her voice harsh. 'All you care about is your blasted pigs. Well, keep your pigs. Marry your pigs, I don't care.' She tugged her wedding ring off her finger and threw it over the wall into the pigsty, and heard the sow squealing out of her sleep. She ran out of the farmyard and down the track towards her mother's house. Ben lumbered after her, stones skidding under his boots as he ran. He caught hold of her and she struggled to get away.

'Let me go, you great oaf!' She pummelled his chest with her fists, aware now of doors opening and of people peering out at her.

Ben was whispering to her with a low urgency, and his hands were wrapped tight round her. 'Come on, Elspeth, stop it now, hush, girl. Stop it now.' He kissed her and she clung to him, all the crying and the madness and the anger spilled out of her like the milk in the shed. 'I hate to see you unhappy,' he said. 'I don't know what to do with myself when you're unhappy. I love you.'

All that was left in her was weariness and sweetness for him. He led her home and his mother stepped away from the shadowy porch and let them through. He took Elspeth up to their room and made love to her, so they were dizzy with each other. And when everything was quiet again, soft and still with the yearning of sleep about it, with the moon peering through the window at them like a nosy face, Elspeth remembered her wedding ring.

They crept down the stairs, giggling, and stepped into their wellington boots in the porch.

They leaned over the pigsty and poked through the swill with long sticks, while the piglets grunted round them. A grey dawn came fingering through the sky and still they hadn't found the ring. When Elspeth went back into the kitchen, Ben's mother was raking the fire ready to boil the water.

'You were up early,' she said to Elspeth accusingly.

'I'm sorry if we woke you.'

'You woke the neighbourhood. What were you doing, stirring the pigsty like a pot of stew?'

Elspeth giggled. 'Looking for something.'

Joan squared her back, ready with questions, but Elspeth would say no more. She carried the porridge pot over to the table.

'You'll find nought in a pigsty,' said Joan. 'Except muck.'

'Plenty of that,' agreed Elspeth. She tapped on the window and Ben came in from the dairy with a mug of milk. His mother tipped his breakfast on to his plate, two fried eggs side by side and shining like cows' eyes, the way he liked them.

After breakfast Ben tried again, this time with the shovel. Ben's mother watched from the window, speechless with curiosity, arms folded.

They eased every bit of muck from the sty into the yard, and then as Elspeth hosed it down Ben turned it all over, peering into it as if he was a gold prospector. At last Elspeth sank down on to her hands and knees and slid her fingers over the mess. She had been so sure she would find it. Now she was tearful, realising what a hopeless task it was. The sty was clear, swilled clean, and the ring had not been found.

'They've eaten it,' she sighed.

'Happen it'll be passed out,' he consoled her.

She giggled, turning her mucky and tear-stained face towards him. 'And would you want me to wear a ring that's been passed through a pig?' she teased.

He shook his head, and she put her arms round him and kissed him. 'Course I would wear it, you softie! But I want no other, Ben, if we don't find it. I love that ring. I love you. And blimey, I love your pigs.'

32

Madeleine was frantic now to talk to Oliver. She felt sure he must know something about Colin's disappearance; after all, Oliver was his only friend. Nothing would persuade her to go up to his caravan again and knock on his door, but she watched out for him among the workers on the site. Every day she grew more anxious. He wasn't there, she was sure of it. How could they both be missing? Was it possible that he and Colin had gone away together?

Then one day she saw him walking down to the village. She hung back, watching him. He was alone, and his face was white and strained.

'Oliver,' she called at last.

He paused for a moment, as though he was thinking of something to say to her, and then he changed his mind and carried on towards the vicarage. She watched him, desperate to know whether he had news of Colin, afraid to ask him.

Colin's mother opened the vicarage door and stared at Oliver, recognising him at once as the young man her son had befriended, the navvy from the site.

'What do you want?' she asked, made cold by his blank expression.

'I've come for the bike, Mrs Hemsley.'

'The bike? What bike?'

'Colin said I could have his bike.' He held a note out to her. She recognised Colin's hand-writing.

'William, will you come here,' she called to her husband. She took the note from Oliver, her hands shaking, and pushed past him into the garden to read it in full light.

'Oliver,' the note read. 'I owe you something. Please have my bike. I won't be needing it any more.'

She stared up at him. Her husband joined her and she held the note out towards him, saying nothing, remembering what Colin had told her about the shaft hole. The vicar read the message aloud, savouring every word as if it was a poem.

'Where is he?'

'No idea.'

'When did this come?' he asked.

Oliver shrugged. 'A few months ago, maybe. It had been pushed under my door.'

'A few months ago! All that time! And why have you only just brought it to us? You must have known we were sick with worry.'

'I haven't been here. I haven't been able to work. I bust my shoulder in a fight.'

The vicar and his wife exchanged glances. They had said nothing to anybody about the confession Colin had sobbed out to his mother. They had never referred to it again to each other, refusing to countenance the idea that their son had tried to kill a man. The vicar couldn't keep the rise of fear out of his voice. 'Where's he gone? What have you done to him?'

'I've no idea where he is. I've come to pick up the motorbike. You see what it says. He wants me to have it.'

'Oh no.' Colin's mother shook her head slowly. 'You're not having it.'

Oliver took the note from her hand and folded it up. 'The fact is, you can't stop me, Mrs Hemsley. You've seen the letter, you recognised the writing.' He took a small ignition key on a piece of string

244

out of his pocket. 'This was with the note, you see. So it's mine now. I knocked on your door out of politeness, but I don't need your blessing to take it.' He turned away and walked round the side of the house to where Colin's bike was parked under its oilskin.

'I've lost my son!' Colin's mother shouted after him, hoarse with grief.

'I've lost my friend,' he said under his breath.

He pulled back the cover and looked at the bike, which was gleaming in the sunlight. He ran his hands over the body, lightly, stroking it, rapturous with longing. He ran his fingers over the coiled springs, chiming them with his nail, as if they were singing to him now. He swung his leg across the saddle and sat astride it, rocking the side stand back. He turned the key in the ignition and kicked the machine into life. It roared instantly and he sat with his head back and his eyes closed. 'Beautiful, beautiful beast,' he murmured. 'Beautiful beast.' He twisted the throttle grip and the machine roared again, and again, still on its main stand, and the sound of its voice echoed against the walls of the cottages and the far hills. Then Oliver turned off the ignition. The beast was silent. He stepped down from the bike, lifted the covers carefully over it again, and walked away from it. Inside the house, the vicar and his wife looked at each other, perplexed.

Oliver went on out of the village to the work-site and joined the tippers at the east shaft hole, where the lining was being filled with cement. The cement was rising slowly, perhaps twenty feet now from the top. He stepped to the edge and dropped the keys down. They rested for a moment on the surface of the soft, muddy sea and then sank from sight. More cement was tipped, more and more, a relentless, swallowing tide, and the hole gulped it down. Within the week it had set, firm and solid as the mountains themselves.

33

The farmers trod the paths they had always trodden, day after day as they had always done; bringing the cows home for milking, rounding the sheep, driving stock to market. The children ran to school every weekday morning and tumbled out at the end of the day, shrieking into the wind, scrambling round the fields and over the stiles, splashing between the stepping stones. And in the back room of the post office shop Dora Proctor and her father Jacob shouted at each other: 'What will we do when the dam's finished? We've got to think of the future. I don't want to. I want it to stay as it is. But it won't stay as it is. It's lost. It's gone. Look at the valley now, how ugly they've made it. It's gone.' And their words were echoed in every household in the valley.

There was nowhere to go to escape the sound of the navvies: their machinery, their voices, their laughter. The work progressed inexorably, the wall of the dam reared up. It completely blocked the morning light from the post office shop. Jacob Proctor drew a curtain across his bedroom window and refused to look at it.

'Will we never get out of here?' Dora moaned to the women queuing up with their ration books. 'This is worse than purgatory. When will our houses be ready?'

'All the things in the garden are starting up again,' Jenny said. 'Lovely little things, while the valley gets uglier by the day.'

'How's your Grace getting on?' Dora asked her, always itchy for news.

'She's coping,' said Jenny quietly. 'But she spends hours on her own, talking to herself.'

'She needs company, poor girl. Not still walking out with the young man from the caravan, then?'

Jenny shook her head and pursed her lips, not willing to be engaged in village gossip when it concerned her family. But the conversation gave her the idea of moving Louise in with her sister.

'It'll be better for both of you,' she said. 'Louise is too big to be sharing with Tommy now.'

'No,' said Madeleine at once. 'No, Mum.

Please don't ask me to do that.'

'It's all right,' said Louise. 'I'll put up with Tommy for a bit longer. But when we move to Dyson's Fields, I won't have to share with him then, will I? Actually,' she said, 'I don't want to be in Grace's room. She hardly ever opens her curtains. She never cleans it out. It's a mess.'

'It was never like that before,' her mother hesitated, looking at Madeleine, 'when there were two of you.'

Madeleine flinched. She ran up to her room and closed the door behind her. It was true that she never allowed anyone to come into it. It smelled musty, even to her. She opened the curtains and the sunlight poured in, lighting up the swirls of cobwebs. Dust furred the golden mirror on the mantelpiece.

'I can hardly see you,' she breathed. 'Grace, Grace, I'm sorry.'

She ran downstairs for a dustpan and brush and cleaned the room vigorously. She wiped the skim of dust from the mirror and her sister emerged, sure and sweet-faced as she had ever been. 'You've come back,' she said.

Downstairs, Jenny Barnes smiled. She could hear Madeleine talking to herself as she worked.

'I won't kill the spiders. I'll scoop them in my hands the way you used to do – ugh! – and let them dangle down on to the honeysuckle outside our window.'

Madeleine opened the window wide and leaned out. It was still early. The dew was still wet on the grass, glinting. She took a deep breath, tilting back her head to feel the sun on her face. The gentle warmth was like a benediction. *Oh Grace, it makes me feel alive! I AM ALIVE!*

She slid down over the sill and jumped into the garden. She could hear the birds singing, every separate note pure and distinct like drops of water. She could see the sunlight touching every leaf, and the way the breeze tossed them this way and that way, with the light coming through them in so many shades of green and gold. Her mother's early yellow roses were blazing like little suns themselves. She wanted to pick one for Grace, but it had to be perfect.

Not a bud, not the closed tight bud that tells me you are dead and stopped.

She watched how the full-blown rose trembled for the bee, how he nuzzled inside it, deep into its darkness, how he tumbled out, full and drunk and dizzy with pollen.

Not the full rose. That would be Elspeth's rose.
I understand these things now.

She found the perfect rose for Grace. It was just opening out like a hand uncurling, with a pure, sweet, wet perfume. She ran home with it and placed it on Grace's side of the bed.

And the curtains will stay open now, so you can see the sunshine and the hills, and watch the light pouring through the leaves. See how beautiful it is. You must never forget how beautiful it is, how the curlew's song trickles out across the moors, how the whole valley is white with the lace of cow parsley. You'll never leave here, my darling Grace. And I'll be both of us for Mum. I want to be both Madeleine and Grace for her now.

Because she had decided not to speak to Oliver again, Madeleine stopped noticing him. She had no idea whether he was still working on the site. She told herself that she didn't care. Sometimes in the evenings she could hear music coming from Marty's farm; she imagined she heard his voice among the singers, his laughter. But her world was full of such things: her sister's voice in the river; her face in the mirror. She no longer knew which was real and which was imagined. Jenny Barnes watched her anxiously, noticing the frown of concentration that told her that her daughter was listening to other sounds than the ones she herself could hear. But she no longer hid herself away in her darkened room for hours on end. Miss Skinner invited her to help in the school again and to everyone's surprise she went willingly. *Grace would have said yes*, Madeleine told herself. *Mum will be pleased because this is what you would have done.*

Soon the seedlings that Sim planted were in full flower. A poppy sprang up out of nowhere, it seemed, and he crouched over it, peering into the opening bud, spying the purple-black heart of it with wonder. When it unfurled he called everyone out to see it. 'I've never seen ought like it, round here,' he said. His voice was soft. 'All the years I've been growing things, and I've never seen nought like this in the garden.'

Louise tried to write a poem about it in her notebook, chewing her pencil as she struggled to think of words to describe its daring blowsiness. Scarlet Dancer, she called it. She wrote down the title again and again, with trails of words floating round it like ribbons. She showed the poem to Madeleine.

'It's for you. I wanted it to be better than this.'

'It's good,' Madeleine said.

'No, it's not. It's stupid. I can't do it. It's too hard. I want to write about the way it dances, and how the red is like a skirt billowing round. I can't do it.' She scribbled across her words, frustrated and angry. 'I wanted to do it for you. And I've ruined it.'

'We could try and paint it,' Madeleine said. 'That might help.' They brought out their paints and spent the morning mixing colours to try to find the exact red. Madeleine frowned at her page with its blobs of orange and crimson and scarlet, as frustrated as Louise had been.

'Grace would be able to do it,' she said in despair.

Louise laughed. 'Do you know what you just said?'

Madeleine stared at her sister, then dabbed again at her painting.

'Mum says it's been harder for you than for any of us.' Louise spoke hurriedly, letting out a tumble of words that she had been holding in her head. 'She said you must feel as if part of you died too, when Maddy died. But she says you're coming through it now. And you are, Grace. Look at you, painting lovely pictures again, and your room is pretty and clean, and sometimes you even smile. Mum said she thought she'd lost you, too, and that was worse than anything. And I've been lonely without you. But you're coming back, aren't you? You're getting better. I want you to be happy again.'

Madeleine seemed not to hear her. She carried on painting, dabbing furiously into the paintbox and on to the page. 'What do you think of this, with that bit of marigold behind it?' she said at last. 'That sets off the red just right, don't you think?'

'It's like the sun,' Louise agreed. 'Can I put that in my poem?'

Madeleine put her brush and paper down. 'My sweet Louise.' She put her arms round her. 'What would I do without you? My little sunshine sister.'

34

The work which had begun at the far end of the valley was swiftly encroaching on the borders of the little village. Safety barriers had been put up to keep the villagers away from the site; now there was hardly anywhere for the children to play except in the meadows by the packhorse bridge. Tommy and his cousins were passing their football to each other at the end of the day when it bounced among a crowd of workmen making their way to the public house up at Dyson's Fields. They teased the boys by passing it from one to another.

'That's it,' Tommy grumbled to Mike. 'We've had it now.'

But the men soon got bored with their game and Oliver emerged from among them, dribbling the ball up to Tommy, and then running past him. Mike tackled him and Oliver expertly dribbled the ball away from him.

'Aw, come on,' Tommy pleaded. 'Give it us. Mum'll want us home for us tea any minute.'

Oliver picked up the ball and started running round Tommy with it, bouncing it, swerving round and backing, while Tommy lunged out uselessly, laughing at first, and then annoyed. The other boys ran off home, fed up.

'What's it worth?' Oliver said. 'Do us a favour and you can have your ball back.'

'OK.'

'Tell that pretty sister of yours I'd like a word with her.'

'Our Louise?'

'Is she Louise now?' Oliver laughed. 'How many names has she got?'

'Can I have me ball back first?' Tommy leapt for the ball and Oliver dodged away from him.

'When she comes.'

'Bloomin' 'eck.' Tommy ran to the house and into the kitchen where Louise and Madeleine were shelling peas.

'That bloke wants to see you,' he told Louise.

'What bloke?'

'That tall bloke from the site.'

Louise giggled and blushed. 'He wants to see me?'

She went to the window. Oliver was still dribbling the ball, weaving round with it in figures-of-eight.

'Show off,' she said. 'It's the man from the caravan.'

Madeleine looked up sharply, pale.

'Are you sure it's not Grace he wants?' Louise asked.

'He asked for the pretty one.' Tommy hopped about impatiently.

'Thanks, Tommy,' the two girls said.

'Hurry up. I won't get me ball back till you go.'

'No,' said Madeleine.

'Louise, you go,' he pleaded. He dipped into the bowl of shelled peas and scooped out a handful.

'I will not. Don't be daft, it's not me he wants. Go on, Grace. Our Tommy's being a pest.'

Madeleine went slowly to the door. She hadn't spoken to Oliver since the day she had given him her name and taken it back again. He had disappeared from her life. She had become calm again, and now, at the sound of his name, her blood was pounding in her veins. She tried to breathe deeply, slowly. She lounged in the doorway, just watching him.

'Bloomin' 'eck,' Tommy said in despair.

'Stop swearing,' she said over her shoulder.

'It's not swearing, that. It's just words.'

She could tell Oliver was looking at her now, darting a glance every now and again in her direction. She was warm for him again, crazy now for the butterfly shiver of his hand caressing her cheeks and her hair, and for the soft touch of his lips. He glanced across at her and smiled and she stepped forwards from the door like someone in a dream. With a whoop of joy Tommy darted past her to claim his football. Oliver waited for her to come right up to him and then kicked the ball away. He held out his hands and took both of hers.

'Hey, Beauty,' he said. 'My beautiful ghost-girl. Why have you stayed away from me?'

'I thought you'd gone away.'

'I've been working on the new houses up there. I wanted to see you. I've missed you. Have you missed me?'

He led her away from the cottages and up towards Marty's farm. Louise watched from the window, narrowing her eyes as she followed their route. Jenny came downstairs from clearing the cupboards and Louise went quickly away from the window, back to the pile of peas still in their shells on the kitchen table.

'Where's Grace?'

'She went out.'

'Where, for goodness' sake? She had a job to do.'

'Our Tommy's lost his ball.' Louise bent forwards so her hair hid her face. *Please, please, don't look out of the window. I want Grace to be happy. She loves him, I know she does. Let her be happy.*

Oliver led Madeleine up towards his caravan at Marty's farm. He had found some paint in one of the barns and had daubed the sides with flowers.

'That's pretty,' Madeleine laughed.

'I wanted you to like it.'

The navvy cook came out of the farmhouse and stood with arms folded, watching them silently as Oliver opened the door of the caravan. Madeleine hung back.

'I'd better not come in.'

Oliver stepped in front of her, shielding her from the cook's stare. 'Why not?'

'Mum wouldn't like it.'

'Mum's not invited. I just want a few minutes alone with you.'

He put one arm around her, the other arm holding back the door, and he folded her round so the going was easy; one, two steps up and she was inside his caravan. She felt him move behind her and heard the soft click of the door. He moved across the room and pulled the dark old sheet that served as a curtain across the window. The inside of the caravan took on a soft glow. It was warm and stuffy. It smelled of him, of his body. Madeleine tried not to look at the buttoned mattress on the floor. There was a book beside it and she kneeled down, leafing through it. Colin's name was on the flyleaf.

'Colin,' she said. She clasped the book in both her hands.

'Aye. He gave it me.'

'Do you know where he's gone?'

He shook his head. 'I've not brought you here to talk about Colin.'

He had to prise the book away from her fingers, then dropped it on the floor. He sat on the mattress and pulled her towards him.

'Don't,' she murmured.

'Do.' He kissed her very tenderly and she felt her whole body softening towards him, yearning for him.

'Please, Oliver.'

'Why not?' he whispered. 'You like kissing, don't you? You like me?'

'I do, but...'

'But nothing, my ghostly Beauty.' His breath was warm and soft and fluttering, and his fingers stroked her neck, her blouse, the curve of her breasts, and the sensation was delicious, and the tender longing for him was deep inside her, dark and wet and secret as a sea. She felt as if her whole body was opening up for him.

'*No!*' screamed Grace inside her head. '*Not him!*'

Madeleine pulled herself away sharply, snapped open her eyes and stood up. She looked down at him, trembling. 'I told you, I don't want to,' she said.

Oliver groaned and sat forwards, his head in his hands. She didn't know what to do with herself. She wanted to touch his hair and say she was sorry. She wanted to run back to the safety of home. She wanted him to stroke her again. She turned and wrenched back the curtain, too roughly, so the cord snapped. The light was harsh and bright, blinding her. She opened the door and stepped outside, drinking in the sharp air, shivering, hugging herself. She walked quickly away from the caravan. Before long she could hear Oliver behind her. She quickened her pace but he caught up with her. She felt angry and hurt and ashamed; confused. She had no idea what she could say to him.

'You won't see me again,' he said, his voice tight and new.

She was silent, and he walked beside her, saying nothing.

'Why?'

'I'm moving on.'

She nodded. Her eyes were hot, burning.

'There's a big construction job down south. There's loads of work. Anywhere. I could go anywhere. I'm leaving tonight.'

She stopped. 'Tonight!'

'You probably don't care.'

'I do care!' She turned her face up to him, tears starting in her eyes.

'Tell me to stay here, then!' His voice was wretched. 'I will if you want me to.'

'I – I don't know,' she stammered. The grip of his fingers was tight on her arm.

'You don't love me, do you?'

'Oliver, don't say that,' she said, helpless. He

262

kissed her again, but this time there was no passion, no tenderness. He was fierce and tight and strong, and she was afraid of him and for him. *I want him. But I don't love him.* The knowledge was clear and true and right, and she looped her arms round him and felt safe now, older than him and stronger. She did not want to hurt him. When he pulled himself away from her, his eyes were wet with self-pity.

'Give me something. A lock of your hair, a photograph. I haven't got anyone, Grace. I haven't got anyone who cares whether I live or die.'

'Wait here,' she said. 'I've got something you can have.'

She went back to the cottage. Her mother and Louise looked at her curiously when she went in, and Madeleine walked past, saying nothing, and went up to her room. She took out of the top drawer the photograph that had been taken at Elspeth's wedding. She was standing apart from the wedding group. She remembered the moment, when all the family members had lined up outside the church. For a second she had allowed the ghost of a smile to play around her lips. She looked so like Grace. It could have been her. Standing next to her was Colin, proud in his best man's outfit. She touched his face. 'Where are you now?' she whispered. 'Where are you, Colin? My heart is so cold.'

She took a pair of scissors out of her sewing box and carefully cut round her image. She put the group photograph back in her drawer, took out one of the lavender-scented envelopes that Louise had given her for Christmas. She put her cut self into it. Then she walked back down through the kitchen.

'Grace? Where do you think you're going, child?' her mother demanded, and the look her daughter gave her told her that the child had grown up, grown away from her.

Oliver was waiting beyond the bridge. Madeleine gave him the envelope and he took out the photograph and kissed it, then put it into his breast pocket.

'I know there's someone else,' he said. 'I always knew.'

'Please take care.' She allowed him to embrace her, wordless, and then she pulled away. 'I have to go,' she said. 'I have to.'

When she went back to the kitchen she took her place at the table next to Louise. Tommy was sent to fetch Sim in from the garden. The meal was served around her. Tommy and Louise squabbled about the last portion of pie, Sim invited everyone to comment on the sweetness of his early peas. Jenny stood up to clear the dishes, and as she did so Madeleine put out her hand and touched her mother's arm. She pushed her chair back and put her arms round her, tight and warm and close as a child in the womb.

35

It was late June. Elspeth was heavy and slow by now as her baby turned and squirmed inside her. Won't be long, everyone told her. Louise watched her with interest.

'Does it hurt?'

'No,' Elspeth smiled. 'Gives me backache sometimes, and the little bunny gives me a right kick to wake me up. But it doesn't hurt, no.' She sighed sleepily. 'It's all I can think about these days, this baby in me. I'm like a balloon, in't I? I feel as I'll go pop any minute.'

'Will she really go back to the right shape again?' Louise asked her mother. 'She's enormous. I don't ever want to be like that. I don't think I'm ever going to have babies, if that's what they do to you.'

'I can remember you saying that you were going to have nine,' Madeleine reminded her.

'That was two years ago. I was just a child,' said Louise. 'I didn't know any better.'

'What's the future for this child?' Ben's mother said, watching Elspeth shifting uncomfortably in her chair as she sewed a tiny garment. The older woman guessed that the birth was close. 'You can't deny what's going on out there.' She jerked her head towards the window.

'I'm not denying it. I just – I just can't think about it.' Ben wiped his hand across his brow in a gesture of helplessness.

Elspeth jabbed the needle into her finger.

'Everyone's been going up to Dyson's Fields, choosing their house,' Joan went on. 'You have to put your name down for the one you want.'

'I don't want one.'

'Ben...we got to do something,' Elspeth murmured.

'You're both the same, you two. You're both the same.' He looked at Elspeth, helpless, too miserable to say any more.

Within a day, the baby came roaring into the world. Elspeth was upstairs when her labour started, gathering up linen for washing. She felt pains rising up in her as if her bones were being pushed apart.

Not today, she said to herself. *How can it be today, when Ben is away over the tops with the sheep and won't be back for hours?*

Joan was below in the kitchen, her sleeves rolled up to her elbows, water steaming in the pot over the fire. She was singing to herself, a low, determined song that was something like a hymn, though she seemed to be making up the words as she went along. Elspeth concentrated on the sound coming up between the floorboards, trying to pick up the tune and echo it, and gradually the pain eased.

'That's better,' she said. 'Perhaps it will go away now, just till Ben gets back. You wait, little bunny. Bide your time.'

She picked up the basket of shirts and night-things she had collected and carried it down the stairs, balancing it on her side. When she was half-way down, the pain came again, rising like a tide deep within her. She gasped aloud, but Joan didn't hear her for the noise she was making herself, squishing water and singing. Elspeth leaned against the wall, unable to move forwards or back-wards, unable to sit, too uncomfortable to stand.

A drench of sweet-smelling water drained down her legs and on to the stairs. 'Sorry, sorry,' Elspeth gasped. She started to weep with pain and excitement, calling out for her own mother.

'Will you hurry with those things,' Joan called out impatiently.

Elspeth tried to move forwards and the basket fell from her hip and tumbled down the stairs, the contents sprawling out as if life had sprung into them for a moment. Joan snapped round, frowning at Elspeth's carelessness, then saw her swaying on the stairs. For the first time ever, a rush of tenderness for the girl came over her. She saw at once, by Elspeth's red, strained face, by the water dripping on the stairs, that the child of her only son was about to be born.

'Lord love us, Elspeth, stay right there,' she ordered. She dried her hands on her pinny and ran up to the girl, putting her arm firmly round her waist. 'Up or down?'

'Don't know,' Elspeth sobbed.

'We may not get as far as your room. Best use mine.' Joan thought briefly about the good mattress that was about to be ruined. She helped Elspeth up the stairs and tried to steer her into her austere white room with its black, frowning beams. Elspeth edged back from the doorway. She didn't want her baby to be born there. 'Ben was born on this bed,' Joan breathed, clucking with greed for the baby that was coming.

'Better now,' Elspeth gasped. 'Eased off.' She thought of Joan snatching her baby from her as if it was her own, and somehow forced herself to lumber down the creaking corridor to the blue rush of light from the room that was hers and Ben's. She tried to sink down on to her bed.

'We'll have that off.' Joan whipped away the patchwork bedcover and eased back the clean sheets and blankets. She ran to the chest and pulled out the oldest sheets and spread them on the bed, then rolled Elspeth on to them. 'How d'you feel?'

'Fine,' Elspeth said, bewildered. The pain had gone. She felt as if she was floating in a blue sea, rocking gently, as if she could sleep. Is the baby not going to come after all? she wondered. Is it curled up and sleeping, waiting for Ben to come home again?

'I want my mum.'

She heard Joan running down the stairs and slopping across the yard to the gate, over the lane and down the track to Madge's farm. Far away on the dam wall was the *chink!* of a mason hammering stone. The sound stopped suddenly, as if the man was listening out for something. In Elspeth's room the silence was like a waiting breath. She lay back with her eyes closed, waiting for the blue sea to wash her away, and then a huge wave engulfed her and her baby was born.

36

Aunt Susan leaned against the sink, dipped her plate and cup into the tepid water and stacked them up on the draining board. She rubbed her hands on her skirt to dry them and went out into the yard, breathing in deeply. The pink stocks by the gate smelled their sweetest at this time of the night, when the air was damp and cool. The cry of an owl shivered across the valley. The moon was behind clouds, and the monster arch of the new viaduct was blackened from sight. Nothing stirred. There were no lights in the farms or the cottages, no lights from the workmen's shacks up on the hill. The thoughts in her head were as clear as crystal.

On such a night as this I used to come out with my father to poach his Lordship's pheasants. On such a night as this I used to slip out of my bed and steal up to the Ghost Woods to lie on the leaves with David. I can feel the sweet warmth of his breath on my cheek, I can hear how he whispered to me that he loved me forever, how he told me he would marry me in the summer. And when he drowned in the terrible flood, only the quiet hills and the black night could give me comfort. There was no comfort in the church, for I was a sinner. And on such a night as this, my baby was born; my little broken bird. I didn't even know about you, little sparrow, till you slipped out. You were only weeks in my belly, too tiny to live outside of me, too weak to breathe on your own. You were a sin. Nobody knew. I scrabbled the earth with my fingers till the hole was deep enough to plant you in, to bury my shame, to hide my sin. I trickled the soil over you, it sounded like rain, like the pittering of rain, and the night was so black that I knew that no one on this earth had seen. 'God bless you,' I said, 'tiny morsel, tiny love-bird.' Nobody knows.

Susan plucked the head of one of the pink stocks and opened the gate. She walked with the hazel stick that Seth had whittled for her, and made for the Ghost Woods, knowing the way exactly. A long time ago a monastery had stood there, and had been destroyed by soldiers. Every generation passed down to its next the memory of the ravaged monastery and the ghosts of the monks who wandered there still. It was there, under the trees in the ancient site, that she had buried her baby. It had seemed a fit place, sanctified once. She had marked the tiny grave with a stone and scratched two letters into it. S D, the S winding round the D like a vine. Over the years she had worked the letters in deeper with a sharp piece of gritstone. Now the trees had gone, destroyed by the navvies. Their tin shacks stood where the monastery used to be. The stone stood alone. Soon it would all be under water.

She sat by the grave that she had dug over seventy years ago, and placed the flower on it. The clouds were racing fast, showing now by the spare moonlight squints the hulk of the viaduct and, beneath it, the deserted Hall, the grey walls of the farm buildings and cottages. She sat on her heels, quite contented, watching how the streaming clouds made the lights and shadows shift and dance.

After a time she was aware of a movement among the stumps of the trees. A tall figure was wandering backwards and forwards. It was impossible to make out any features, yet he seemed to be a man. Every now and then the figure put out his hands, reaching out to touch something invisible. Susan watched, wondering, a catch of fear and not fear, thrill perhaps, in her throat. She stood up as the figure approached her, yet it was clear that he hadn't seen her. He walked straight past her, slowly, steadily, and went on towards the navvies' huts. He paused as he reached the first hut, touching the sides soundlessly. Then he turned and came back down to Susan. She thought he was going to walk straight into her and sprang back, alarmed. The figure stopped and reached out towards her and her senses flitted away from her in fright.

'Who's this?' he said.

She knew the voice. Her confused mind was a muddy pool again, and there were no names there, but she knew the voice.

'I'm minding the baby,' she whispered, her own voice fluttering in her throat.

The ghost figure dropped his hands to his sides. 'Susan, is it?' he asked.

'Little Susan Sorrel. Doing no harm.'

He crouched down and his hands groped to the stone, his fingers tracing the letters. 'Now I know. S D. S for Susan, is that it? Is something buried here? Is it your baby, Susan?'

But surely she knew the voice. 'She's all right. She's fast asleep,' she whispered. Then the wonderful knowledge came to her. 'It's David, isn't it!' she said, laughing now, blithe as a girl of eighteen. 'Come to find me, haven't you? I knew you'd come soon.'

'D for David. I always wondered. Come on, Susan. I'll see you home.'

She jumped up and linked her arm in his and they walked together down the hill, she smiling up at the blank, closed face of the young man at her side, and the moon dipped and flashed as the clouds washed across it and made their shadows dance.

They stopped by the door, under the deeper shadow of the viaduct straddling the garden on its huge legs. It cut a black swathe across the stars. The owl shivered its cry into the night.

'I'm tired now, David. Leave me be.'

'I'll see you in.' Don't break into her dreams. Everybody in the village knew that. Old Susan's playing with the fairies.

She leaned on his arm as he led her into the house. She paused by the mirror, glimpsing her reflection. She allowed herself to be lowered into her patched settee and she sank back, eyes closed, completely weary. The dancing world stilled again. She felt quite calm.

I am myself again. I lost my self and now I've found her.

'I don't mind the thought of my cottage going now, going to the water, fishes floating through the doors and windows like bees on summer night,' she said. She opened her eyes. The dying fire flickered light across the young man's face, and she knew him. 'It's all right, Seth. I shall be all right.'

He bent down to her. 'Your secret's quite safe,' he told her.

'Oh yes. Quite safe. Under the earth, under the water, under the moon. Quite safe.' She leaned forwards and touched his face. 'I know myself by my old face in the mirror. How do you know yourself, Blind Seth?'

He went home quietly, uncertain. For a time he had been lost himself up there in the Ghost Woods without his familiar guiding landmark trees to touch. For the first time in his life he had felt himself to be a stranger in his own valley. He went quickly back to his own cottage and pulled the door to behind him, reaching out for the old comfort of his grandfather's armchair. The sound of girls' laughter came to him, the sure grasp of hands in his own, the wild dancing on the hillside.

After a time Susan edged herself up out of the settee and went over to the table. She turned up the lamp. Her tubes of paints and her brushes lay in an untidy heap. She pulled her sketchbook towards her and turned the pages one by one, looking at her paintings of the Hall, the river, the valley in summer, the valley in winter, lambs in the fields, ewes being dipped, old Jacob and Ted on the bench under the chestnut tree. 'You've not been a bad painter, girl,' she chuckled. She closed up the book and wrote in pencil across the front 'For Madeleine', and then she frowned. Was that right? 'I still get mixed up,' she muttered. 'Should it be for Grace?' She put the pencil down and went back to her chair, and sank down in it, exhausted. She closed her eyes again. 'It is right,' she said.

It was Madeleine who found her the next morning. Something about the perfect stillness of the room as she opened the door told her that Susan Sorrel was dead.

37

It seemed to happen so quickly in the end. The hill farms were already empty. The sawmill was closed down, and the men who had worked there took jobs on the dam site. Prisoners of war awaiting repatriation were put to work alongside them and up at Dyson's Fields, building the filter house for the reservoir and finishing the new housing estate. Before the summer was out, the first houses at Dyson's Fields were ready. Dora was the first to move in, crowing with excitement. You'd have thought she had been made the Queen of England and was moving into Buckingham Palace, the fuss she made of it all. She walked back down to the post office shop the next day and held court there.

'You press a switch, and a light comes on! Wait till you see! You turn a tap and hot water comes out of it! And the lavatory! Wait till you see the lavatory!'

'Can we move in soon?' Louise asked her mother. 'I can't wait!'

'We have work to do here yet,' her mother told her. 'When the Hall is emptied we can go.'

'But surely it was emptied ages ago!'

'That was only the furnishings. No, me and your dad and your Auntie Madge want to see it through. We worked there all our lives, pet. We can't just let it be pulled to bits. It's got to be done right.'

The families from the mill cottages moved up to Dyson's Fields next. Gradually the farms lower in the valley were run down, the stock sold off. The younger farmers found jobs on the site or in Hallam. The older ones like Jacob resigned themselves to never working again. Sim was cruelly attacked with arthritis in his spine. He knew he would never find proper work again. Crouching down to do gardening was one thing; he could take his time over it. But he would never manage heavy manual work, and the walk down to the railway station at Joansford would be slow and painful.

'What will I do?' he asked Jenny in despair.

She shook her head. 'I'll find a job, easy. We'll have a little garden up there,' she promised him. 'You can grow things.'

'I can grow old,' he said, bitter. He went back to the Hall, working slowly round the gardens there as he did every day, unable to stop himself until the time came to go.

'Why bother?' Tommy asked him, when he was called to help with something his father couldn't manage.

Sim shook his head. 'Queer, in't it?' he said. 'I can bear the thought of it all going under water, just. But I can't bear the thought of it running wild, after all I've done for it. I can't watch it happen.'

One by one the families moved out of the valley, until it was like a ghost village, with just a few scattered homesteads clinging on till the last minute. At night the lights glowed from their windows like warm, comforting signals. The vicar announced that a final service was to be held in the church, a service of thanksgiving and farewell. All the people who had already moved up to the estate came back down for the service. As soon as the church was full, and before the service had even started, Dora Proctor stood up in her pew.

'We want to know where the graves are going,' she said. 'Are they to be left here, to be under the water?'

Madeleine looked up in alarm and her mother squeezed her hand, tears starting up in her eyes. The silence in the church was so thick that you could touch it. There wasn't a single member of the congregation who didn't have relatives buried in the churchyard.

'Surely they'll come up to Dyson's Fields?' asked Madge. 'There's plenty of room in that back field. There's only a couple of houses there yet.'

'Can't be done,' said Farmer Gilbert, who had been looking into these things. 'It's against the law for a new burial ground to be constructed near houses. Isn't that right, Vicar?'

The vicar sighed. It was most irregular to be holding public conversations like this in church. And besides, he had been saving this bit of news for the sermon. It was his final gift to the parish, after months of worrying and negotiating.

'I am pleased to tell you,' he said, 'that the matter of the graves has been resolved. I have been in long consultation with the bishop, and with the vicar of Joansford. It has been agreed that the burial ground at Joansford will be extended to house the remains of our dead.'

Jacob stood up, his mottled old hands quivering on the back of the pew in front of him. 'We live here, here in this church. From font to grave, and we take a few steps away from it for the time in between. I'd thought to be buried here, same as all my kin. Now not even the long dead can bide in peace.'

'Oh shut up, Dad,' said Dora. 'I suppose you'd have me swimming out here with a bunch of flowers for your grave every week?'

A rumble of laughter went round the church.

'This is not a time or a place for argument,' said the vicar's wife. 'Or for laughter.' Everyone turned to her, amazed to hear her speaking out in this way. 'We're here to say goodbye to our beautiful church, and to thank God for giving us this lovely valley to live in for a time. I have been very happy here.' She sat down abruptly, overwhelmed.

'Amen,' said Madge softly, and the rest of the congregation repeated, 'Amen.'

The choir stood up to sing: Louise, Gilbert, Seth, Madge, Dora and Ben. Miss Skinner played the opening chords of the anthem, and glanced round at Ben. He nodded and cleared his throat and stepped forwards to sing, the sheet music trembling in his big red hands, and the rest of the choir took up quietly behind him. The music swelled out, and the congregation joined in, their throats tight and their eyes wet. Baby Winifred murmured in Elspeth's arms. Madeleine sat with her head bowed, letting the music swell over her, listening to the raw beauty of the untrained voices as if she was a member of an audience, not one of them. Then she stood up and began to sing with them, pitching just right, listening to the sweet breathy sound of her own singing voice. She hadn't heard it for two years. It was her own voice.

After the service, the bells peeled out bravely. The vicar stood on the steps of the church and shook hands with all his parishioners. He was too upset to speak. Jenny Barnes stayed in the church, last to leave, gazing at the glowing stained-glass window.

'My darling Madeleine,' Jenny whispered.

Madeleine paused in the doorway and looked back at her mother. Her loneliness then was so deep that it was like black water engulfing her.

The next day, the work began. Canvas sheets were slung across the churchyard like newly washed linen on a line, to protect the business of opening up the graves from the curious eyes of visitors. The relatives of the dead who were buried there grieved again. The remains of two hundred and eighty-five people were transferred to Joansford and re-interred. For some families, it was the release they needed. Now they were ready to go up to Dyson's Fields.

Madeleine stayed in her room. She could see the churchyard from her window, she could see the canvas sheets, and she could guess the movements behind them. Jenny had left her to it. She had her own awakened grief to cope with. She kept busy, packing and sorting, cleaning out cupboards as if new families would be moving in after they left. Only when the canvas was removed and the churchyard lay with its soil bare like a newly ploughed field did she turn to Sim and allow him to hold her and give and take comfort.

'She's gone now,' Jenny said quietly. 'There's nothing to keep me here.'

Sim put his hand on her shoulder and led her away from the window. 'It's two years since she died. Hard to believe. Two whole years.'

'It brings it all back. That nightmare. The thought of leaving her behind was terrible, Sim.'

'I know,' he said. 'It's a good site they've chosen up there. I shall ask the Joansford vicar if I can keep the graveyard tidy.'

'So can we go?' asked Louise, who had tiptoed silently into the room, into the holiness of her parents' tenderness for each other.

'When the Hall's done,' Sim said.

When the cottagers and farmers on the far bank of the river had moved up to Dyson's Fields, the ancient packhorse bridge was removed. The stones were lifted off one by one and carefully numbered. The children watched in wondering silence.

'What will the trout do now?' Louise asked. 'They like to shelter from the sun under that bridge.'

'They'll have to follow it back upstream,' Miss Skinner said. 'The men are going to rebuild it beyond the dam, where the river will flow into the reservoir.'

'Why?'

'It will be a kind of memorial to the village. When people walk over it, years from now, they'll be able to remember that there used to be a village here in the valley.'

'It's going to confuse the fish. And the king-fisher. And the dipper. And the heron.' Louise took out her notebook, chewing her pencil as she watched the men prising the stones away from their tight balance and laying them on the embankment.

'What are you going to do with all these stories you're writing?' Miss Skinner asked her.

'They're not stories. They're true. It's an important record. It's a kind of goodbye book.'

'Am I in it?' Tommy asked.

'Course you are. Everybody's important, even you.'

Tommy grinned, driving his hands so deep in his pockets that the lining ripped.

'And you'll give it to your grandchildren so they'll know what it was like when you were a girl,' Miss Skinner smiled.

'My grandchildren!' Louise screwed up her face. 'I'm giving it to the world!'

In a rush of excitement the children prepared items to place in the four canisters that would go under each of the pillars of the dam. A man came with a camera to take a photograph of all the class standing in front of their old school. When he put his head under the black cloth Tommy started them all giggling. They were excited and nervous; it was really happening, they were really going now, after all the waiting and talking. They would never come to this school again, never sit at those desks that were scratched with the initials of their parents and grandparents, never see Miss Skinner again. It was as if something that had been hanging around them for months had descended like a net from the sky, catching them all up in its meshes. They felt that the moment the photographer squeezed the trigger their childhood would be frozen forever. They couldn't laugh or move or speak; they could only stand in rigid silence, staring at the black-robed camera as if it was a huge mouth that would swallow them all up. And then Tommy started giggling and it was too much for them; they laughed hysterically, clutching their stomachs, howling with laughter, eyes streaming. It was not what the photographer wanted but he took the picture any way, and, when it was developed, the photograph was rolled up and put inside the canister, along with school reports and the day's newspaper, coins and stamps.

And on that day, the village school was closed. Miss Skinner kissed all the girls and shook hands with all the boys. She refused the offer of a lift on Gilbert's cart to Joansford station and walked proudly out of the village carrying a holdall with the only belongings she wanted to keep. She climbed up the long hill out of the village and never looked back, though she could still hear the voices of the children. "Bye Miss Skinner!' they were calling. "Bye!' For years to come the high, bright voices chanted to her in her dreams.

38

The vicar looked round at the ruins of the few buildings yet to be demolished.

'The ravages of war could not have made this place more desolate,' he said. He held his wife's hand, like a small child in need of comfort. 'Soon it will be the church, and then we will have finished here.'

'It's all happening so quickly now,' his wife said. 'Have you found out where we're going to go?'

'No,' he said, abrupt. 'But there will be no new parish for me. I am too old, Emma. The bishop has told me that.' He had not mentioned it to her before. He loosened his hand, sensing the tightness of her fingers. 'So, so.' He tapped the ground with his foot; his thinking habit, one of the small irritations which his wife always chose to ignore. 'So, so. Still things to do. Everything must be sorted before we sort ourselves out. Everything must have a home. I must speak to Grace about the window.'

He knocked on the door of the Barnes cottage. Madeleine was on her own, stirring a pan of plums for jam. She did not hear him coming in, and for a moment he stood in the doorway, watching the way she nudged the hair from her cheek with the back of her hand, her face lovely with the blush of heat from her cooking.

'You're a young woman now,' he said, hardly realising that he was speaking his thoughts out loud. 'You'll be finding a husband soon.'

She looked up at him, startled and embarrassed, and in both of them the memory of the vicar's lost son rose and swelled and faded. *Colin. Where are you? The ache in my heart is unbearable.*

'I'm sorry. I didn't mean to startle you. The men are beginning to move things from the church. I came to ask you about the window.'

'The window?'

'Your sister's window. It has to go somewhere.'

'No,' Madeleine said, panic rising in her at the thought of the window being removed.

'Surely you'll want to have it?'

'No. I don't want it. It belongs here. It's hers.

Please don't make me take it. I want to think of it here, under the water, with her.' He watched her, alarmed and surprised at the strength of her emotion. *After two years her grieving should be done. You get used to things, as I have got used to Colin's absence now. The pain lessens. One cannot live with pain. One has to move forwards.*

'My dear,' he said softly. 'Your sister is at peace in Joansford churchyard.'

'The window must stay,' Madeleine insisted. The jam bubbled in the pan and she drew it away from the heat, stirring slowly and steadily, calm again now.

The vicar retreated. A car had drawn up outside the church, and a young man stepped out, tall, as his son had been, blond-haired. But the vicar recognised him at once as the sexton of Joansford church, who was to receive the vestments and the chalice on behalf of his vicar. He hurried to meet him.

'Come for the spoils!' he said, falsely jovial, shaking the young man's hand.

Together they watched the medieval baptismal font being carried away, the men sweating and grunting as they half heaved, half rolled it down the path.

'Take care of that! It's hundreds of years old!' the vicar shouted. 'I don't want it smashed up for rubble.' He turned to the sexton. 'Please take the font too.'

'We already have one.'

'You could put it in your churchyard and grow flowers in it,' Mrs Hemsley said. Her husband shuddered and she smiled up at the young sexton, her eyes blue with concern.

From the vestry the two men collected the embroidered garments and altar cloths. The vicar unlocked the treasury and walked out of the church and down to the sexton's car with the precious chalice cradled in his arms. He had used it every day of his working life, and now he turned it over in his hands as if he was looking at it for the first time.

'Nice, this,' the sexton said. 'What's the things carved on it?'

'A phoenix on one side, a turtle on the other,' said the vicar. His face was grey with misery as he watched the man swathe it in a blanket and place it behind the driving seat of his vehicle.

'The symbols are fitting,' the vicar's wife said suddenly, startling her husband's reverie.

'What?'

'The turtle is a creature of water. The phoenix rises from the ashes. So the memory of the village lies under the water, yet it will rise again in Joansford.'

'Nonsense,' said her husband. He strode away from her, thinking about her words, taking comfort from them.

And after that, the church was demolished. It was almost more than the vicar could bear, but he stayed until the men had finished their work. Only the bell tower was left standing, and, in it, the little stained-glass window.

The vicar and his wife could not even bring themselves to return to the vicarage that night. They had their bags packed ready and they sent for a taxi, a thing that had never been done before in the valley, to take them to Joansford station. They would spend the night at the station hotel in Hallam. They still had no idea where they would go after that, where they would spend the rest of their lives. The vicar closed his eyes as the taxi pulled away.

'Goodbye, goodbye,' he murmured. 'Valley of my heart, goodbye.'

Goodbye, Colin, they both said, soundlessly.

'I've always fancied Scotland,' said Mrs Hemsley, when they were sitting on the train.

For once her husband opened his mind to her words.

'Scotland it is, my dear,' he said.

Amazed, she turned to look at him. 'I think this is the first time you have ever listened to me,' she said.

'Is it, by Jove!' He allowed the ghost of a smile to play across his lips before settling himself behind a newspaper.

'Do you know,' she said. 'It's a very strange thing, but I feel happy. I actually feel happy.'

39

At last work began on the demolition of the Hall. Jenny and Madge had their last instructions, to supervise the removal of all the woodwork that they had so lovingly polished and dusted, to remove the shrouds from the windows and to watch it all go. Now they stood in the lane and watched the beautiful oak panelling of the walls and the ceilings being removed, Seth's carved door, the floorboards, the stone steps, the iron gates, the balled towers of the gateways, the lions. Bit by bit it was dismantled, and the Water Board took the lot and sold it on. Then the demolition men moved in, and the great walls came thundering down.

'Still looks magnificent,' said Sim, hoarse with emotion. 'Even in ruins.'

'Now,' said Louise, slipping her hand into his, and he looked down at her.

'Yes. Now we can go.'

When all the boxes were packed and their old cottages no longer looked like home, Jenny and Madge decided to go to the village of Eccles on the navvy bus and look for work. They went on a whim, too restless to stay in the valley. All their jobs were done. They knew that as soon as they moved out, their homes would be demolished. Sim and Tommy started to load up the traps, and the women tried to help and were told to go, it would be easier that way. At the last minute they persuaded Madeleine to go to Eccles with them. She was white-faced and silent on the bus, refusing to look at the houses in Dyson's Fields as the bus trundled past them.

They found work at a small button factory immediately, and were told they could start work the next week. It couldn't be easier. From the new house they could walk down to the train station at Joansford and be at work twenty minutes later. They would be bringing good money home every week.

Madge was hugely excited. 'I've never done anything except look after the Hall and the children,' she said, when they arrived back at the cottage, full of excitement, to tell Sim their good news. 'And now I've got a good job. I never thought this would happen to me, never. I can't move up there fast enough now. It's a new life starting.'

'Everybody's ready to move, I reckon,' said Jenny.

'Except poor old Ben! He's done nothing about selling those pigs, Elspeth tells me. I think he's going to be walking them up to Dyson's Fields and shoving them in the back bedroom. And he's got such a glum face on him, there's no talking to him.'

Louise was sitting at the table writing in her notebook. She was making records of each family as they moved out of their houses and cottages. There were only four left now: the Barnes', Madge and her children, the Glossops, and Blind Seth. She looked at Auntie Madge and frowned. Wasn't there something, long ago, that someone had told her about Joan Glossop? She flicked back the pages and sucked her pencil thoughtfully. Then she closed her notebook and stood up.

'I'm just bobbing over to cuddle baby Winifred,' she said. As soon as she was outside she ran like the wind to Ben's big farmhouse. Joan Glossop was on her own in the kitchen, having a quiet minute with her grandchild. Louise stood in front of her with her feet planted apart and her hands behind her back. She took a deep breath.

'I've got a wonderful idea,' she said.

40

'Ben, I'm going to go with Grace to that factory,' Elspeth said the next day. She and Joan were baking in the kitchen and Ben was standing with his hands in his pockets, staring out into the yard. 'One of us will have to get work.'

'I'll find something,' Ben muttered.

'You're not doing anything about it,' Elspeth said. 'We've got to be practical about this. We've got to think about what to do next.'

'I'll tell you what's going to happen next,' Ben said. 'I'll have to sell my pigs and go into the army.'

'He's right,' his mother said. 'If he's not farming, he has to do his National Service.' She kneaded her dough in a slow, careful rhythm. 'I'll look after baby Winifred, Elspeth will work in the factory, and Ben will be a soldier.'

'Don't,' Elspeth snapped, fear in her throat. 'I wouldn't see him for months on end.'

'I'd rather be a soldier than not farming,' Ben said. 'There. I've said it. Stop arguing now.'

'How can you say that?' said Elspeth, shocked. 'You'd leave me and Winifred, and this new bunny—' she pressed her hand against her stomach. 'There, now you know there's another one coming.'

'You don't understand me, do you? I don't want to leave you. I never want to leave you. But I can't bear the thought of spending my days up there,' he nodded in the direction of Dyson's Fields, 'and doing what, Ellie? I can't think about it and that's the truth.'

'Have you arranged to sell the pigs yet?' his mother asked. And, 'Have you, Ben?' when he didn't answer.

'Monday market,' he muttered. The baby started crying and he bent over and lifted her out of her cradle, and stood rocking her in his big rough hands. 'Not you, little Winifred. Not taking you to market. Who'd have you, anyroad? Pretty little nose like that, they'd say. Too good for a farmer's daughter. Who'd buy you?' His voice was breaking up. Elspeth went over to him and took the baby out of his arms.

'Go on, see to your pigs,' she said softly. 'Frighten the life out of her, you would!'

When Ben had gone out to the sties the two women worked in silence for a time. Joan was deep in thought. Elspeth lifted the tins of dough on to the window ledge to rise in the sun's warmth and turned to see Joan standing with her hands clasped together like a young girl.

'I'm going out for the day,' she said, as if she had suddenly made up her mind about something.

Elspeth was surprised. The morning's work was nowhere near finished yet. There was a heap of fruit to be picked over and stored.

'I'll see to the plums,' she said. 'I'll bottle this lot, shall I? And jam the rest.'

'I want you to come with me,' Joan said. 'It's a fair walk, over the tops, so wrap little'un up warm. We'll take turns carrying her.'

'Where to?' Elspeth asked, but Joan pursed her lips and shook her head. She went outside and tied on her boots, and stood with her arms akimbo watching the snuffling piglets, till Elspeth joined her with Winifred bundled in her arms. They walked in silence up past Marty's farm and the workmen's shacks. On the ridge Winifred woke up and cried for food, and the two women rested while Elspeth fed her.

'I guessed you might have another one coming,' Joan said.

Elspeth smiled to herself. 'I only just know. Ben didn't know till just now. He didn't say anything, did he?'

'That's his way.'

They looked down on the valley, ugly and torn as it was, with the cranes stretching their long necks like prehistoric monsters over the broken walls of the deserted farm buildings.

'Those beautiful houses,' said Elspeth. 'Just look what they've done to them. It's a crime.'

'It's an eyesore,' Joan said, grim. 'The sooner it's all under water, the better.'

Winifred lapped her lips and settled herself, red-cheeked and sleepy-eyed, her head lolling. Joan made her shawl into a makeshift carrier round her shoulders, and took the baby from Elspeth.

'She's heavy, mind,' Elspeth laughed.

'She's a true Glossop. Ben was a big baby,' said Joan, and said nothing more as they trudged on, down into the next valley and up the next hill. Elspeth had never been this way before. She took the baby again after they had rested, and a mile or so later they swapped her round. Now they came

303

over a stony edge where the boulders were twisted savagely into strange shapes, sculpted by the wind into cupped hands, chariots, mushrooms, and all manner of wonderful shapes. They dropped down into a lush and lovely valley, and stopped at the gate of an ancient farmhouse. 'Old Booth Farm' was written in peeling paint on the gate. The sun gleamed on its old walls and mullioned windows. A litter of piglets squealed in their sty, roused by the women's footsteps into expecting food.

'Blooming pigs,' Joan snorted. Then she raised her voice. 'Are you there?' she shouted. 'Laurie Pigman, are you there?'

An elderly man came out of the house. He pushed his cap back away from his eyes and peered at Joan.

'By, you've aged,' she said. 'White whiskers all over your face!'

He stared at her, incomprehension in his milky blue eyes, then he barked a laugh. 'It's bloody Joan!' he hooted. 'Bloody Joannie Glossop! You've put a bit of weight on tha hips, Joannie, but it dun't suit thee bad. This your daughter?' he peered at Elspeth, chuckling. 'And a grandchild.'

'She's my son's wife. I have a son, Benjamin. You'll have heard. Named after his father.'

'Aye, I heard. And then old misery blasted off with a fancy woman, I heard that too,' the man chuckled. 'I'm saying nowt, Joannie. I'm saying nowt.'

'I'm not asking you to.' Joan jerked her head towards the cottage. 'Give us the little'un, and go and have a neb inside,' she told Elspeth. 'Be sure to look in every room, mind.'

'Is that all right?' Elspeth asked doubtfully.

Laurie shrugged his shoulders. 'Reckon Joannie's boss,' he chuckled. His eyes glinted. 'She han't changed much.'

Elspeth held the sleeping baby out towards Joan. To her surprise the man took her, rubbing his whiskery chin over the baby's head. 'They're just like piglets, babies are,' he muttered.

'Go on,' Joan told her, and Elspeth went uncertainly into the house. Laurie seemed to live in the huge downstairs room. It was clean enough, clean but bare and uncomfortable, with a bed at one end and the fireplace and table at the other. She could imagine the room with curtains the colour of sunshine, and knitted red rugs thrown over the threadbare sofa to liven it up, and a bright rag rug across the floor stones. As she climbed up the twisting staircase Elspeth could tell that it was a long time since he had been up to that floor. She explored each room cautiously, longing to fling open the windows and let out the musty smell. Old yellowing wallpaper ballooned from the ceilings, and the windows were grey with the lace of dusty webs.

At last she came downstairs again. Joan and Laurie were sitting companionably under the apple tree, the baby asleep in the man's arms.

'What do you think of Old Booth?' Joan asked her.

'It's beautiful,' said Elspeth, surprised. 'I think it's the prettiest house I've ever seen.'

Laurie nodded, smiling happily.

'Could live here, could you?' Joan asked.

'Now hang on,' said Laurie, his smile disappearing into his beard.

Joan tutted. 'You'll be an old man soon,' she said. 'You can't manage here much longer. Your eyesight's going. And your knees.'

'It's my home,' he said gently, as if he'd never thought of it before. 'What you on about, Joannie?'

She pressed the palms of her hands together, as if she was praying in the village church, and then smoothed them across her cheeks. The gesture seemed to make her young again, almost a girl, coquettish. 'I'm about to move into a brand-new house,' she said prettily. 'Nice little kitchen. Indoor toilet. New windows. No damp. No woodworm. Electric lights.'

The silence was like a night's full sleep. Into it, the black cockerel crowed, and as if he had just woken up, Laurie said, very shy, 'Joannie Glossop, are you asking to wed me?'

She shook herself like one of the hens, feathers fluttering. 'There's two bedrooms,' she said pertly. 'Reckon we're a bit old for oojimiflips.'

'Wey.' He sucked in his lips. 'I need to think about this. It's come like a flash of lightning, this has, Joannie.'

Elspeth let out her breath at last. 'Ben's a good pigman,' she whispered. 'We've got saddlebacks and curly tails.'

'So I've heard.'

'He wants to breed them. It's his ambition to have a place like this, with a copse of trees for them to rootle round in. He wouldn't bother with cows and sheep, 'cept for our own needs. He loves pigs like he loves me and Winifred.'

'Better,' Joan said.

Laurie chuckled and rubbed his chin.

'And I'd love this house like a palace – better than a palace. I'd polish the wood and put sunshine curtains up, and grow flowers and vegetables in the garden, and I'd fill every room with children.'

Winifred opened her eyes and stared at her, blue and wondering and impish.

'It'd still be your place, Laurie. They'd be tenant farmers, and they'd look after it like you used to look after it yourself.' Joan paused and Laurie turned to look at her, waiting. 'And I'd look after you like I've always wanted to,' she added, a red blush starting at her neck and rising to her cheeks. Elspeth began to move away, more than a little embarrassed, but Laurie put his hand on her arm.

'I've not struck such a good bargain since I sold my last suckling pig at the Marquis market,' he said. 'I want you to witness this, Elspeth. Will you marry me, Joan Glossop?'

'You know I will.'

'You should have said yes years ago, Joannie.' His voice was tender and wistful then, the teasing gone.

'Never mind that.' She stood up briskly, brushing her hand just lightly against his as she did so, allowing her glance to meet his, just; allowing herself to smile, full and warm. 'If you can get that old jalopy of yours to work and consent to drive us back home, I'll give you a good ham supper and plum crumble.'

'Now you're talking business,' Laurie said. He took her arm and led her to his van, and Elspeth followed, turning back with every other step to look at the sun glinting on the windows of her new home.

41

It took no time to evacuate the big farmhouse in the valley, for Joan to move up next to Dora and Jacob Proctor, and to make arrangements with the vicar of Joansford for the quiet wedding. Laurie and Ben moved the pigs and the other stock over to Old Booth Farm. Madge and the Barnes prepared to move up to Dyson's Fields at last. Seth was still in his old cottage halfway up the hillside, refusing to move until the last minute.

'Will you come up? Your house is ready now,' Sim Barnes said to him the day before his own family moved up. 'We can move your stuff up with ours.'

'I'll come soon,' Seth said.

'Are you all right?' Sim asked awkwardly.

'I'm fine. I'm happy. I've a job to finish first.'

'I'll call round in a day or two,' Sim told him.

'You have to go then, Seth. The last of the cottages will be coming down at the end of the week.'

'I'll be ready,' Seth promised him. As soon as Sim had gone, Seth went back to his table, where he had been working. He had a set of wood-carving tools, tucked in their own pockets in a roll of green felt. He had inherited them from his grandfather. On the table he had a large piece of wood, and every now and then in the last few months he had been chipping away on it, fashioning shapes. Now he worked on it feverishly, day and night. He must finish it before he left. It was a relief map of the valley, his valley as he knew it: the folds of the fields, the rise of the hills, the curve of the river, and the raised outlines of all the buildings. He ran his fingers over it, easing up the rough splinters, smoothing the wood; naming the parts.

Sim went back to the house and helped Madge and Jenny to load their belongings on to carts. Much of their furniture was too big and heavy to move up to the new houses; it was built in the cottages; it would stay there. Madeleine went up to her room to pick up the bundles she had made of her clothes and belongings. The golden mirror was still on the mantelpiece. She lifted it down

311

and stared into it. 'Is it you, or is it me?' she whispered to her reflection. 'Are you there, Grace?' The room was absolutely silent.

For Jenny Barnes and Madge the move, after all, was quick and simple. The time was right. Jenny closed her door, and Madge closed hers, and they just walked away. Tommy and Mike and the little ones ran shrieking in front of them in an ecstasy of excitement. Sim put his hand on Louise's shoulder. 'It's done,' he said. 'It's over.'

A few hours later they were relaxing in the electric splendour of their new house.

'I don't like to think of Seth down there on his own,' Jenny said anxiously.

'He's always on his own,' her husband reminded her.

'You know what I mean. Alone in the valley, with all the buildings being brought down and that. Besides, it's not safe for him.'

'He'll come soon. We couldn't have left a moment before we were ready,' Sim said. 'Ready in our minds, I mean. And now we're here, it seems like home.' He looked round at the cushions and curtains that Jenny had made, at Tommy arranging his toys, at Louise sitting under the electric light, writing in the notebook. Her favourite cat, Pudding, was curled up on her knee.

'Grace hates it,' Louise said. She finished writing and drew a line under the last words. 'There, my book's finished now, for a bit,' she said. 'I'll have to add something when the King comes to open the dam, when all the work's finished. But that won't be for a couple of years yet, will it? And then, the water will come flooding over the houses. Won't that be exciting, Pudding Cat!'

Next day, Madeleine disappeared. She went to the factory that morning with her mother and Madge, and during the day she put down the piece of machinery she was handling and slipped her work apron off. She walked out of the building some-how without being noticed by anyone. It was some time before her mother noted the empty place on the production line.

'Where's Grace?' she mouthed to Madge over the clatter of the machinery, and her sister shrugged and shook her head. They looked for her in the toilets in the yard at the end of the day, and then hurried to the station. She wasn't there. There wouldn't be another train out to Joansford that night, and they had to take it, grim with worry and fright though they were.

'She'll find her way, you'll see,' said Madge. 'She'll be at home cooking a meal for you all when you get in.'

42

Seth had almost finished his carving. He straightened his back and ran his fingers again over the board. There was one last thing he wanted to check up on. The packhorse bridge had been taken away and rebuilt, but the stepping stones were still there. Strange, he thought, he'd never counted them. He'd stepped over them every day of his life, and he just knew that the one that rocked was the last one on the far side. He went down and crossed them carefully, counting as he went. The stream was running swiftly. He kneeled down, balancing on the rocking stone, and trailed his fingers in the water, chuckling at its icy coldness. He had always heard voices in the stream; as a little boy he had told himself that it was the pebbles singing under the water, the tiny fishes whispering, the reeds sighing. He knew all the sounds. And there was another sound that came again now, that chilled him as it had chilled him years ago, that froze his heart. It was Madeleine's scream, the moment her sister had died.

He stood up and instinctively made his way down the empty lane between the deserted cottages. He pushed open the wooden gate to the Barnes cottage and went up the path where untamed flowers sprawled. The door was slightly ajar. He stood in the hallway, listening to the uncanny silence, then went slowly up the stairs to the room that he had visited only once before, the day he had followed Colin down from the slippery stones. In the room he could hear the sound of steady breathing, and knew that she was there. Cautiously he walked over to the window and kneeled down. Her breathing had changed. She was awake now, watching every move he made. His knees creaked as he crouched next to her.

'You must go home,' he said. 'You can't stay here.'

Madeleine held her breath.

'We all have to leave something behind,' Seth said. 'I know every inch of this valley. I can walk round here as freely as anyone. But I have to let that knowledge go. Up there, I'll be trapped in my blindness again. I'll have to be led round like a child,

316

learning. But I can't stay here, can I? I can't swim.'
He chuckled and she smiled with him, nervously.

'Madeleine, go home,' he said softly.

'I'm not—'

'You see, you're caught in a trap too. You've made a prison for yourself. But you can get out of it. Not like me. It's in your power. Tell your mother, and you'll have opened the door of your prison. Doesn't she need to know? You'll feel better. You can't carry this burden with you for the rest of your life. Let Grace go, Maddy. She's a free spirit. Let her go, and you'll be free, too.'

'I can't leave her behind,' Madeleine whispered.

'Grace isn't here. You know that. Grace is dead. Say it.'

'Can't.'

'Let her go. Set her free. Now's the time. Let her go, and free yourself.'

He felt for her hand, and sat, offering no other comfort, and the touch of his hand on hers released the grief that had been dammed up inside her.

'Grace is dead,' she whispered. Her words shivered in the silent room. 'Grace is dead.'

She cried for the first time since her sister had died. Every bone and nerve of her body cried out

317

with sorrow. He held her hand and when at last the crying stopped he put his arm round her and eased her head against his shoulder, and let her sleep.

A curlew swept across the valley, pouring its song out. There was a roar of falling masonry. A wall in Ben and Elspeth's farmhouse slid to the ground. At last Madeleine woke up again; dazed, calm.

'Ready to go home?'

'Ready.'

They went out of the cottage together. The sun was setting, blinding in last brilliance. Madeleine put her hand across her eyes, shielding them from the light, and saw her mother coming down the track that led from Dyson's Fields.

'Grace!' her mother called. 'Grace, is that you?'

Seth squeezed her hand and Madeleine moved away from him, slowly at first, then running, gasping her way up the slope till her heart was pounding. She didn't stop until she reached her mother's arms. And then she told her.

'It's not Grace,' she said. Her breath was bursting from her. 'Grace died. It's Madeleine. Mum, I'm really Madeleine.'

43
Two years later

Fifty thousand people came to watch the King opening the dam. They came from all over the country, and they brought with them all the colour and excitement and noise of a carnival. Bands were playing, flags were flying; mounted police stood guard, their huge horses restless with the jostle of the crowds.

'Nobody was bothered when we told them we was losing our valley,' Jacob Proctor said, peering out of his window. 'Nobody cared, not even newspapers. And now it's all over, they come flocking to neb at it.'

'Oh, give over grumbling, Dad,' Dora said. 'You like it up here, don't you?'

'I do,' he agreed. 'It's grand.'

'Then get your shoes on and come and have some fun.'

'Fun!' he muttered. 'That's for kids. And I don't

want getting squashed, neither.'

She kneeled down and tied his laces, helped him out of his chair, led him to the door. All the families of the estate were hurrying to get places on the new viaduct.

'The King's dressed as the Admiral of the Fleet!' Louise told them. 'He looks wonderful!'

'I'd like to know what he thinks he's going to do in that get-up,' Jacob rumbled. 'Sail across ruddy watter?'

'...a depth of one hundred and thirty-five feet,' the spokesman for the Water Board was saying. Numbers floated from his mouth like bubbles in the air, filmy and brilliant, incomprehensible. 'It will hold sixty-three thousand million gallons of water. One thousand tons of concrete went into its construction.'

Louise tried to scribble the numbers into her notebook and gave up, lost in a bubble storm of noughts.

'One million tons of earth. One hundred thousand tons of puddled clay. A triumph of construction. An inspiration to British engineering. Three hundred and twelve men working here. The designers, the contractors, the labourers ...'

'And part of English history is lost for all time,' murmured the vicar, who at the last moment had been unable to stay away, and had travelled down from Scotland for the final view of the valley he loved so much. The eyes of all the former villagers were on the ravaged valley, the stunted footings of their homes, cottages, farms, church, the Hall, shop, mill, the school. Elspeth clutched a toddler in her arms. Ben stood with his arms looping Winifred. She held up her hand and he hoisted her up on to his shoulders so she could see. The toddler started crying, frightened by the crush of people around her.

'Hush, bunny,' Elspeth crooned, burying her face in little Susan's hair. 'It will be all right. Bless you, everything will be all right.' She couldn't take her eyes off the place where the fountain would start.

A young stonemason handed his mallet to the King. His Majesty turned the wheel which would send water roaring through outlet valves into the weir pool hundreds of feet below, and a plume jetted into the air with a gush that was like the collective sigh of the entire crowd. The cheer rose, fifty thousand people waving their arms in the air and shouting. Jacob lifted up his stick like a baton and the band started playing. Fireworks whooshed into the air.

Sim shook his head, overwhelmed. He dug his hands in his pockets and turned away. Jenny dabbed her eyes and looked round at her daughters.

'All right, Madeleine?' she shouted into the noise.

Madeleine nodded and laughed. She caught Louise's hands and danced with her to the music. 'Fine, Mum. It's OK. I'm fine.'

44

It took more than a year for the slow creep of water to fill the valley completely. At first the villagers couldn't resist going down to the viaduct bridge, gazing down to watch their old houses drowning. After a time even the children lost interest. Their new lives, their new homes, took over.

Louise followed her mother and Madeleine to the factory as soon as she left school, and then Madeleine went to art college. Now she was twenty the course was finished, and she was thinking that perhaps she would train to be a teacher. Louise was saving up to go to a college of journalism. There was plenty of work for Sim Barnes as gardener and odd job man; too many houses in Joansford had lost men to the war. Tommy left school early and became a plumber's apprentice. Old Jacob Proctor died in his sleep, and Dora astonished everyone by falling in love with a police sergeant and moving into the police house on the estate; the first house to have a little nine-inch television set. And still the waters rose, as imperceptible now as breath in the air.

One evening in the late summer of 1951, Madeleine and Seth walked to the viaduct together. They leaned on the parapet, turning their faces to the warm glow of the late sun.

'Tell me what you can see today,' Seth said.

Madeleine rested her elbows on the parapet and cupped her chin in her hands.

'All right. But tell me what you see first.'

'What I can see?' he chuckled. 'A kind of serenity. Just quiet. Grey maybe, if that's the name of the colour. But I see better with my skin and my hearing. I can feel a soft, cool air lifting off the water. I can feel that on my face. I can hear the curlew. I can hear birds flying across the water, swallows chasing after flies. But they'll be gone soon, won't they? Ah, now I can hear a waterbird of some sort. Is it a coot? Little sweet piping sound it makes.'

'It is a coot. There's a pair of them by the bank. And, yes, there are swallows skimming the top of the water. You heard them before I saw them, Seth. The water is perfectly still today. There's a lovely silver light on it right at the far end. And here, the hills are perfectly reflected in the water. Tipped upside down. They're absolute images of each other, as if you couldn't take one away from the other, as if you couldn't say, this exists on its own.'

They were both silent, taking in the idea. It's like a sky mirror, Madeleine thought. *The birds and the clouds seem to fall in and out of it. Another world, that you can't go into.*

A man was coming down the road towards the viaduct. He stopped when he saw the two figures, and made as if to turn away. Then he seemed to make up his mind and came slowly towards them. He stopped again when he was within earshot, turning his face away from them, looking at the stretch of light, at the greens and purples of the hills in the glassy water.

'But the image in the water couldn't be there without the other one,' Seth frowned, trying to put Madeleine's words within the context of his own experience. 'Like an echo can't exist without a source.'

'You're right, but the reflection's always there, under the surface. Just waiting to show itself. And it is like an echo. Exactly like an echo.' In her memory she heard the voices of two young girls singing together, the one voice trailing the other in exact imitation, like pealing bells. 'The heather's still out, Seth. It's a deep colour called purple. The hills are cloaked in it. The grass is light green where the sun's slanting across it, a kind of golden-green. And because it's a double image, it's twice as beautiful as the single image would be. I wish I could paint it. You know, Aunt Susan would have loved this! It's so beautiful. She always said water is the hardest thing to paint. She would have loved it so much. And I wish you could see it, Seth.'

'Wish, wish, wish!' he gave his quiet chuckle. 'But I can see it. You've painted it for me.'

'Words won't do it justice. Maybe Louise could find the words, but I can't. Ah, I didn't tell you. Right across the other side I can see where the village was. You can still see the spire of the church reflecting itself. It's pointing up, and it's pointing down.'

The stranger turned towards them and came a few steps closer. 'Who'd have believed that we'd be standing here one day,' he said, 'admiring this reservoir like this?'

Madeleine looked at him sharply, not knowing him. But Seth recognised his voice immediately.

'Colin!' he started forwards, his hands held out.

Madeleine stared again at the young man. His hair was cropped to a dark stubble, and he had a moustache that was almost ginger. She took in his eyes and his hands, the line of his mouth under the moustache, the gaunt cheekbones, the weathered skin.

'Is it?' she hardly dared say it. 'Is it really Colin? But you look totally different. And yet you look the same!'

'I could say the same of you. You've changed a lot. Your hair is short!' he laughed. You're a woman. You're lovely, he wanted to say. There had been so many times in the last few years when he had tried and failed to bring her image into his mind; there had only been the ghost of her, a young girl shaking her hair loose, laughing up at him, her hands to her mouth; the grieving twin, turned away from him, sorrowing. And now, seeing her again at last, it was like meeting a new person who had her voice and her smile, her eyes, her grace, but the childlike essence of her had slipped away. He couldn't take his eyes off her, wanting to know her again.

'I never thought I'd come back here, ever. But there's something you need to know, Grace.'

'Ah, Colin, there's something I have to tell you,' she said, her voice catching for a moment in her throat.

'I'll go back,' Seth said. 'You have a lot to talk about, you two.'

'I'll see you across. There's a car coming.' Madeleine took his arm and guided him down the steep step of the pavement and led him over the road. Once he was on the other side and up on to the pavement she let go of his arm. He caught hold of her hand for a moment, held it in both of his, and kissed it. Then he walked steadily in the direction of Dyson's Fields.

Madeleine crossed back to rejoin Colin. 'I can't get over you!' she said. 'I thought I'd never see you again. Where did you go? What about university?'

'Listen,' said Colin. 'I want to get this over. I want to tell you about Oliver.'

'*Oliver?*' Madeleine felt the blush rising to her face. 'Oh, how is he?'

Colin turned away. He couldn't bear the light in her eyes. 'I never thought I'd come back here,' he repeated fiercely. 'When I left, it was for good. I had no idea where I was going.'

Madeleine watched him carefully while he was speaking, trying to find the boy she remembered in his face. *He's cruder and rougher than he used to be*, she thought. *Much thinner. But he's still there, like a shadow, like a reflection waiting to come through. The old Colin is still there.*

'What did you do?'

He laughed. 'I got a job on a building site! There was loads of work, repairing war damage. Still is. I loved it, working outdoors, moving round the country when I felt like it. I felt strong. I felt I was doing something important. Then they started calling us up for National Service, and I went and registered. I could have got away with it, maybe. The authorities didn't have any address for me. Or I could have said I had a university place – that would have deferred it a couple of years anyway. But, you know, lads of my age had gone out and got themselves killed when the war was on. It felt the right thing to do, so I did it. I must say, I never really thought I was going to be putting my life at risk. But, as it happened, I did get sent out on active service. They sent me out jungle-bashing in Malaya. You've heard what we're doing out there, fighting the terrorists.'

'Was it awful?' It was a hopeless thing to say. She watched the flash of something like incredulity in his eyes; pain and horror and sorrow.

'Of course it was awful.' *How could she know?* he told himself. *She's just a country girl.* How could anyone who hadn't been out there even begin to imagine what it was like; the intense, ceaseless monsoon rain, the heat and the sweat of hacking through that impenetrable jungle, the stench of the leech-infested swamps and always, everywhere, day and night, the terror of walking into a guerrilla ambush.

'But it's over now!' she said, awkwardly breaking into his silence 'You did come back. And you're safe and well.'

He laughed, and it was a mature, ironic sound, without humour. 'I still don't know why we had to do it, why they sent a bunch of kids five thousand miles away from home. Yes, I'm safe and well.'

Madeleine turned away from him, a start of tears rising. She looked over the water, waiting for its calmness to soothe her before she spoke again. 'As you said, it's amazing to think we're standing here and saying how beautiful the reservoir is. I never thought I'd ever think that, let alone say it.'

'I didn't come back to see this. I came to see you. I came to tell you something.'

'About Oliver.'

He glanced at her again, and again felt the old jealousy flaring up in him. 'Before I left here, we had a fight, me and Oliver. I tried to kill him.'

She remembered then, with the strange vividness of a dream, running down from Oliver's caravan with his jacket round her shoulders, and Colin stepping towards her, smiling to see her. She remembered letting Oliver's jacket slide from her shoulders to the ground, and turning away from Colin, too upset and confused to speak. That was the last time she had seen him.

'Instead of that, I nearly killed myself. I nearly went down one of those shaft holes. Oliver saved my life. He grabbed hold of me as I was sliding over and I don't know how he held on, or how he dragged me up. He could have gone down with me. We could both have died. I wanted you to know that.'

She stared across the water, saying nothing. The sun was dropping fast behind Black Tor.

'I never even thanked him. I couldn't face him again. I couldn't face Dad, I couldn't face myself. I ran away. Like a coward in the night, I ran away.'

A swallow dipped, swooping down to its perfect image and away again in an effortless curve of flight.

'I couldn't forget about it. You can't leave your past behind you, that's what I've learnt. It's all you've got. Well, as it happened, I saw Oliver again a couple of years later. He was called up, and by chance he was sent out to Malaya too. We were there together.'

'And you made it up.'

'We should never have been sent out there. Jungle warfare. You've no idea what it's like. We weren't properly equipped.' His voice was beginning to break up. He turned away from her, remembering how he had felt when he had come face to face with Oliver. Colin had been sent to meet a new unit sent out from England. When the men stumbled out of the helicopter, dazed by the wash of heat and rain, Colin had recognised Oliver instantly. They had looked at each other warily, in disbelief. It was Oliver who had lifted his hand first in the slightest gesture of acknowledgement. Colin had forced himself to go over to him, to try to blurt out an awkward apology . . .

'Look – Ollie – that night—'

'Forget it.'

'I don't know what came over me.'

'I said forget it.'

'Trouble is, I can't.'

He stood back. The men were being handed their heavy kitbags. Oliver struggled to hoist his bag over his shoulder. 'Funny, we used to josh about taking off and travelling round together. Seeing the world. Seeing life.' He put his hand out awkwardly and, just as awkwardly, Colin took it. 'I'm glad we're in this together.'

They fell silent.

'Do you believe in God?' Oliver asked suddenly.

'What?'

'You always say that.' Oliver grinned at Colin. 'Wouldn't it help, here, if you did…?'

Madeleine held on to the parapet; her knuckles were small white shells, her heart was a slow throbbing drum, beating the agony of dread. She knew what Colin was trying to tell her.

'We were – tracking bandits, guerrillas. They were slaughtering all the jungle villagers in terrorist attacks. Our job was to drive them into the jungle, round them up, capture them – or kill them. But we were a poor match for them. These bandits, they come without a sound. They slide up to you like snakes, and before you even know they're there they kill everyone in sight. You're listening out for them all the time; every sound you hear could be a terrorist. We were hacking our way through thick jungle every day, hardly making any progress. We were tired to the bone, every one of us, but it's impossible to sleep properly, you're listening and listening with every nerve of your body. In the end you kind of drown with exhaustion, in spite of the rain, in spite of the mosquitoes and the snakes, in spite of the terror. But someone's always on guard, and the night they attacked us, it was Oliver.'

Madeleine felt weak, her limbs dissolving as if there was no substance to her body now.

'He heard them, but it was too late. He gave the alarm, and we hauled ourselves out of our stupor, and opened fire. But they got him for it. Oliver's dead.'

She forced herself at last to turn round to stare at Colin, wanting him to say the words again, to say them differently, to unsay them.

'I managed to drag him away from them. I'd have done anything, anything to save him. But I was too late. And that's why I've come here. Somebody had to tell you.'

Madeleine was silent. That she had never really, deeply loved Oliver was something she had realised and whispered to herself many times. That she might never see him again was something she had made herself believe. But she had never imagined that he might die, that his fine young flesh, the hands that had stroked her, the mouth that had kissed her; breath, voice, laugh, song; the joy of him might savagely cease to be.

'I want to go to Seth,' she murmured.

'Of course.' Colin lowered his head. 'I understand.' He listened to the sound of her going, knowing that she was in that desperate place called loneliness. He had never been able to reach her there. In his mind's eye he saw her in Seth's arms, releasing her tears, and the blind man rocking her and soothing her as he himself would like to do, as he had dared to imagine himself doing.

Twilight had gone from the reservoir; the night's darkness had risen. The moon was like two tipped boats, ready to rock themselves across the twin surfaces. Its light silvered the hills so their ghostly shapes shouldered up through the water like strange monsters of the deep. At last Colin picked up his kitbag and slung it across his shoulder. He was weary. He started to walk back over the viaduct to the main road. He could hitch a lift in either direction. He could soon be miles away from this place. And yet he stood in a daze on the corner of the viaduct. A lorry thundered past. Another. He made no attempt to stop them. He couldn't bring himself to leave. Not yet. There was a bewitchment in the still air.

He saw the lights of the public house on the edge of the Dyson's Fields estate. A beer would set him up. He recognised some of the men in there, old farmers from the valley. Though they turned round when he came in, nobody recognised him, and he was glad. He knew how much the last few years had changed him. He didn't want to talk to any of them. He asked if he could take a room for the night and went straight up to it. The loud voices and laughter drifted up though the floor-boards. He took an envelope out of his pocket, and immediately the horror of his last sight of Oliver came back to him.

The voices in the downstairs bar stopped, the farmers left, and the publican closed the doors for the night. Colin lay taut and still on the lumpy mattress. He could sense with every nerve of his body that she was near-five minutes' walk away, in one of the estate houses; maybe Seth was comforting her.

'I shouldn't have stayed,' he said aloud, wretched with himself. 'There's no place for me here. I should never have come back.'

He drifted into an uneasy, tortured dream, and woke up in the night drenched in the sweat of the jungle, imagining the humid green sea of rain swamping down from the canopy of trees hundreds of feet above his head. He could hear again the unearthly shrieks and howls of night creatures. He could hear the furtive rustle of a terrorist bandit sliding through the darkness, a knife between his teeth, murder in his heart. He heard Oliver's hoarse shout of alarm, and the moonlit skirmish of bodies, blood and gunshots. He saw himself run screaming towards Oliver, kicking away the bandits, covering Oliver's mutilated body with his own, then dragging him away where he couldn't be harmed any more. And in Oliver's eyes he saw a flicker of recognition, of wordless thanks. It was all Colin could do. It was the least, and the most, he could have done for the man he loved like a brother. In the green light of dawn he and another soldier had run through the jungle carrying Oliver's body on a bamboo stretcher and had placed him in a clearing to be picked up by the army helicopter. But it was too late, it was all too late.

The other soldier, on a whim, had kneeled over Oliver and gone through his pockets. He handed a bloodied envelope to Colin. 'Your mate, wasn't he?' And when Colin opened the envelope, there was the strange, cut out photograph from Ben and Elspeth's wedding picture; the sad, sweet, unsmiling face.

45

Colin opened the windows and the air was soft on him; the curtains whispered like the trees of his childhood. He sank back into a sweet sleep and, when he woke, the morning sun was pouring into the room and the air outside was bright with bird-song. The landlady brought him a breakfast tray and he ate hungrily.

'Will you be leaving this morning?' she asked him when he took the tray downstairs.

'Yes. I thought I'd take one last look at the reservoir before I go.'

'Beautiful, isn't it,' she said. 'Do you know, there's a village underneath it. Isn't that an eerie thought? Strange to think of that, now. It just feels as if the lake was always here.'

Just as Colin was making his way down to the reservoir Madeleine was coming out of her house at Dyson's Fields. She called out his name but he didn't hear her, and she followed him quickly. He started running, and she ran to catch up with him. He crossed the viaduct and ran to the end of it, and then ducked under the railings and went right down to the water's edge. He stood with his hands on his hips, breathing deeply, calmed by the quiet loveliness of the sight of the familiar hills of home folding down into their own unfamiliar embrace.

'Colin!'

He turned round, startled, as Madeleine slithered down the pebbly slope towards him.

'I'm so glad you're still here,' she said.

'Are you?'

She tried to steady her breath. 'There's something I've got to tell you.'

He bent down and picked up a stone, skimming it over the water. It bounced into three perfect rings before it sank.

'You don't have to tell me. It's all right. I know. It's all right.' The rings of water touched each other, absorbing one another. 'I understand. I was insanely jealous of Oliver. But I'm pleased about Seth. He deserves someone like you.'

'Seth?' she laughed, surprised. 'What are you talking about?'

340

He crouched to pick up another stone, balancing on the balls of his feet. The stone was smooth as an egg in his palm, a perfect, wonderful thing. She stooped down next to him and sat with her arms looping her knees. He could smell soap on her skin. There was no sound except the soft lingering sheesh, sheesh of the lapping water.

'You went away,' she said softly. 'And Oliver went. And then Elspeth. Seth became my friend, my lovely, dearest friend. Like a cousin, or an older brother, that's what Seth is. I think he might be a distant cousin, actually, on Aunt Susan's side. I do love him. But not *that*. Not what you think.'

He tossed the egg stone gently from one hand to the other. 'So that isn't what you wanted to tell me?' He turned to look at her. 'Then what is it, Grace?'

'I'm not Grace.' She let the words sink as the skimstone had sunk, home to a deep, dark place. 'That's what I wanted to tell you. I did a terrible thing. I lied. When Grace died, I couldn't let her go. I wanted to die with her. I wanted to tell myself she hadn't died. I took her name. I don't know what I thought I was doing. I told Mum that it was Madeleine who had died, and after that it was too late. I didn't know how to take it back. I began to believe it myself. I didn't ever want to take it back. It was safe. It was Grace who died.'

There was a long, deep, fathomless silence. The ripples of her words spread and looped and touched one another.

'I'm sorry. I'm sorry, Colin. Seth helped me to let her go. Believe me. I'm sorry. I'm sorry. I'm Madeleine.'

He let out his breath in a long sigh.

'I needed to tell you. I'm so glad I was able to tell you before you went.'

'I'm glad you told me.' He straightened up. 'I feel as if I've just come through a dream. Madeleine, Madeleine, Madeleine.' He jogged on the spot, shaking his arms and legs, loosening his limbs. 'Madeleine. Maddy.'

'You won't go yet, will you? Please don't go yet.'

'No. I don't want to. I don't think I was going anywhere, not yet. I don't think I could have left here without seeing you again.'

She ducked her head, smiling, too shy to look at him.

'Can we walk round this thing?'

She laughed. 'It's a long way. It'd take us all morning. Longer.'

'That's all right. I'm not in a hurry. Can you?'

She shrugged, smiling. 'I expect I can.'

'Good.' He was still not looking at her. 'We've got a lot to talk about.'

'I could show you where they've put the pack-horse bridge, right at the top end of the reservoir.'

'Let's do it. Tell me everything that's happened since you became Madeleine again.'

When they stood on the little packhorse bridge at the head of the valley, far away from any sound of traffic, it was as if nothing had changed. The quiet river trickled beneath it; dippers bobbed on the boulders.

'I'm glad they brought it here,' Madeleine said softly. 'It seemed crazy at the time. But I'm glad they did it.'

'I'm glad I came back,' said Colin. 'It seemed crazy at the time.'

Madeleine smiled at him.

'I've thought about you all the time I've been away,' Colin said.

'Are you sure it was me?' she teased.

'Sure. Quite sure. Does it hurt, Maddy, to think about Grace?'

She shook her head. 'Not any more; not in that hopeless, anguished way. Oh, I miss her terribly. I think about her all the time, about how lucky I was to have her. I loved being "we". But I'm a separate person now. I know that. I've become myself. I'm me.'

They began to walk on, round the track. Colin slid his hand into hers and they walked on in a silence that was spinning with thoughts. They stopped when they came to the place where the track ran down right into the reservoir. It was the old road. At one time, it would have led over the packhorse bridge to their village. Now all that could be seen of it was the church tower.

'I'm sorry we teased you so much,' Madeleine whispered.

Colin unlaced his shoes and stepped out of them, pulling off his socks. 'Come for a swim with me?'

She laughed up at him. 'Are you serious?'

'Come on. See if we can get as far as the church.' He pulled off his jacket. 'Close your eyes. The trousers are coming off too.'

They were both laughing. She kicked off her shoes and tucked her dress up and ran ahead of him, screaming and shouting as the ice-cold water touched her skin, and he ran past her, grabbing hold of her, dragging her in with him, gasping and shouting and laughing. They struck out towards the church, and gradually settled into slow, sure strokes, swimming side by side.

'Where will you go next?' she asked. 'Is your university place still held for you?'

'I'm not doing the course,' he said. 'I'm not cut out for the ministry. Oliver made me realise that. "Do you believe in God?" he kept asking me. And I still can't answer that question. I don't know. I don't know anything. I believe in hell.' He ducked his head down and came up again, blowing out air and water. 'I've just come from there. But man made that, not God.'

'So now what?'

'I've traced my parents. I shall go up and see them in Scotland. Tomorrow, probably.'

He swam on for a bit, turned over on to his back. The sky was a perfect blue. He felt as if he would see the curve of the earth.

'And then – America.'

'America!'

'A new start. A new life. It's a new world, Maddy.'

He turned over again and struck out steadily for the church. Madeleine kicked up speed and drove herself after him. They reached it together, each with a hand on the spire, breathless with triumph and wonder, dizzy with effort. The hills were spinning round them.

'Maddy, Maddy, Madeleine!' Colin chanted. His voice sang back to him. 'I'm happy again. Being here. Being here with you! I'd forgotten how to be happy.'

'Me too.'

'I'd forgotten lots of things. I'd forgotten how beautiful you are. How could I forget that?'

Madeleine oared the water with both arms, splashing him so he turned over, spluttering and scooping water over her, showering it over her head so the water streamed through her hair.

'You know what I want?' he said. 'What I've always wanted?'

'Don't ask me yet,' she laughed, teasing him, dancing away from him in the water. 'I hardly know you.'

'When? When can I ask you?'

'Shall we find Grace's window first?'

'All right.'

'Deep breath.'

'Deep breath.'

Down and down they plunged, away from the light, solemn in the water's thickness, and hand in hand. Their fingers touched the window at last, traced the outline of the girl in the field, the river, the stepping stones. And then up they soared, flying fish, out and up, and burst into the sunlight.

'Yes,' Madeleine gasped. 'Yes, oh yes, Colin. I will.'

46
Fifty years later

The earth is caked dry in the summer of long drought. The great reservoir is laid bare, like an open, hungry mouth revealing at last the snaggled teeth of the crumbled walls of long-deserted buildings. People have come from miles around to see this wonder, the drowned village brought to light again. Among the sightseers is an old woman who has come with her daughter and her grandsons. The boys whoop among the stones, searching for keepsakes. The two women stand, trying to make sense of the tumbled remains.

'That was the church,' one of the women says. 'The school. The packhorse bridge was over there.'

'There was the Hall. That's easy to tell. It must have been grand.'

'Oh, it was. It was a beautiful place.'

'And that would be Susan's cottage, right opposite?'

'My lovely old Aunt Susan. She lost her mind when all this happened.'

'And Blind Seth's would be up there on the hill. I feel as if I know it all,' the younger woman said. 'It's all in Louise's book. Dora Proctor's shop, right? And who lived over there, next to the church?'

'Louise did. With Auntie Jenny and Uncle Sim. And the twins.'

Her daughter nods, remembering the strange story.

'Maddy should come back from America and see all this, before it all disappears again. Now, wait till I show you this.' Elspeth steps cautiously over the stones, pausing now and then with a frown, shaking her head, and then leads her daughter surely through a wrought-iron gate that stands half open, the few stones of its path leading seemingly to nowhere. She stops by a mound of stones all in a swathe of caked mud that is wrinkled and cracked like old skin. 'These are the pigsties. Where your dad proposed to me.'

'No harm in being romantic!' Winifred smiles. 'He hasn't changed much, has he?'

'Him and his blessed pigs.'

'Does it make you sad, Mum, coming back?'

'No. Not sad. Strange. I feel very strange.' Elspeth looks round, lost for a moment. 'It seems like another life that somebody else lived, not me.'

The youngest boy crouches by them, poking into the dry mud with a stick. He brings up a cake of mud and crumbles the earth away with his fingers. 'Hey!' he says. 'I've found treasure.'

'Let's have a look!' His grandmother takes the mud-rock from him and turns it over in her hands. Where she rubs it, a band of blackened gold gleams through, a spark of diamond light.

'It is treasure!' the child says, excited. 'It's gold. You can just see it. Can we take it to Grandad?'

Elspeth stands with her hands cupped round the rock, her eyes closed tight. At last she gives it back to the child. 'Bury it, bunny,' she says. 'It belongs here. Bury it.'

The child tosses it aside and runs off, whooping again, to his brothers. Their mother follows them and the older woman stays where she was, naming the cottages, naming the people who'd once lived there; naming the ghosts.

'Granny!' One of the older boys comes running back down to her from where the Ghost Woods used to be. 'There's a queer stone with writing on!' he shouts, his hands cupped round his mouth to make his words carry.

Elspeth smiles. 'The S and D stone.'

'What's it for?' he shouts, and she shakes her head.

'I don't know,' she says. 'I never did, and I never will. It's one of the mysteries of the valley.'

At last her daughter comes back to her and tucks her arm in hers. 'Time to go, Mum,' she says. 'Look at the sky. It's starting to rain.'

'So it is.' Elspeth stands as if transfixed, watching how the huge raindrops spatter on to the earth like bubbles bursting.

'No, you were right, Maddy,' she says. 'You were right, not to come back.'

Thunder rumbles round the purple hills, and at last the rain streams down, coursing over the stones, rushing down from the slopes, seeping back into the hungry earth; drowning its secrets.

Author's note

The story is loosely based on the building of the Ladybower reservoir in North Derbyshire. The characters in my story are completely invented and the relationships and happenings among them are entirely the work of fiction. Engineering details and the timescale of the Ladybower project have been altered for the purposes of the story. In actuality, two villages, Ashopton and Derwent, were both submerged when Ladybower was constructed (1935–1945), to support and complement the existing reservoirs of Derwent and Howden. The church tower was demolished in 1947 to stop people swimming out to it. A few miles away an earthbank reservoir (Dale Dyke) had collapsed in the previous century, causing the Great Sheffield Flood.

I have lived in the vicinity of Ladybower for most of my life, have marvelled at the beauty of the reservoir, have walked among the ruins during the 1986 drought, and have wondered about the families who once lived there and who were rehoused at nearby Yorkshire Bridge. For many years I have been haunted by the idea of the disappearance not just of homes, not just of a community, but of a way of life.

Acknowledgements

In researching for *Deep Secret* I read:

Water Under the Bridge
© V. J. Hallam, E. Evans, 1979

The Silent Valley
© V.J. Hallam, Sheaf Publishing, 1983

Walls Across the Valley
© Brian Robinson, Scarthin Books, 1993

Derwent Days
© Yorkshire Arts Circus, 1998

The Lost Villages of Derwent and Ashopton,
a pamphlet written and published by
© Harry Gill, 1969

And talked to the late Jack Elliot about his childhood in the Derwent valley.

Berlie Doherty

Abela

BERLIE DOHERTY

Two girls.

Abela lives in an African village and has lost everything. What will be her fate as an illegal immigrant? Will she find a family in time?

'I don't want a sister or brother,' thinks Rosa in England. Could these two girls ever become sisters?

Abela is the powerful and moving story of a true heroine who overcomes great hardship. Double Carnegie-winning author Berlie Doherty writing at her very best.

Shortlisted for the Manchester Book Award, the Coventry Inspiration Book Award 2009 and The Blue Peter Book Awards.

'Excellent . . . what could be an unbearably sad tale is made compulsively readable by a writer of grace and skill.' *Independent*

HBK 9781842706893 £10.99
PBK 9781842707258 £5.99

Holly

STARCROSS

BERLIE DOHERTY

'Do you know who I am?'

Holly has never really thought about it. But then her internet friend Zed asks her name, and a mysteriously familiar man starts driving around and asking after her. She is going to have to explore the long-forgotten life her mother ran away from eight years before, and find out who she really is.

'A beautiful, moving story with characters to believe in and a sense of the uniqueness of every human life.' TES

BERLIE DOHERTY is twice winner of the Carnegie Medal.

9781842709306 £5.99

The GREAT DEATH

JOHN SMELCER

When white strangers visit, they leave a deadly sickness of red spots and fever. Only thirteen-year-old Millie and her younger sister Maura survive. The two girls embark on an epic trek through the harsh Alaskan winter wilderness in search of fellow humans.

An extraordinary story of courage, endurance and survival.

'A must-read by an exciting new novelist: definitely one to watch.'
Jake Hope, *Bookseller's Choice*

'An outstanding piece of writing and undoubtedly my favourite novel of the year.'
Lindsey Stainer,
Bookseller's Choice

ISBN 9781842709191 £5.99

OVER A THOUSAND HILLS I WALK WITH YOU

HANNA JANSEN

'At its heart the Rwandan tragedy was profoundly personal. This novel captures with great poignancy the terrible cost to the youngest and most vulnerable.'
Fergal Keane

'This is an extraordinary and devastating book. Like *The Diary of Anne Frank*, I will never forget it.'
Emma Thompson

Jeanne is a typical school girl: bickering with her little sister, teasing her brother. Then, in one horrifying night, a torrent of violence is unleashed. Jeanne's family flees their home and tries desperately to reach safety. They do not succeed. Jeanne is the only survivor of her family's massacre, and this is her story as told to her adoptive mother. A story that makes unforgettably real the events of the 1994 Rwandan genocide.

ISBN 9781842706732
£6.99

Learning to Scream

Beate Teresa Hanika

Sensitively handled and beautifully written, this is a best-selling German novel.

Malvina is thirteen. She and her best friend, Lizzy, have taken over an abandoned villa, raised a pirate flag and waged war on the boys from the local estate.

This is Malvina's story about last summer, but she has another story that's intertwined, a story she's ashamed of. She can't quite tell it yet, not to anyone, not even Lizzy, or her big brother Paul. But Granddad knows her secret, he says it's just between them and no one else would understand. And then she meets a boy. A boy she can trust; a boy she thinks she could fall in love with. But first she needs to learn how to scream!

'A courageous and heartbreaking book, written in the unbelievably light and poetic language of a thirteen year old.' *Die Zeit*

9781849390606 £6.99

The Unfinished Angel

SHARON CREECH

'Peoples are strange!
The things they are doing and saying – sometimes they make
no sense. Did their brains fall out of their heads?'

Angel is having an identity crisis when he meets Zola –
a talkative young girl who moves into Angel's tower
high in the Swiss Alps. 'This Zola is a lot bossy,' Angel
thinks. But out of their bickering an unexpected
friendship forms, and their teamwork is about to benefit
the entire village . . .

Sharon Creech won the Carnegie Medal and the
Newbery Medal, and was shortlisted
for the Costa Award. She has sold
over one million copies of her
books worldwide.

"Inventive, sassy and gutsy . . . The
Unfinished Angel . . . is an endlessly
witty and life-affirming read."
Booksellers' Choice,
The Bookseller

IISBN 9781849390835 £5.99